THE MEGALODON MIX-UP

A CHARLIE RHODES COZY MYSTERY BOOK FOUR

AMANDA M. LEE

WINCHESTERSHAW PUBLICATIONS

To Linsey, Augusta, Jenn, Boyd, Pam, Lee, Dan, Ricardo, Elizabeth, Franklin, Alison, Cindy, Joe, and Emma. What happens at tiki, stays at tiki.

ONE

"So ... it's a nice night."

I nodded like an idiot, my mind going a hundred different directions at once. It was a nice night. It was a beautiful night for a first date. A first date with my co-worker, who was technically my boss when it came to security issues with the Legacy Foundation, a group of paranormal monster hunters seeking answers to the big secrets.

I was the newest member of the team and had a big secret myself, one that Jack Hanson wasn't aware of. All he knew is that I was Charlie Rhodes, gung-ho and headstrong, mouthy and opinionated, and occasionally moronic and brash. He decided to ask me out anyway, something that made my heart palpitate as my thoughts went hazy.

Jack was handsome in a bad boy way, dark hair brushing the tops of his shoulders and dark eyes that could pierce the soul of monsters and humans alike. Of course, he was a non-believer working with a lot of believers. That made him cagey when it came to searching for answers on cases. That also made him dangerous when he found out about me ... and he would have to find out the truth eventually. I was the type of thing the Legacy Foundation searched for — a psychic with a hint of telekinetic ability — and I was hiding in plain sight. If I ever wanted a relationship with Jack to work, I would have to tell him.

Eventually. That didn't need to happen tonight, which was a minor relief.

For now, we simply had to get through the world's most stilted first date.

"It is a beautiful night," I agreed, my eyes traveling to the lake. Jack picked a restaurant an hour away from our office because he didn't want to risk running into our co-workers. Part of me wondered if I should be offended by that. The other part simply accepted that it was the smart thing to do. The last thing we wanted was to be studied by people we had to spend inordinate amounts of time with when we were still feeling our way around each other. "Extremely beautiful."

Small talk wasn't exactly my strong suit. I had no problem talking, don't get me wrong, but that often came across as babbling. Jack, on the other hand, was ex-military. He was often taciturn, occasionally introverted, and spontaneously sweet and romantic when he managed to remove his head from his hindquarters. That happened the night he asked me out, which occurred after a head injury that prohibited him from seeing a man turn into a huge werewolf and his daughter into a much cuter version of the mythical beast.

I kept that secret, too.

I had a lot of secrets.

Hmm. Maybe this was a bad idea.

"What kind of food do you like?" Jack was clearly struggling as he tried to find topics for us to discuss.

I was trapped in my own head — worry, excitement and excessive hormones warring for supremacy — and wasn't offering him much help. That needed to change. "This is awkward," I said after a beat, smoothing the front of my dress. I'd gone all out, dipped into my savings and selected a pretty lavender dress to wear because I wanted to look nice. I wasn't much for dresses, though, so I felt uncomfortable even though I hoped I looked cute. No matter how hard I tried to be demure and flirtatious, my mouth always managed to get ahead of my brain. I was a blurter of the highest order, and that was on full display tonight.

"Very awkward," Jack agreed, heaving a sigh and staring at me with unreadable eyes. "I wanted to take you to a nice dinner, someplace that you would always remember and maybe even impress you a little. I didn't realize how weird that would be."

I took a moment to glance around the patio where we sat. It was filled with older people — well, older than us — who had money and means. They were used to wearing evening gowns and suits. Jack wore a suit, going the extra effort to dress up for me, but he looked as uncomfortable as I felt.

"I don't think this is our scene," I said finally. "I would've been fine with McDonald's and a walk around the lake."

Jack pursed his lips. I couldn't tell if he was amused or annoyed. "You know what? You're right. This isn't us. Come on."

He pushed back his chair and extended his hand, causing my eyes to go wide.

"Where are we going?" I asked, a bit breathless. "Is that it? Is the date over?"

"This isn't a date. Not yet, anyway." He linked his fingers with mine and signaled to the hostess. "I'm taking you somewhere else. We can't be ourselves here, and that's the point of a first date. We're never going to get anywhere if we can't relax."

"Where are we going?"

"Someplace else." Jack dug in his wallet to hand the hostess money. "We also need to change our clothes. Are you comfortable in that?" He eyed the dress speculatively.

I shrugged. "I don't know. I bought it for the date."

His eyes softened. "It's pretty. You look pretty in it. If you want to keep it on, that's fine."

"Keep it on?" Instantly I turned suspicious. "We're not going to a hotel, are we? I thought we were supposed to talk to get to know each other first." Suddenly I was extremely nervous. "I shaved my legs, but I'm not ready for that." Seriously, was shaving my legs the wrong message to send?

Jack shook his head, his eyes lighting with mirth rather than annoyance. "Yeah. That's not what I meant. You're allowed to wear whatever you want. There's a Target store right around the corner. I thought we could buy some bum-around clothes. As for shaving your legs, the effort is appreciated. We are not, however, going to a hotel."

"Whew." I mimed wiping my forehead. "That's a relief."

"Oh, yeah?"

I nodded as I followed him toward the exit. "I think I would've passed out if I had to get naked in front of you."

He snickered. "I love that you say whatever comes to mind. I never have to worry about you hiding your feelings ... or lying."

That wasn't exactly true. A lie of omission was still a lie. Now was not the time to dwell on that, though. If things went well, I would have to tell him. He wouldn't believe me at first — that was to be expected — but when I eventually did show him what I could do, we would face a true test of the bond that seemed to be growing.

We weren't there yet.

"That's me." I twittered nervously. "Speak first, realize how stupid it was later."

"I actually like that about you." Jack was sincere. "Most of the time."

"I like that about me, too. Most of the time."

"Come on." He gripped my hand tightly. "Let's do this date the right way. There's no sense getting off on the wrong foot."

IN THE END I HAD to agree with Jack's assessment. Dinner at the expensive restaurant he selected was a nice idea, but we both would've felt too nervous and on display to relax. Instead, we selected cheap and comfortable clothes, picked up takeout at Burger King (the only nearby fast food restaurant we could find), and selected a park on the lake to get to know one another in a more intimate way.

Er, not *that* intimate. Nothing got dirty except our bare feet.

"Wait a second ... that can't be right." Jack bent over at the waist thanks to irrepressible laughter. "You participated in a beauty pageant?"

"You don't call them beauty pageants any longer," I argued, dipping a fry in ketchup. "They're scholarship programs."

"Did you wear a bathing suit?"

I scowled. "Yes. It was a respectable one-piece with a lion's face on the butt."

Jack laughed so hard I thought he would start crying, wiping the back of his hand over his cheek to swipe away invisible tears. "Oh, please tell me there are photos."

"There are no photos."

"I don't believe you."

I didn't blame him. Sadly, there were photos, but I had no intention of showing them to him. "It was the only thing I could think to do," I explained. "My parents left me a little money for college, but it was hard to spread it to cover everything I needed. I thought the scholarship might help."

Jack stilled, sobering. "That must have been hard on you." He was quiet as he moved back to the picnic table. "You were awfully young to be on your own."

I shrugged. I wasn't sure we should be talking about something so heavy on a first date, but I brought it up, so I couldn't complain. "I was on my own before that. They adopted me, took me in, raised me as their own. I like to think that I had a limited amount of time with them, that they saved me because they somehow knew that, and I'm better for the time I had with them."

Jack arched an eyebrow. "That sounds really healthy."

"It should. I was forced to see a therapist after my parents died because there was worry I wasn't adjusting well. I wasn't an adult, so I had no choice."

"Well, it's still healthy." Jack snagged one of my fries and popped it in his mouth, his own dinner already devoured. "Why did you choose this? I mean ... why did you decide to focus on hunting monsters and the unknown?"

I'd chosen it because I could move things with my mind and see into other people's heads when their defenses were down. I'd chosen it because I was different and desperate to find out why. I'd chosen it because I needed a way to understand why I was so different from almost everyone else I'd ever met.

"I've always liked the idea of unexplained things – entities I guess – being out there," I replied. "When I was a kid about eight or so I saw this show on television. It was about the Loch Ness Monster.

"They had that video, the one shot a long time ago — you know the one I'm talking about, right? — and I remember being fascinated," I continued. "I was a fidgety kid. I bounced from one thing to the other, one adventure to the other. That documentary ignited my imagination in a way I didn't realize was possible at the time."

It felt whimsical reminiscing, and Jack appeared truly interested.

"After that, I started watching every show I could on the strange and unexplained," I said. "I watched shows on Bigfoot ... and yetis ... and those ghost hunter adventures. My parents thought I was nutty, but I couldn't stop myself. I was obsessed."

"I don't think that's so bad." Jack kicked out his feet under the table, placing them on either side of mine. It wasn't a particularly sexy gesture, but there was something intimate about it all the same, warm and inviting. I could feel the heat radiating off him. "You have a curious mind, Charlie. That's not always a good thing, because it can get you into trouble — and often does. But it's not a bad thing. You want to learn. You want to experience everything life has to offer. I would rather you be enthusiastic about things that probably aren't real rather than jaded to what is real."

It was an interesting statement. "What about you? Why are you working for the Legacy Foundation when you're clearly not a believer?"

"What makes you think I'm not a believer?"

"I've met you."

Jack smiled. "That doesn't mean I'm not a believer."

"I've been on several missions with you," I reminded him. "You always lean toward humans as culprits."

"Have I been wrong? I mean ... did Bigfoot kill people in Hemlock

Cove? Did the Chupacabra eat people in Texas? Did werewolves rip apart campers?"

He had a point. Bigfoot most certainly hadn't been killing people in Hemlock Cove. Real witches were hiding among fake ones to cast curses, though. Werewolves did not kill the campers, but they were definitely real. I saw two people shift with my own eyes. Jack was knocked out at the time, and I couldn't tell him because I'd made a promise to the family. As for the other ... .

"I saw the Chupacabra," I reminded him. "I saw it before I lost consciousness."

A muscle in Jack's jaw worked as he stared me down. He didn't like being reminded of what had happened in Texas. I almost died. He almost lost it trying to find me. We were separated when I saw the Chupacabra, too. "You *think* you saw it," he said finally, his voice soft. "You were injured, Charlie. You took a bad fall. You wanted to see the Chupacabra, so that's what you saw right before you lost consciousness."

I didn't believe that. "Jack ... ."

He held up his hand to silence me and shook his head, firm. "No. I don't want to argue about this. You were hurt and it makes me sick to my stomach to think about what you went through. So, if you think you saw the Chupacabra, you saw it. I believe you."

I searched his face. "You do?"

"Yeah. I believe you."

We held each other's gazes for a long time, something electric passing through us. I finally broke the silence. "I ... um ... ." I honestly had no idea what I was going to say. Luckily, I didn't have to think of anything. At that exact moment, lightning split the sky and caused me to jolt.

Jack flicked his eyes to the west, furrowing his brow. "Storms."

"Yeah." I followed his gaze. "I guess that means the date is over." As if on cue, the rain started falling in a steady sheet, causing me to laugh as I hastily collected the remnants of our dinner so I could toss the wrappers in a nearby trash receptacle. "Wow. That was quick."

"Let me help." Jack double-checked to make sure we had everything, and when he joined me by the trash container his handsome face was wet from the rain. He didn't move to scurry for cover, instead taking a step closer to me and staring directly into my face. "How was our first date?" he asked after a beat, his voice low and throaty.

My pulse tripped at our proximity. We weren't touching, but I could feel his heart beating in rhythm with mine ... and it was a fast rhythm. "It was good." I wasn't sure how I found the right words. "It was really good."

"Yeah." His fingers were gentle as they slipped a strand of my long hair behind my ear. I'd worn it up when I donned the dress, but took it down when we changed into comfortable clothing. It was important to be normal. That's what Jack wanted — what I wanted, too — so I went for my own brand of normalcy.

"How are we going to handle this with everyone at work?" I asked, ignoring the way the storm ramped up around us. "I don't know that we should tell them right away. I ... think that would be weird."

Jack nodded, solemn. "Yeah. I never thought I'd be in this position, but I've given it some thought. I think you're right. We need to keep it quiet ... at least until we know if it's going to stick."

His words broke through the fuzz that his proximity was creating in my brain. "You don't think it's going to stick." It was a statement, not a question.

"I don't know," he hedged, clearly uncomfortable. "I know that I'm attracted to you. I know that you make me laugh. I also know that you make me crazy. We don't know each other all that well."

"Isn't that why we're dating?"

"Yes, but the fact that we work together adds a layer of difficulty that most dating couples don't have," Jack replied. "I'm good at my job. I believe in being professional. That doesn't mean we can't date. It simply means I don't think we should date at work."

That was interesting. "Meaning we pretend we're not involved while on the clock?"

"Exactly."

Hmm. "That's actually probably a good idea. If the others find out

— especially Laura — things might get uncomfortable. That could ruin both our working and personal relationships."

Laura Chapman, another co-worker, recently developed an interest in pursuing Jack. He shut her down quickly, but she showed no signs of giving up. She wouldn't react well if she knew Jack and I had embarked on something new.

"So, you're okay with us keeping this on the down low?" he asked. "You're not going to make a thing about it?"

I shook my head, my wet hair flying from side to side. "I think keeping it a secret is a good idea. This is my first real job. I want to be professional. It's important to me."

"Good." He leaned closer, lightning flashing and illuminating his eyes. "So, we have a plan." His lips were close to mine. "We're dating but no one at work needs to know we're dating."

"That's the plan," I agreed. "I ... ."

"Shh." I could feel his breath on my face. "No more talking. Just ... hold still."

He pressed his lips against mine and I completely forgot what we were talking about. The kiss was simple, soft and sultry. It didn't devolve into a teenage make-out session and there were no wandering hands.

It was still the best kiss of my life and my lips went numb at some point. I think my brain went a little numb, too.

"This will work," Jack whispered when we finally separated. "We'll be calm, cool and collected. We're professionals. How hard could it be?"

TWO

I woke late.

The first thing I remembered was the kiss, which made me feel girly and ridiculous, but I basked in the memory.

It didn't last long because my phone started beeping with an incoming message. It seemed we had a new job and I was expected at the airport. I had to shower, dress and pack for the Florida heat – and do it fast.

My hair was still damp by the time I arrived at the airport. My boss, Chris Biggs, collected my suitcase and loaded it himself. His face was lit with excitement, joy practically oozing from every pore, and he hurried me onto the plane before I could get a question out.

The Legacy Foundation was financed by Chris's family, so even though the monster-hunting portion of the business was dealt with on the sly, we were well-funded and had a private plane at our disposal.

There was an open seat next to Jack, but remembering our agreement from the previous evening I opted to sit next to Millie Watson. She used to be married to Chris's uncle Myron and continued working for the company when the relationship fell apart. She was older, often bawdy, and I felt comfortable with her from the moment we'd met.

She was also the only person in the group to know my secret. She witnessed me unleashing my powers and I had no choice but to confide in her. Surprisingly, despite her prominence in the group, she not only embraced my secret but actively encouraged me to test my abilities. While I was still getting used to my place with the foundation and the others in the group, I had faith Millie was someone I could rely on.

"What's going on?" I asked, fastening my seatbelt. "Why are we in such a hurry?"

Millie, always shrewd, didn't immediately answer. Instead she took a long time to look me over. "Why are you so shiny?"

The question caught me off guard. "I'm not shiny."

"You most certainly are."

"I am not." My hackles rose. "I'm sweaty. I overslept and had to get ready on the fly. Sweaty is not the same thing as shiny."

"If you say so."

I opted to stow the conversation, waiting until we were in the air at cruising altitude and I could remove my seatbelt before speaking again.

"So ... what's going on?"

"What's going on is that we have a new job," Chris replied, rubbing his hands together. The seats were arranged in such a way that we had no problem hearing him. "It's probably the biggest job we've ever had ... and I'm not simply saying that because of the size of the creature we're hunting."

Oh, that sounded promising. "We're going to Florida, right? What kind of creature lives in Florida? Ooh. I've read about certain swamp hominids. Are we looking for one of those?"

Chris shook his head. "Think bigger!"

"A crocodile species that dates back to the dinosaurs and is eating people?"

"No, but you're getting closer."

Jack made an annoyed sound in the back of his throat when I

opened my mouth to offer another guess. "Why don't you just tell us, Chris? The flight is less than three hours. We need time to discuss things, plan. At this rate, Charlie will still be guessing when we land."

I shot him an annoyed look. He met my gaze evenly, his expression bland. He clearly wasn't worried about me being angry. That was par for the course when it came to us working together, so apparently our plan was in full swing.

"Fine. Jack clearly doesn't want to play this morning." Chris shot the tempestuous security head a fond look. They had an odd relationship, work brothers who never saw things in the same manner, but they were fairly close. "We're looking for Carcharocles megalodon."

I simply stared, dumbfounded. Jack was the first to speak.

"You mean the huge shark that went extinct millions of years ago?" He was flabbergasted. "You can't be serious."

Chris straightened his tall frame. "Carcharocles megalodon was a prominent species years ago. We have evidence that it survived, and is roaming the Gulf of Mexico."

Instead of being impressed, Jack rolled his eyes and smacked his hand to his forehead. "Oh, geez."

I decided to take pity on Chris. "Why do we think the Megalodon is hanging around the Gulf?" I asked.

"Carcharocles Megalodon," Chris corrected.

"Honey, I love you, but no one is going to spit that out every time we talk for the next few days," Millie noted. "I know you like proper names, but let's go with Megalodon on this one to save everyone some headaches."

Chris let loose an exaggerated sigh. Even though Millie was no longer his aunt because of the divorce, he loved her all the same. They were unbelievably tight. "Fine. Megalodon."

"Megalodons are extinct," Jack barked. "They've been dead for years. I don't care what movies and fiction books say. They're gone."

"Unless they're not." Chris was back to being excited as he slid a glance to Hannah Silver. She was a brilliant scientist who knew a lot about almost everything and who happened to look like a model. She was also easy to get along with, personable, and could double as an angel if she chose to put on wings and a halo. On paper I should hate her. She was too nice to hate, though. She and Chris had recently admitted their feelings for one another and were in the middle of a very public courtship. They were constantly petting and gazing into each other's eyes. I had a feeling that was only one of the reasons Jack was so adamant about keeping our relationship secret.

"I don't want to dampen your enthusiasm, sweetie, but I have to side with Jack on this one," Hannah said. "Megalodons are extinct."

"Unless they're not." Chris clearly wasn't ready to let it go. "We have evidence to suggest that a Megalodon attacked and killed a woman in the waters off St. Petersburg."

I wasn't familiar with Florida geography, so I asked the obvious question. "And that's on the Gulf side?"

Jack nodded. "Close to Tampa."

That still didn't mean anything to me. "How close is that to Disney World?"

Jack sighed. "Hours away."

"Oh." That was a bummer. No Mickey Mouse for me. "Well ... why do we think it's a Megalodon again?"

"We don't think anything," Jack cautioned. "Chris is the only one who thinks it's a Megalodon."

I didn't like his tone. "It could be a Megalodon."

Chris beamed at me. "Thank you, Charlie."

"Great," Jack muttered just loud enough for me to make out the words. "Now there are two of you."

"Yes, it's fantastic," I agreed, grinning. "So what happened to make the police think a Megalodon killed this woman?"

"The police don't think a Megalodon did it," Chris replied quickly. "They're calling it a shark attack. The file was flagged, though, because the wound pattern is far too big to belong to any shark that cruises the Gulf."

"And what types of sharks would those be?" Laura asked. She'd been quiet since takeoff, sucking down coffee and casting the occasional look toward Jack when she thought no one was looking. She wasn't a big believer either, but she liked the paycheck and travel associated with the gig.

"Bull sharks," Jack replied quickly. "Tiger sharks, Blacktip sharks, Nurse sharks and Great Hammerhead sharks, too. Bull sharks are the biggies. They're also more likely to attack humans than most other sharks, including Great Whites."

I stared at him, confused. "How do you know that?"

Jack shrugged. "I watch *Shark Week*."

"Me, too!" I was impressed, and a little giddy. "I watch it every year."

Jack's eyes momentarily softened. "Yes, well, it's great. We can talk about *Shark Week* later. Right now our concern seems to be Megalodons, which are extinct. There's no way a Megalodon attacked a woman in the Gulf of Mexico."

"Unless there is," Chris pressed. "I present you with Shayne Rivers." He held up his tablet and displayed a photograph of a young woman, impressively pretty, with big brown eyes and a demure smile. "She's a romance author who was discovered in the waters directly behind a resort. She was caught in a shark net ... what was left of her, that is."

I pursed my lips. "Obviously that shark net wasn't working."

"Maybe because the shark that went through it was so big it couldn't hold," Chris suggested, tapping the side of his nose. He was clearly getting into this. "Shayne was discovered by two fishermen on a pier. They saw something in the water and investigated. That's when they found her. Evidence of a shark attack was clear."

I cringed at the words. I had a reoccurring dream of being attacked by sharks. I was both intrigued by and terrified of the creatures. Other than being burned alive, that had to be the worst way to go.

"Okay, I'm calling bull on this one," Jack started. "Not necessarily bull shark, but bull all the same. Megalodons had a bite radius of about six feet across. Maybe a little smaller, but you get what I'm saying. A Megalodon would've eaten her entirely."

"Unless it was an accident," Chris argued. "I watch *Shark Week*, too. Sharks don't attack people because they taste good. They attack people because they mistake them for something else ... like seals and turtles."

"I've always thought it would be cool to be a turtle," Millie offered. "I like the idea of carrying your house around on your back and being so ugly you're cute."

"That is neat," I agreed.

Jack scorched me with a look. "If we could come back from Turtle Land, there's no way a Megalodon mistook a romance writer for a turtle and only ate part of her. That is the most ridiculous thing I've ever heard."

"And yet that's what we're dealing with," Chris said. "I know it's difficult to hear the details, but they're necessary. The victim's bottom half was missing, suggesting the shark ate that. Along her chest, right across this ridge, she had two deep gashes that have been identified as indentations from shark teeth.

"Now, a normal shark's tooth is about two inches in length," he continued. "The largest Great White tooth on record is three inches. Would you care to guess how big the wounds on our victim measured?"

I was both fascinated and horrified. "How big?"

"Seven inches."

"Seven inches isn't all that big," Laura drawled, earning a dirty look from Jack for the double entendre. "I prefer nine inches myself."

Chris, oblivious, barreled forward. "There is no shark in the Gulf big enough to have caused the injuries our victim sustained." He said it as if it were fact and we should all acquiesce, grab some scuba gear and start looking for a prehistoric shark without further delay.

"Chris, I know you get into this stuff, but I need you to be reasonable." Jack adopted a pragmatic — and mildly condescending — tone. "A Megalodon wouldn't go unnoticed. They were, like, sixty feet long and ate everything in sight. The marine population in the Gulf would be decimated if a Megalodon was present." He was trying to sound reasonable, but I recognized the bite to his words. "There's no way it was a Megalodon. I might buy that a Great White found its way into the Gulf, though that's unlikely. Maybe it was a large Great White. Even if it was, I don't see how this is a case for us."

"It is if it's a Megalodon."

"It's not!"

"Unless it is." Chris was like a shark with blood in the water. When he believed something with his whole heart, he refused to concede defeat. He clearly had no intention of letting go of this. "If you don't want to be part of the team investigating this, Jack, you don't have to. You can go back on the first flight out if you want to be excused from this assignment."

Jack's eyes darted to me, as if silently asking if I wanted to abandon the trip. Even though I wasn't convinced it was a Megalodon — although, how cool would that be? — I wasn't ready to abandon ship. A Megalodon was unlikely, but perhaps there was another giant shark out there waiting to be discovered. The possibility was exciting.

"Where will we start when we land?" I asked, my voice small. "Are we staying in the same resort the victim was staying?"

Chris nodded, his eyes still on Jack. "Those staying with the investigation will have rooms there. It's called the Gulf Winds Lodge. It's huge, seven different restaurants on the premises, a spa."

Laura brightened considerably. "You had me at spa."

"Do we still have you, Jack?" Chris asked pointedly.

Jack nodded, his posture stiff. "I will do my job like I always do."

"I know you will." Chris's easy smile returned. "You always do, even when you think I'm being a loon."

"Well, since you put it out there, I think you're definitely being a loon this go-around," Jack supplied. "In fact, I think anyone embracing this theory is being a loon."

I felt his gaze on me but refused to make eye contact. "How will we approach things when we land?"

"I have vehicles waiting. It takes about thirty-five minutes to drive from the airport to the resort. We'll check in and then go from there."

"What do we know about the victim?" Hannah asked. She was the rational sort. She was a believer, but always looked to science for confirmation.

Chris turned his attention back to his information packet. "She's a romance author. She's married and has five kids, all under the age of ten."

My mouth dropped open. "She looks twenty in that photo you showed us. How can she have five kids?"

"Her age is listed as thirty-one," Chris replied. "Maybe she simply looks young. That happens."

"I still get carded," Hannah offered helpfully.

"That's because people mistake you for an angel," I said. "I'm barely old enough to drink and never get carded. I must look old. That's not good, right?"

Jack cracked a smile and shook his head. "You look fine." He caught himself quickly. "I mean ... you don't look old or young. You look like Charlie."

"Yes, which means you look like a circus freak," Laura sneered.

This time the look Jack shot her was murderous. "If you don't have something nice to say, Laura, maybe you shouldn't speak."

"I agree." Chris focused on his file as he chimed in. "Don't make things difficult, Laura. We'll have a tough enough time gathering information."

"Whatever." Laura petulantly folded her arms over her chest and turned to stare out the window. "This is going to be a stupid trip."

I rubbed my forehead and glanced at Millie, finding her watching me with a thoughtful gaze. "What?"

"Nothing," Millie replied hurriedly. "Do you have a headache?"

"Soon."

Her lips curved. "Well, we're hunting a Megalodon. You'll forget all about that headache soon."

"That would be nice."

"What else do we know about this woman, Chris?" Jack prodded in an effort to get the conversation back on track. "What was she doing at the resort?"

"There's a writer's conference there. Fiction Writers Incorporated, I believe. The victim arrived yesterday, but the conference is still going for another few days."

"So we're dealing with a bunch of writers," Jack mused. "That seems like a dramatic group."

Curious, I leaned forward. "What makes you say that?"

"They're artistic souls. That means they overreact about everything. Maybe our writer wasn't killed at all. Maybe she jumped off the pier, cracked her head while falling down, and was eaten because the shark was attracted by the blood. And when I say shark, I mean bull shark."

"A bull shark could not have made the wound our victim suffered," Chris persisted. "We've been over this."

"Yeah, well, I want to see the autopsy report myself," Jack said. "I'm guessing there's some wiggle room in your interpretation. Not to be insulting or anything."

"I'm not insulted." Chris's smile was easy and quick. "You never believe. That's why I enjoy having you on my team. When I find proof, your apology will mean the most."

I pressed my lips together to keep from laughing at the ridiculous look on Jack's face. Millie shook with silent laughter next to me, and a quick glance at Hannah told me she was fighting the urge to break out into hearty guffaws.

"Well, if that happens I will gladly apologize," Jack said finally. "Until then, I'm leaning toward accidental death and bull shark scavengers."

"That's completely up to you. As for the rest of us, I have photographs and hunches. Let's get started."

THREE

The Tampa airport was small, which made it easy to navigate. I ended up in a vehicle with Chris, Hannah and Millie. That left Jack, Laura and Bernard Hill, our equipment guru, in the other vehicle. I tried not to dwell on the fact that I was certain Laura would spend the entire drive flirting with Jack and instead focused on the case.

The hotel was beautiful, featuring an ornate lobby with a Starbucks located smack dab in the center of things. I headed that way while Chris sorted out the room situation, ordered an iced green tea, and watched the people milling about the open area.

The banner hanging over the lobby touted the conference, and the people standing in small groups wore lanyards with their names emblazoned across them. That would make identifying who we were talking to much easier, although I had no idea what I should expect when dealing with authors. I assumed they were like actors, full of themselves and oblivious to real-world issues like Megalodons and Chupacabras, but I had nothing to base that on other than movies and television.

"Do you like pimento cheese?"

The question seemed so out of the blue I could do nothing but stare at the woman who claimed the stool to my left as she fixed a friendly smile on her pretty face. She wore a lanyard. The name read "Sarah Hilton," and she wore the most ridiculous cat T-shirt I'd ever seen. The feline in question had a horn (like a unicorn) and there were sparkles flying out of its butt.

"Um ... what was the question?"

"Pimento cheese," she repeated. "Do you like it?"

"I don't know that I've ever tried it," I said after a beat. "Should I like it?"

"Absolutely. I have some up in my room if you're interested. Two-twenty-seven."

"Okay." The word "odd" didn't begin to describe her. She seemed nice enough, don't get me wrong, but inviting me to her room seemed weird. "I'll see if I can free up some time."

"Great." She took the drink she was waiting for from the barista and happily shuffled away from the counter, heading toward a small group of women who looked to be cackling and having a good time.

"Who was that?" Jack asked as he appeared at my other side, hoisting himself onto a stool and signaling the barista for a tea to match mine.

"Sarah Hilton," I replied. "I think she's an author. I'll have to look her up."

"What were you talking about?"

"She asked me if I wanted pimento cheese and then invited me to her room."

"Hmm." Jack's gaze was thoughtful as he watched the woman cavort with her friends. "Maybe she was hitting on you."

That hadn't even occurred to me. "Why? Is pimento cheese code for something I don't know about? I said I would think about it. What if she thinks I mean it and waits for me to join her in her room?"

Instead of being upset, as I expected, Jack merely chuckled. "Something tells me you'll be okay. As for the room situation, we're not going to be in regular rooms this time. Apparently the resort is sold out."

"What does that mean? We're not sleeping on the beach, are we? I've heard horrible things about crabs crawling into certain cracks and crevices if you sleep on the beach."

Jack arched an eyebrow. "Ah, you must be talking about the notorious ass crab infestation of 2015. I think we're past that."

His sense of humor reared itself at the oddest of times. "I didn't say ass crabs."

"Yes, well, that's what I heard."

"Whatever." I sipped my tea. "What are we going to do about the rooms?"

"They have timeshare condos. We're getting two of those."

"Two?" I did the math. "How many rooms?"

"Four."

That sounded a little too cozy for my taste. "So ... how is that going to work?"

Jack shrugged. "Chris and Hannah will take one room. We'll put Laura in the condo with them to punish her. Then you and Millie can share a room in the other. Bernard will take the second room and I'll sleep on the couch."

"Why do I have to share with Millie?"

"Because it's either her or Laura."

He had a point and still ... . "Why can't you share with Bernard and I'll take the couch?"

"Because I'm not sharing with anyone. Bernard is a great guy but we're not sharing a bed."

I loved Millie dearly, but I didn't want to share a bed either. "I'll sleep on the floor ... or I guess I could sleep on the couch in the other condo."

Jack blew out a sigh. "Do you really want to share a roof with Chris and Hannah the way they're ... all over each other?"

I understood what he wasn't saying and shrugged. "I think it's kind of cute."

"It won't be cute when they lose control in the middle of the night."

"How do you even know they're sharing a room?"

"Because Chris flat out told me. He seemed to think I would frown on it, but it's not my business. That doesn't mean I want to share a roof with them. That's why Laura is being punished. No one likes her. And at least she won't be under our roof fouling things up."

He had a point. "I guess it doesn't matter who is sleeping where. What are we going to do once we drop our stuff off in the condos?"

"We're heading out to the pier to look at the scene."

That sounded exciting. "It's nice out. I love the beach. I haven't been in a long time ... but I love the ocean ... and the waves."

"And the Megalodons," Jack added.

"Don't get snide," I chided, wagging a finger. "I don't like your attitude. It could be a Megalodon."

"Megalodons are extinct."

"There was a fish that was thought to be extinct but discovered alive," I argued. "I can't remember its name but I know it exists."

"I know what fish you're talking about, and that's a completely different situation. That fish grows to be, like, six feet long, not sixty."

"Still, we haven't seen everything in the ocean. It's too vast. Maybe the Megalodon was living in a deep trench and lost its food source and had to come to warmer waters or something."

"You saw that in that Jason Statham shark movie. I saw it, too."

A smile flew to my lips, unbidden. "I think it's kind of funny that we both like bad shark movies."

"We'll have to have a movie night when we get back."

I glanced over my shoulder to make sure no one from our group was eavesdropping and lowered my voice. "We're doing okay, right? Although ... maybe you shouldn't be sitting with me if we're trying to fly under the radar."

"We spent time together before we started dating," Jack reminded me. "If we completely stop hanging out they'll be suspicious."

"I think Millie is already suspicious. She said I was shiny this morning."

Jack chuckled. "You did look a little shiny."

"You look shiny, too."

"Men don't look shiny."

"Oh, yeah? How do you look?"

"Studly and brave." He puffed out his arms enough to make me laugh and then sobered. "We can't stop interacting. We can't interact too much. It's a balancing act. We'll feel things out until it slips into place."

"Luckily Chris and Hannah are so caught up in each other they won't notice. Laura will figure it out, though. Millie will, too."

"They will. By then, hopefully we'll have everything figured out ourselves."

"That would be great."

"So ... we'll work toward that."

THE CONDOS WERE BIGGER than we thought, which was a blessing. That didn't change the fact that we were practically on top of one another.

"Why do I have to share with Chris and Hannah?" Laura complained as we walked toward the pier an hour after stowing our gear and getting the lay of the land. "Why was that decided without me?"

"We have limited options," Jack replied, his gaze pointed ahead as Laura matched his pace. She was being rather obvious with her attempts to keep close to him. "Two women will have to share a room. That means it's either you and Charlie, you and Millie or Millie and Charlie. I can't see you coming out of the situation alive if you're paired with either of them, so I figured this was the best option."

Millie, who was walking beside me, laughed. "He's got you there. If you want to share a room with me, that's fine. Just be prepared for a gag ... and maybe a bullet."

Jack shot Millie a warning look. "Don't threaten her. If you're not careful we'll have to attend another one of those 'don't threaten your co-workers with death' seminars. You know how annoying those things are."

"Well, if she wouldn't constantly make me want to threaten her we wouldn't have been forced into the previous two. This is really on her."

"Yeah, yeah." Jack waved off the comment. "What were we talking about again?"

"The fact that I don't want to share a condo with Chris and Hannah," Laura replied without missing a beat. "They're going to be doing it all night. You know it and I know it. Why can't Millie and Charlie sleep in the second room in that condo?"

"Because Millie is Chris's aunt and doesn't want to hear that." Jack was prepared for Laura's arguments and it was fairly impressive the way he laid things out. "She can't hear that – it's gross when you're dealing with family members – and she has to room with Charlie."

"Then what about Bernard?"

"I need Bernard in the other condo with me," Jack replied. "We're going to be dealing with a lot of equipment issues — boats, nets, tran-quilizers and all that other stuff — and I prefer him close. Besides, I don't want things to get uncomfortable with me being the only man in the condo. It makes sense for Bernard to share with Millie, Charlie and me."

Laura was in no hurry to let things go. "Why can't you and Bernard go into Chris and Hannah's condo?"

"Because I need my rest as the head of security. It's my job to keep everyone safe. I can't do that if I don't get a proper eight hours of sleep. I'll never get eight hours in that condo."

"In other words, you're saying I'm the sacrificial lamb."

"Pretty much," Jack agreed. "I've already gone over room assign-ments with Chris. You can try to talk to him, but I made it clear how things would be going and he agreed to let me have the final decision. If you don't like the sleeping arrangements, you can sleep on the beach."

"With the ass crabs," I offered, earning a snicker from Millie as Jack tried to hide his smile.

"I hate all of you," Laura hissed, increasing her pace so she could reach the end of the pier before us.

"She's a peach of a girl," Millie said, making a tsking noise with her tongue as she shook her head. "I don't know why some fine sociopath hasn't snapped her up and taken her to his lair."

"Don't push her too much on this trip," Jack warned. "She's going to be absolutely psychotic after spending a night with the twitterpated duo."

"A *Bambi* fan, too?" Now I was doubly impressed. "You're full of surprises."

"I'm a multifaceted guy."

ONCE WE REACHED THE end of the pier — a longer than expected walk — Jack excused himself to talk with Chris and the police officers handling the scene. That left Millie and me to stare at the water, including the tattered remains of what looked to be a net as it was collected in small boats and replaced with a new panel.

"That must be the shark net," Millie mused, narrowing her eyes. "It doesn't look very strong, does it?"

I'd been thinking the same thing. "No, but I get it. If it's too heavy, the sharks will have something to fight and it will be easier to break. By having it thinner, with more give, the sharks have less chance of getting trapped and dying. They also have less chance of breaking through."

We watched as two men on a nearby boat held up a ripped piece of net, one man gesturing wildly as the other shrugged and held up his hands to signify he didn't have the answers the other gentleman was looking for.

"You don't think it was a Megalodon, do you?" I asked out of nowhere. It seemed a ridiculous question to lob in her direction, but I was genuinely curious.

"No." Millie shook her head. "I don't think it's a Megalodon."

"Chris does."

"Chris has always had an imagination as big as his heart." Millie's smile was fond. "I spent a lot of time with him when he was a kid. It wasn't that his parents were negligent, mind you, but they weren't exactly hands-on.

"We would take adventures," she continued. "I made him watch *The Goonies* and we looked for pirate ships. We sat on the lawn at the big house and talked about adventures in outer space. He always wanted to believe no matter what, even when his parents told him he was being ridiculous."

"I always wanted to believe, too," I admitted. "I always thought ghosts were hiding in my closet ... and monsters were under my bed ... and evil was around every corner. I don't know why I thought that. My parents tried to break me of it. They were always calm, always rational. They explained things in ways I could understand. I still believed despite their best efforts."

"That must make what's going on with you and Jack difficult."

I wasn't sure I heard her correctly. It was windy on the pier. My ears could be playing tricks on me. "W-what?"

"Oh, don't do that." Millie's smile was sly. "Honey, I know what's going on with you two."

"How?"

"For one, you just told me."

"But ... ."

"Don't worry about it. I won't tell anyone. It's nobody's business."

I sucked in a breath to calm myself, hoping the panic fluttering through my heart didn't show on my face. "If you didn't know, how did you guess?"

"Little things. I first noticed in Michigan, when Jack took off after you the night you disappeared. He was convinced you were in danger."

"He's head of security. It's his job to keep me from danger."

"There was more than duty going on that night. He was afraid in his heart."

I swallowed hard. "He got hurt that night. It wasn't life-threatening, but he got hurt going after me. I feel bad about that."

"Don't. He wanted to go after you. He never would've forgiven himself if he didn't make it to you in time. I'm curious about what happened after he got hit on the head — I think it was probably magical — but I know better than to pressure you. You won't share someone else's secrets."

"No," I agreed, thinking back to the things I had seen, the things Zoe Lake-Winters told me. "It was an informative trip."

Millie laughed, genuinely amused. "I bet." She patted my arm. "I also happen to know you and Jack went on a date last night."

I was floored. "He told you?"

"No, and lower your voice," she ordered. "If he thinks we're talking about him, he'll get edgy. He's absolutely no fun when he's edgy. The Megalodon talk makes him antsy enough as it is. You don't want him to go off the rails, do you?"

Definitely not. "If he didn't tell you, how do you know?"

"I saw him on his computer earlier in the week," Millie replied, matter-of-fact. "He was looking at expensive restaurants outside of town. I was intrigued. I figured he had a date. I didn't know it was with you. I thought maybe he might fight his attraction a bit longer. I give him credit for not being a typical man. He stepped up to the plate right away."

"Just because he was looking at restaurants doesn't mean they were for me."

"Yeah, but I heard him make a reservation, and you came in looking shiny this morning. I'm not an idiot. In fact, I'm a fairly good investigator. I know exactly what's going on with the two of you."

I didn't like her smugness. Not one bit. "For your information ... ."

"Don't bother thinking up a lie." Millie waved a dismissive hand. "You're bad at it and it doesn't matter. I won't tell anyone. I think you guys are cute together."

"He doesn't want anyone to know," I stressed. "We both want to be professionals. We're keeping our personal relationship away from the job."

"That'll never work, but I think the attempt will be funny, so I'm willing to sit back and watch."

I balked. "Why won't it work?"

"Because matters of the heart are never that easy," Millie replied simply. "You'll figure that out going forward. For now, it's your life.

You guys are allowed to move at your own pace. I'm guessing this trip will be funny, though."

"It will be professional," I stressed. "We have everything under control. There's nothing to worry about."

"If you say so."

FOUR

*J*ack and Chris got into an argument not long after the guys on the boats hauled up the shark net.

They didn't call it an argument, of course. Jack said it was a debate and then pointed for me to walk toward the beach when I said it sounded like an argument. With nothing better to do, I acquiesced.

Millie went with me, mostly because Laura would not stop whining and refused to let go of the idea that someone should trade bedrooms with her. I was entertaining the idea of sleeping on one of the loungers on the back patio, so I understood her pain. That didn't mean I was interested in relieving it.

"This is cute." Millie's eyes lit with excitement as we walked over a small hill and discovered what looked to be the world's cutest tiki bar. "This is ... magical!"

I slid her a sidelong look. "Magical?"

"It is." Millie bobbed her head, refusing to back down. "It's rum runners at your fingertips. It's ... sandy beaches, cute bonfires, hot bartenders. This is like heaven at the end of a licorice whip."

I had no idea what that meant. "It's a bar on the beach."

"It's better than a bar." Millie gave my shoulder a little shove. "This is the grand momma of all bars."

"Uh-huh." Millie was a big fan of bars. She didn't care if they were inside, outside, dive or high class. She simply liked all of them and I could tell this tiki bar, which was a three-minute walk from our condominiums, was going to be a regular haunt. "Just don't swim in the ocean if you get drunk. There's a Megalodon out there."

Millie tilted her head as she regarded me. "You don't really believe that, do you?"

Her tone told me what she thought about the possibility. "That it's a Megalodon?" I searched my heart. "No. I think that's unlikely. I'm not entirely ready to discard it, though. Several creatures have been discovered after being declared extinct. There's a species of elephant, for example, that was saved thanks to trades between countries."

Millie didn't immediately respond, instead blinking in rapid succession. Finally, when she did find her voice, it was full of derision. "And what does that have to do with the fact that we have a tiki bar in our backyard?"

"Nothing. I was talking about the Megalodon."

"Right. Here's the thing, Charlie: A Megalodon is too big to hide."

"Not it if hid in deep underwater trenches where we can't go."

"I read that book, too." She patted my arm and made a clucking sound with her tongue, reminding me of the mother I'd lost when I was a teenager and momentarily causing my heart to ping. "This isn't like the other stuff we've dealt with. A Megalodon can't hide behind a tree or in the basement of an abandoned hotel."

"But ... ."

"No." She shook her head, firm. "Megalodons are well and truly gone. I draw the line at that."

"And I'm fine with that." I meant it. "What if it's a giant hammer-head? Or maybe a huge Great White ... or a mutant bull shark? Are any of those possibilities less exciting than a Megalodon?"

"To Chris, yes. To me ... I don't really care. I found my home with this tiki bar. I don't ever want to leave again."

I quietly followed her to a small table. She ordered a rum runner without delay, snickering when I requested an iced tea, and then turned her full attention on the busy tables.

"Do you think these are all writers?" she asked, her eyes bouncing from group to group.

"Most of them are wearing those lanyards I saw," I offered. "I think that means they're with the writing conference."

"None of them look alike. I would think writers would look alike."

"Why would writers look alike?" I was genuinely curious.

Millie held her palms out and shrugged. "I don't know. Stephen King is pale ... and kind of looks like a serial killer. Mark Twain looked like Colonel Sanders. Charles Dickens looked like he was allergic to the sun. These people look ... normal."

I cringed when I realized the pimento cheese girl had noticed me and was heading my way. "They're not normal. Trust me." I pasted a fake smile on my face for the woman. Sarah Hilton, I reminded myself. I didn't want to slip up and refer to her as the "pimento cheese girl." It was doubtful she would find that complimentary.

"It's you." She pulled up short and stopped in front of me. "Did you change your mind about the pimento cheese?"

Seriously. That had to be code for something. I needed to explain things to her or she would never take the hint. "I don't want pimento cheese," I said finally, enunciating clearly. "I don't need any cheese. Not any type of cheese. Okay?"

Sarah merely nodded. "Okay. Maybe later. You remember my room number, right?"

I didn't, but I was opposed to the idea of her repeating it. "Absolutely."

"Okay." She waved before heading to the bar.

When I risked a glance at Millie I found her shoulders shaking with silent laughter as she wiped tears from her eyes. "What was that?"

I didn't know how to answer. "She keeps offering me pimento cheese."

"You've been here barely two hours."

"And that's the second time she's offered me pimento cheese." My voice skyrocketed a notch. "It's weird, right?"

"It's ... I don't know what it is. I've never heard of terrorism via pimento cheese."

That made two of us. "Let's talk about something else."

Millie's smile twisted into something I couldn't quite identify. "Let's talk about you and Jack. How was your first date?"

I didn't want to talk about that. Well, in truth, I couldn't talk about that. I wanted to blab to someone about what happened, but it most certainly couldn't be a co-worker. Jack would melt down. I needed to find a friend so I could talk about my feelings. I hadn't made any outside of work since moving. Hmm. The pimento cheese girl was starting to look appealing. That was a scary thought. "I ... ."

Luckily I didn't get a chance to finish what I was going to say (even I didn't know what it was), because Jack picked that moment to pick his way across the busy bar and join us. I didn't miss the way several heads tilted in his direction, his rugged good looks calling to anyone with a hint of estrogen.

"Are you guys done on the pier?" I asked, thankful for the interruption.

"We are," Jack confirmed. "What are you two doing at a bar?"

"I'm having iced tea. Millie is ... having something else."

"Thank you, Little Miss Tattletale," Millie drawled, rolling her eyes. She clearly wasn't embarrassed at being called out because she took a long sip of her drink. "It's hot. I'm old. I need to keep refreshed."

Jack rolled his eyes. "Yes, I'm sure rum runners will help with the dehydration problem."

"How did you know she was having a rum runner?" I asked. "Is that like a superhero power or something?"

"I know lots of things," Jack replied. "We're heading to the medical examiner's office to look at the body. I thought you should know in case you were looking for me."

"And why would I be looking for you?" Millie teased, clearly enjoying herself. "Unless ... were you talking to someone else?"

Jack's eyes briefly narrowed as they snagged with mine. "I was talking to both of you."

"Right." Millie didn't look convinced. "Have fun at the medical examiner's office."

"I want to go with you," I said, hurriedly getting to my feet. "I want to hear what they have to say about the bite marks."

Jack shifted from one foot to the other, uncomfortable. "I don't think that's a good idea, Charlie."

"Why not? I've been to a medical examiner's office before."

"This is different."

"Why?"

He heaved out a long-suffering sigh. "Because this body will be in rough shape compared to the others we've found."

"He's saying the body was partially chewed, Charlie," Millie offered. "Do you really want to see that?"

I most definitely didn't want to see that. I had to if I expected to get a possible reading off the body, though. "I'm fine seeing it." I hoped I sounded more convincing than I felt. "I'm part of the team. You can't just cut me out of this."

Jack looked caught. "Fine," he said finally, shaking his head. "But if you pass out I'm not carrying you back to the hotel."

"I'm sure I'll manage."

"I guess we'll see."

I WASN'T A BIG FAN of morgues.

That should probably go without saying, but visiting the cold laboratories where dead bodies went to be ripped apart when something suspicious happened was the thing I liked least about my job. It was necessary. Occasionally I could see things in my head when I touched things — people, objects, corpses — so I had no choice but to make the attempt, no matter how shaky the prospect left me feeling.

"We're still trying to ascertain exactly what happened," Dr. Peabody explained, forcing a smile as he led us through the sterile room and toward the wall of refrigerated drawers. "I understand you're with the Legacy Foundation."

"We are," Chris confirmed, remaining close to Hannah. They didn't hold hands or anything, which was a relief, but Chris's protective instincts were on full display as he kept her pinned to his side.

Jack, on the other hand, didn't crowd me, and offered only one sentence of advice before focusing on the medical examiner. "Don't touch anything ... or break anything ... or throw up on anything."

Jack wasn't the warm and fuzzy type, so I couldn't exactly hold it against him.

"I've heard great things about the Legacy Foundation," Peabody enthused. He'd decided upon meeting us that Hannah and Chris were worth his time and Jack and I weren't. Since then, he'd completely focused on them while jabbering away and ignored us. "You must think something interesting is going on here if you took time out of your busy schedule to visit."

"It's weird enough that we thought we should check it out," Chris agreed, pulling up short when we reached the drawers. "We need to see what happened to the victim if we expect to move forward. There's no way around that."

"Thank you for letting us see the remains," Hannah said, her smile friendly and warm as she snapped on plastic gloves and prepared to go to work. Her inner scientist was on full display.

Peabody sent her a charming grin, perhaps responding to her latent sexual appeal. Hannah had no idea how pretty she was (something I found unbelievably annoying), and she merely smiled back and waited for him to open the drawer.

"Last chance," Jack whispered, taking me by surprise when he sidled up behind me. "You don't want to see this, Charlie."

I ignored his admonishment and focused on the drawer.

I don't know what I expected. Peabody was all business as he opened the drawer and tugged on the retractable gurney. Hannah was intense as she stepped forward to draw back the sheet. Chris was professional as he stoically looked over the remains.

What was left of the body wasn't only vaguely human. The first thought that entered my head was that the body was too short. Of course, there was a reason for that. Everything below the chest had been eaten.

A body left in water loses color, bloats and other gross things that I don't want to discuss. Shayne Rivers suffered from every horrendous thing water could do to a body ... and perhaps ten that I never considered.

"Oh, wow."

"If you're going to throw up, head to the bathroom now," Jack growled. He remained close to me instead of with the body, but I had a feeling that was because he was convinced I would screw things up and embarrass him.

"I'm not going to throw up." I squared my shoulders and took a deliberate step forward. "I can handle this. You don't have to worry about me."

"I can't seem to stop myself from worrying about you."

The statement wasn't a compliment, and yet it warmed me. "Thank you."

Jack merely shook his head, although a small smile played at the corners of his lips. "You're welcome. Now ... shh."

I was happy to let the others do the talking as I focused on the body ... and calmed the nerves that threatened to overwhelm me. I sucked in a series of relaxing breaths as I willed myself to keep from losing it.

"How long do you think she was in the water?" Chris asked as Hannah poked her gloved fingers into the woman's body. I had no idea what she was looking for but she seemed to have a basic idea what she was dealing with.

"We're looking at between midnight and two," Peabody replied. "I'm leaning toward two."

"That would be about the time the bars close down," Jack noted.

"Do you think that has something to do with this?" Chris asked, intrigued.

"Probably not the way you think," Jack hedged. "It's just ... there's a tiki bar on the beach. That's where I picked up Charlie. You can see the pier from the bar. It would've been dark, so visibility wouldn't have been great, but it was still a pretty big chance to take."

"What was a big chance to take?" Peabody asked.

"Killing her," Jack replied without hesitation. "I'm assuming she was murdered on land and then dumped in the water to cover it up."

Peabody scrubbed his cheek. "I guess that's possible. We haven't found proof that's what happened, though."

"What was the cause of death?"

Peabody shrugged and pointed toward the body. "Pinpointing a cause of death won't be easy. Most of her major organs are gone. Even those that you might think are there — like the heart — didn't survive what happened to her body."

"What can you say with any certainty?" Chris asked.

"She was definitely gnawed on by sharks," Hannah answered for Peabody, straightening. "There are bite marks here and here." She indicated the lower part of the body, the skin I was desperate to keep from seeing. "What type of shark is beyond my expertise. There's also no way of knowing if she was dead when she hit the water or if that came after."

Jack made a disgusted sound in the back of his throat. "You're going to keep thinking this was a Megalodon, aren't you?"

I tuned out Chris's answer and tentatively stepped forward, the courage I'd been trying to gather finally taking shape. It helped to think of Shayne Rivers as a prop, something that I was looking at through the lens of a camera, like being trapped in a movie. When I tried to think of her as a person, the pain I was convinced she must have felt as she was being ripped apart in the water became almost too much to bear.

"What are you doing?" Jack hissed, moving to cross to the other side of the metal table to stop me from getting up close and personal. "Charlie ... don't!"

It was already too late. I couldn't stop myself. I raised my bare hand and drew the corner of the sheet that was obstructing my view.

Things happened quickly after that.

Jack yelled, as was his way.

Chris barked at both of us to be quiet even though I hadn't said a word.

Hannah warned that we shouldn't jostle the body because it wouldn't hold together long if we damaged it.

Peabody gave me a look that reminded me of a middle school teacher I loathed. He always thought I was giggling because I liked being disruptive. In truth, I was simply nervous all the time and giggling was my way of coping.

As for me, I only wanted one thing. To stay on my feet as the noises I heard in my head assailed my senses and threatened to bring me to my knees.

"Charlie!"

I heard screaming ... and swearing ... and yelling. There were angry voices, accusations and a loud noise I couldn't identify. It sounded like the chomping of giant shark jaws. Of course, that could've been my imagination playing havoc with my low level of practicality.

My mind went black, my knees weak, and I was already halfway to the floor when I realized I was about to lose consciousness. Somehow Jack managed to catch me before I hit, probably those superior reflexes of his, and my head miraculously didn't smack against the hard cement floor.

The last thing I remembered was looking into his freaked eyes as he clutched me against him.

Then things went quiet in the real world and the screaming ramped up in the visions I could no longer stop careening through my head.

It was terrible ... and every circuit I had overloaded.

FIVE

I didn't lose consciousness, which was a blessing.

The noises in my head simply overwhelmed me. It was one image after the other, a cascade of shadows and raised voices. I couldn't make out the words – they were muffled – and the faces were too rounded to be recognizable. Then there was running and darkness and the sound of water on the shore. The one thing I managed to pick out of the din was terror, and I was fairly certain Shayne Rivers was the one screaming as the terror turned to despair … and ultimately death.

Jack freaked out. He was barking orders, demanding I look at him, and when someone waved a plastic container full of foul-smelling liquid under my nose I jolted back to reality.

"I'm going to kill you," Jack announced when I finally focused on him. "I told you this was a bad idea."

He assumed I lost it because of the body. In his defense, that was a definite possibility. That wasn't what took me down, though.

"I'm okay," I said automatically, recovering. "I ... I'm fine. It was a momentary thing."

"I told you not to come," he hissed.

Hannah, who was much more pragmatic and sympathetic, shot

Jack a warning look as she knelt in front of me. "It's okay." Her smile was serene. "Seeing a body in this condition has brought three-hundred-pound men to their knees. There's nothing to be ashamed about. People pass out when looking at bodies all the time."

I furrowed my brow. "Have you passed out?"

"No. But I'm different. You didn't attend medical school, take classes on autopsies or even flip through random medical journals."

Because those classes – and, yes, the periodicals, too – sounded gross. "I'm fine. I just started thinking about what it must have been like to be eaten alive and my head went a little ... woohoo."

That was a ridiculous lie. That wasn't what I saw in my head. Sadly, the images I did see were fleeting. It was the noises that brought me down, the anger and resentment, the overpowering terror. Ultimately it was the fear that caused my head to implode. "I'm fine."

I moved to sit up, but Jack kept a firm grip on me. "Don't even think about it." He inclined his chin toward Peabody. "Do you have some water? I want to make sure she's solid before I let her up."

"Of course." Peabody's expression was sympathetic when he returned with a bottle of water seconds later. "You scared ten years off me, young lady. I'm not used to the living going rigid in my laboratory."

That was a weird thing to say. "Well ... at least you'll have a story to tell at your holiday parties this year," I offered, tilting my head up so I could accept the water Jack insisted on pouring down my throat. I drank half the bottle before speaking again. "So ... we're definitely thinking it was a big shark, right?"

Jack scowled. "No."

"Yes," Chris countered, bobbing his head. "It was definitely a big shark. We're in the right place. This is going to be a monumental discovery, Charlie."

He was always glad when I joined his side in an argument, so I flashed him an enthusiastic thumbs-up. "Awesome."

"It's definitely going to be awesome."

. . .

JACK WAS LIKE A MOTHER hen during the drive back to the hotel. Chris and Hannah took the back seat so they could stare soulfully into each other's eyes and whisper things they thought we couldn't hear. Unfortunately for them, Chris's voice carried even when he thought he was being quiet, so their plans for a moonlit beach stroll were essentially public knowledge.

Jack helped me from the rental when we hit the parking lot, shaking his head when Hannah and Chris scurried away. He looked frustrated, angry even, and I braced myself for a blow-up. Instead, when he was certain we were alone, he ran his hand over the back of my head and stared into my eyes.

"Are you sure you're okay?"

The change in his demeanor took me by surprise. "You're not going to yell?"

"Oh, I'm going to yell. I want to make sure you're okay first. You dropped fast, Charlie. Like ... out of nowhere. I didn't know what was happening. One second you were standing there and the next you were falling. I think my heart stopped."

It was a stirring admission. "I'm okay."

"Yeah?"

"Yeah."

"Great." He gave me a quick kiss that was soft rather than sexy. "I'm glad you're okay."

I relaxed. "Me, too. That body was something, right? Have you ever seen anything like that?"

"No, and I didn't want you to see it because I knew it would be too much." His voice took on an edge. "Why don't you ever listen to me?"

"Oh. This is the part where you're going to yell?"

"Yes."

"Can we do that inside? I want another green tea."

"Fine." Jack was resigned as he ran his hand over my hair to smooth it. "We're back to being on the clock. You scared the crap out of me."

"I'll try not to do that again."

"That would be a nice change of pace."

.   .   .

ONCE JACK WAS CONVINCED I wasn't about to pass out, he left me to my own devices in the lobby and disappeared to track down Bernard. Apparently he was trying to get a feel for the currents in the Gulf — which I thought was a waste of time because a Megalodon was strong enough to ignore currents — but he clearly needed a little space to collect himself.

I planted myself at one of the tables in the lobby and watched the writers. The conference seemed to be set up in such a manner that various classes were going on at the same time. When the classes were in session, only a handful of writers remained in the lobby. Most seemed excited to attend the classes, but it was the ones who remained at the tables while the others were learning that truly intrigued me.

"Are you an author?"

I shifted to study the woman who took the chair to my right. She sat without invitation, a bottle of water clutched in her hand, and seemed legitimately interested in my answer.

"No, I'm here with a different group," I replied after a beat.

"I thought the hotel was full of mostly writers. That's odd."

"We're staying in one of the condos on the property. We're here because of the death."

"Oh, Shayne." The woman made a clicking sound with her tongue. "That is some awful business. I can't tell you how stunned I was to hear about all of that this afternoon. Are you with the police?"

"Not exactly." I was never sure how to describe our group to strangers. "We're looking into the possibility that marine life was involved in the death." I chose my words carefully. "It's a possibility and we need to be sure."

"Of course. I'm Leslie Downs, by the way. I write thrillers and mysteries."

The declaration took me off guard until I realized other authors would be interested in that information. She was simply speeding along the "get to know you" process. "Charlie Rhodes." I extended my hand. "Have you been an author long?"

"Well, I've been writing a long time," she said. "I went the whole traditional route first. You know, querying an agent and trying to find a publisher. I did that for twenty years before I realized it was never going to happen for me if I kept trying to force things."

The woman looked to be in her sixties, which meant she spent a third of her life chasing what turned out to be the unattainable. She also looked to be bucking for a keynote speaking position at an Aqua Net convention, but that was a whole other issue. "So you don't write?" I was confused.

"I'm an indie. I publish the books myself."

"That must be fun." I meant it. "That means you can write what you want without having anyone else dictate to you. If I was a writer, that's how I'd want things to be."

"It has its ups and downs," Leslie hedged. "Some indie authors hit it out of the park and understand exactly what they're doing. Others ... well ... others struggle."

I couldn't help but wonder which category she fell into. It felt invasive to ask. "Would I know any of your books?"

Leslie preened at the question. "I write the Anderson Dawkins books."

That didn't sound right. I recognized the name of the series. In fact, Jack often read them when we were on planes. "I thought a guy named James Sanderson wrote those books."

"Oh, not *those* books." She flashed a tight smile. "My books are a spinoff series."

"How does that work?"

"They're in the same world. We came to an agreement so I could write in his world. I'm not doing it illegally or anything."

The way she said it made me think she probably got accused of something nefarious regularly. "Okay, well ... ."

"We were supposed to write the series together," Leslie explained, launching into a tale I wasn't remotely interested in hearing. "I met him at a writing conference. I paid a lot of money to be there. We hit it off right from the start. Our eyes met across the room and it was as if we recognized each other from a great distance."

Her moony tone made me instantly alert. "I'm not sure I understand. You're involved with James Sanderson? I thought he was married. I only know because I've read the back of his paperbacks. My friend reads them all the time. He seems to like them."

"You should point him toward my books, too."

"I'll do that."

"As for James we're friends not ... you know ... *friends*."

The way she said the second "friends" had me biting back a laugh. "Yes. You're not romantically involved. I get it."

"Exactly. We're not romantic soul mates, but writing soul mates."

That sounded a tad delusional, but she was determined to tell her story so I simply nodded.

"Anyway, we were at this writing retreat," she said. "He set it up so we could learn from him. I told him an idea I had for his characters and he liked it a lot. He suggested we collaborate, that I write a series set in his world."

"Would he get money from that?"

"Of course, like a licensing fee."

"So you essentially pay him to write in his world," I said. "I get it. I don't know that it sounds fun because I think the appeal of writing is making up your own characters, but if you really love his characters it was probably a good idea."

Leslie shot me a withering look. "I can think up my own characters."

"I didn't say you couldn't."

"My world is even better than James's," she stressed. "You have no idea what you're talking about."

"Okay." I held up my hands in capitulation. I didn't start this conversation. She sat down with me. How was I suddenly the bad guy? "Let's talk about something else."

Leslie ignored my suggestion. "We were supposed to have a meeting with his publisher when he suddenly cut off contact. I kept calling and calling ... and then something weird happened that forced him to change his phone number. I had to track down his agent and follow her into a bathroom stall to get her to listen to me. She made the mistake of thinking I was a random kook and was trying to protect him – which I get – but it took me forever to plead my case to her. I knew he had to be worried because he hadn't heard from me."

Wow! Leslie Downs was clearly a stalker. She probably didn't realize it, but she was. "Um ... so ... did you meet with his publishers?"

"No. Apparently they changed their minds about us collaborating. They didn't think it was a good idea. Like they would know a good idea if it bit them on their behinds."

"Uh-huh." I desperately scanned the room for an exit. "That sounds terrible."

"It was. James was so embarrassed he disappeared again. He was mortified and blamed himself, and went into hiding. I kept calling, but he was too upset to return my calls."

I very much doubted that was why he didn't return her calls. "Well, you obviously got in touch with him again because you're using his characters."

"I am." Leslie brightened considerably. "I found him on a fishing trip. I remembered an interview he once gave. He said he had a fishing cabin he visited in Minnesota for a month every year. July. I wasn't sure if it was the beginning of July or the end of July, so I showed up in mid-June, just to be on the safe side.

"I got a hotel room and watched his cabin," she continued. "I had to pull documents from the clerk's office to find out where the property was located. You should've seen his face when he arrived and realized I was already there."

"I can imagine." Holy crap! She was definitely a stalker. The pimento cheese girl was starting to look sane compared to this lady. "Did he call the cops?"

She knit her eyebrows. "Why would he call the cops?"

"I don't know. It was just a question." I didn't want to upset a woman with stalker tendencies, so I pretended I was confused. "He allowed you to use his characters, right? That means he's a good guy."

"He is," Leslie agreed. "He finally agreed to allow me to use his characters, and once the restraining order was processed and I agreed not to return to his fishing cabin, we signed off on everything and now I'm allowed to publish two books a year in a spinoff series."

"And how is that going for you?" *Please say good. Please say good.*

"Not great." Leslie's scowl returned. "There's a group of trolls out there who want to take me down. They're jealous that James and I are so close. They don't understand that I'm really the superior writer and he sees that so he's helping me attain the heights I deserve. I get a lot of bad reviews and complaints from his readers because they're jealous he chose me."

That didn't make much sense. Jealousy was one of those things that I believed should've died out as soon as a kid hit thirteen. It was such a middle-school word. "Well, you can't do anything about jealous people. Haters gonna hate, right?"

Leslie nodded. "Definitely."

I took advantage of the momentary lull. "I should probably be going. I have a death to investigate, after all."

"Not until I grab a book for your friend. I want you to give it to him. He'll definitely love my books if he likes the others. Mine are better."

"Oh, well ... ." I tried to picture Jack's face when I gave him the book. It would be easier to deal with than her face if I told her no. "I would love a copy of one of your books."

Leslie beamed. "I'll be right back."

I considered running when she scampered away but I'd already told her we were staying in condos on the property. I worried she would track me down and turn thriller book killer crazy if I didn't give her the adulation she so desperately needed, so I opted to wait.

That turned out to be a mistake because the pimento cheese woman found me seconds later. "I see you met Leslie," she said, shining an apple against her cat T-shirt. "She's a real nut job."

If it wasn't for the pimento cheese thing, I'd really like Sarah Hilton, I decided. She had an amiable personality and an infectious smile. The cheese thing was definitely weird.

"She's making me wait for a copy of one of her books," I explained.

"She seems determined to make sure I don't leave without it. I figure it's best to wait for her to come back."

"Yeah. You don't want her tracking you down. Just ask James Sanderson."

"She mentioned something about that." I plowed ahead with the obvious question. "So ... he's still alive, right?"

Sarah barked out a laugh. "He is. He allowed her to write in his world if she agreed to sign a voluntary restraining order and keep at least two-hundred feet from him. That story was the talk of the conference last year."

"At least she hasn't killed him."

"No, not him. I've thought maybe she killed Shayne Rivers, but that's probably too easy of an answer."

My interest was officially piqued. "Why would she kill Shayne Rivers?"

"You'll find the author community is a very ... weird ... group."

That wasn't really an answer. "But why would she want to kill Shayne?"

"Everybody wanted to kill Shayne," Sarah volunteered. "She was essentially the most disliked woman in the literary world. I mean ... people hated her. They doxxed her online and threw Facebook parties simply to attack her."

I didn't know what to make of that. "Facebook parties to attack her?"

"Totally lame, but funny. Basically a big insult-fest. I got a lot of ideas for future series from it."

"I see. Why did Leslie hate Shayne?"

"Shayne was trying to pursue a partnership with James Sanderson, similar to the one Leslie has," Sarah explained. "The thing is, if Shayne managed to sign a contract, it was pretty obvious Sanderson would back those new books and not throw any publicity in Leslie's direction."

"Was he throwing publicity toward her at all?"

"No, but it wouldn't be as obvious if she was the only one. If there were two of them and one was getting all the love ... ."

I picked up quickly on what she was saying. "So Shayne Rivers was essentially threatening to take away Leslie Downs's livelihood."

"In a nutshell."

That sounded like soap opera stuff, and not in a good way. "Huh."

"Yeah, we're a very complicated and interesting group." Sarah rested her elbows on the table and leaned forward. "I wasn't kidding about the pimento cheese. You need to try it. Your life will never be complete if you don't."

Oh, geez. Talk about complicated.

"I'll pass for now. Thank you for the offer, though. As for the gossip … I greatly appreciate that. I now have a place to start looking."

SIX

*J*ack found me at the coffee bar an hour later. He looked more relaxed than when I'd last seen him, although his eyes were keen as they scanned the lobby. I could almost see his sigh of relief in the way his shoulders relaxed when our gazes finally caught, and he immediately set out in my direction.

"I wasn't sure you were still here," he said as he joined me at the bar. "I was about to text you."

"It's been an interesting afternoon." I told him about my run-in with Leslie Downs, gifting him with the book she gave me upon her return. "You'd better read that or she'll hunt me down."

Jack flipped over the paperback and shrugged. "I'll give it a try. I don't see what it could hurt." He turned serious. "The other stuff, though, how did you find that out?"

"You'd be surprised what these authors are willing to volunteer," I replied. "The pimento cheese girl told me most of it, but that chick over there, the one with the curly hair, she told me a few additional things."

"Like?"

"Like Leslie Downs has been kicked out of three different conferences — apparently there's no end to writing conferences held here and abroad — because she's so intense and makes other authors feel uncomfortable."

"Huh." Jack rubbed his chin as the barista approached. "I'll have what she's having." He pointed toward my drink.

"No problem." The barista, who boasted the chest of a stripper and the butt of a Kardashian, offered him a flirty smile. "Are you one of the authors?"

She'd barely noticed I was alive, let alone a paying customer. Jack was another story. She couldn't fall over herself fast enough to wait on him.

"I am not." Jack's return smile was pleasant but not open. "We're here investigating the death."

"Oh, right." The woman, whose nametag read "Andi," grew more interested by the second. "I heard a special group came in for that. You're staying in the condos, right?"

"We are."

"Once your co-worker is down for the night, you should head to the tiki bar. It's right around the corner."

I hated the way she referred to me as a "co-worker." Of course, I technically was. However, I was much more than that. She didn't know that, though. Jack and I could have passions on top of passions for all she knew. "Thanks for the tip," I said dryly.

She ignored me and remained focused on Jack. "I'll get your iced tea."

"Thank you." Jack waited until she was at the other end of the counter to focus on me. "There's no reason to get riled. I won't go to the tiki bar without you."

"I don't care about that." Mostly. "It's just ... have you ever noticed the way women look at you?"

His smirk told me he had. "No. How was she looking at me?"

"Like you were the last pimento spread on the shelf and she had all the crackers."

Jack barked out a laugh. "Oh, geez. That was funny."

It didn't feel funny to me. "Women throw themselves at you all the time, don't they? I mean ... I've seen it. I never really gave it much thought. You're like a Jonas brother."

Jack's smile slipped. "What's a Jonas brother?"

"Hot boy-band dudes."

"Take that back."

I enjoyed the way his eyes darkened. "No. You're totally like a Jonas brother."

"And this conversation is done." He squared his shoulders and straightened his back. "So, I was thinking, Chris is all caught up doing research with Hannah on Megalodon migratory patterns. How anyone could possibly know anything about that since they've been extinct for millions of years is beyond me, but it doesn't matter. With them caught up with each other and Millie fascinated with the tiki bar, I thought we might be able to slip away for a private dinner."

The suggestion caused my stomach to roll — in a pleasant way — and my cheeks burned. "Really? I thought you wanted us to act like co-workers while at work."

"Dinner is not work. We've worked all day. I've even checked online. There's a seafood place right down the road. It has great reviews. Since it's offsite, we have less chance of running into the others."

I liked the idea. I was still leery. "I'm kind of worried that you're going to shut down if people find out," I admitted after a beat. "I think Millie already knows." I was certain Millie already knew, but I didn't want to freak him out.

"I'm sure she does," Jack agreed, unruffled. "She's good at reading people. She won't say anything. She might torture us, but she won't spread the word."

That was it? That's all he had to say about it? "So, you're okay with that?"

"Eventually people are going to find out. I'm not stupid enough to pretend otherwise. I simply want us to get to know each other first, make sure it's worth pursuing. We might find we don't actually like one another."

From my end, I doubted that was true. "As long as you're okay with it."

"I'm fine with it. I think a private dinner will be good for us. In fact ... ." He trailed off, his eyes going dark as he looked to the other side of the coffee bar.

I followed his gaze, disappointment rolling over me when I realized Laura was staring directly at us. She looked annoyed, as if she hadn't expected to find us together. She also looked determined ... and she wasn't alone.

"That's everybody," I said, trying to tamp down my disappointment. "I don't think they were as caught up with the research and other stuff as you thought."

"Apparently not," Jack muttered.

"There you guys are," Laura announced as she rounded the bar and planted herself as close to Jack as possible without climbing onto his lap. "We've been looking for you. We made reservations at the Italian restaurant here at the resort. We thought we would have dinner as a group and discuss a few things about the investigation."

Jack pursed his lips. For a second I thought he might argue, but we both knew that was a bad idea. "Sounds good," he said finally. "I love Italian food."

THE RESTAURANT WASN'T large, but there was plenty of room for seating. We were directed toward an outdoor table, which was in the shade, and when everyone settled into their seats I found Jack had managed to claim a spot on my left. Unfortunately, Laura was so determined she took the spot on his left.

"So, we've been conducting research on the Gulf," Chris said once the waitress took our orders and delivered our drinks. "I don't think the idea of a large predator being able to survive in these waters is unthinkable."

"I'm almost afraid to encourage you, but why is that?" Jack queried. "A sixty-foot-shark would gather attention. There are oil rig platforms all over the Gulf. People essentially live on them. Someone would've seen something."

"Only if they were looking at the right time."

"But ... ."

"I know you don't believe it's a Megalodon," Chris said quickly. "I'm not sure I do either. We need more proof before I can commit to that line of thinking. I do think we have a large predator in these waters. You saw the body. Heck, Charlie passed out when she saw the body."

Laura snickered, derisive. "You passed out?"

"I didn't pass out. I ... got a little shaky." There was no way I could explain what had really happened. In fact, I was still trying to figure that out myself. It was better to let them think that I was an idiot who couldn't handle a shredded body rather than a psychic who caught a glimpse of the past but was so shaken by what she couldn't make out that she almost fainted like a total girl. "I'm fine now."

"And she learned a valuable lesson," Jack noted. "I told her not to come, but she didn't listen. I bet you'll listen next time, huh?"

That was highly unlikely. "Sure." I averted my gaze and grabbed a breadstick from the basket at the center of the table. "What did you learn about the Gulf that makes you think a Megalodon could be living here?"

"Well, the waters are fairly deep in some places." Chris enjoyed talking about scientific topics, so he embraced the conversation without hesitation. "The average depth of the Gulf is roughly five-thousand feet. There are parts that go as deep as fourteen-thousand feet ... although some people dispute that and say the maximum depth is twelve-thousand. That doesn't matter. What matters is that it's plenty deep for a large predator to hunt and hide in."

"Okay, I know you believe I'm always the naysayer, but I think this must be brought up," Jack said. "If Megalodons somehow managed to survive, they would've been seen by now. By cruise ships ... or oil rig workers ... or submarine pilots. Heck, they're big enough to be sighted from satellites in space. They would've shown up on Google Earth cameras or something."

Instead of arguing, Chris merely sighed. "The Loch Ness Monster has gone years without verifiable proof, but we all know it's real."

"I don't know it's real," Jack countered. "In fact, I think it's something the locals have kept in the news because it draws tourists. The weather isn't great in that area, so a monster makes for a big catch of looky-loos."

"Hopefully we'll get a chance to visit and I'll prove you wrong," Chris said. "The Loch Ness Monster is hardly our concern right now."

"Right," Jack drawled, annoyance obvious. "Megalodons are our biggest concern right now."

"Precisely." Chris nodded, ignoring Jack's tone. "We need to get out on the water before the animal heads back to open sea."

"Let's say I'm willing to concede this was a Megalodon attack — which I'm not," Jack said. "What makes you think it hasn't already disappeared? Why haven't more animals turned up dead? Why aren't the other creatures that live in the Gulf reacting to the presence of a huge predator? Why are we assuming it's one shark instead of multiple sharks? I mean ... there are too many questions."

"There are," Chris agreed. "We'll start answering those questions tomorrow. I've rented a boat."

"Oh, geez." Jack smacked his hand to his forehead. "I can't believe this is happening."

"I'm not sure a boat is a good idea," Millie hedged, drawing everyone's attention to her side of the table. "No boat we could navigate would be big enough to hold off a giant shark." She shot a guilty look toward Jack. "Not that I think it's a Megalodon."

"I can't even ... ." Jack was beside himself.

"I thought about that," Chris admitted. "When I made my calls, the biggest ship I could get was sixty feet. If the shark is sixty feet, that's a little too iffy for my comfort. That's why I placed a call to Uncle Myron. He arranged for a private cutter to take us out. It's a salvage unit with a huge shipping company. It'll be at our disposal the entire day."

I had no idea what to make of that. "What happens if we see the Megalodon?" I asked the obvious question. "It's not as if we can trap it.

We can't kill it because it's a modern marvel. What do we do if we see it?"

"I'm going to pee myself," Laura offered, looking to Jack for a laugh. He ignored her.

"We're going to document it," Chris replied simply. "We'll take photos, maybe find a way to track it. I have some shark experts coming because this is not my area of expertise."

"You can't know everything," Hannah said, patting his hand as he smiled at her adoringly. "I think a day on a ship that size will be educational and enjoyable. That's why I love this job."

"Thank you, Hannah." Chris beamed at her in such a goofy manner I couldn't help being a little charmed. "Just for the record, everyone is expected to be on the ship. No arguing. We leave first thing in the morning."

"I can't wait," Jack muttered, shaking his head. "We're going to spend the day looking for a Megalodon. How could that possibly go wrong?"

HE WAS STILL IN A BAD MOOD when we slipped out of the condo to walk the beach after dark. The air remained humid, almost stifling, but there was a nice breeze as I carried my flip flops and splashed my feet in the water.

"You need to get over it," I said finally, his dark mood bringing me down. "Chris is in charge. He gets to decide what we do with our time."

"Yes, and looking for a Megalodon seems a great way to waste an entire day."

I shrugged as I squinched my toes in the sand. "It could be worse. We'll be on a boat. The Gulf is beautiful. We'll have food and water ... and we'll be able to see dolphins and other animals. It's not the worst thing that's ever happened."

Instead of firing something nasty back, he tilted his head. "You're a glass-half-full person. Occasionally you have a bad day, but most of the time you're an optimist."

"Is that bad?"

"No. Simply an observation. You know I'm a pessimist, right?"

Ah, so that's what was bothering him. "You're not a pessimist."

"I am so."

"You're not." I was firm. "You're a realist with an optimistic streak. Otherwise you never would've bothered to ask me out."

"What makes you say that?"

I shrugged, noncommittal. "I don't know. It's something I feel. I had a crush on you long before you admitted to having feelings for me. I didn't want to admit it because I thought you were kind of a wank, but it was there. I couldn't escape it. The thing is, I thought nothing would happen because you wouldn't allow it. You took me by surprise when you decided to take a chance on moving forward instead of holding back."

Jack's mouth dropped open. "That was ... almost profound."

"I'm more than just the annoying new member of the group."

"You're only annoying fifty percent of the time." He lowered himself to the sand and removed his shoes, taking a moment to rub the soles of his feet. "And even then you're so cute it's hard to find you annoying."

I was glad it was dark because my cheeks burned so hot I knew they were bright red. "That was kind of nice."

"Yeah, well, I'm a kind of nice guy." He flicked his eyes to me, his smile soft. When he suggested we go for a walk to get some time alone, I jumped at the chance. The disastrous dinner left everyone on edge, especially Jack. I wanted him to relax. "Come here." He held out his hand to me.

I took it as I moved closer, laughing as he tugged me down to sit next to him. He slid his arm around my back, making sure he didn't move too fast but anchoring me close, and smiled as he stared out at the rolling ocean.

"It's pretty here, huh?"

I nodded, trying not to focus on the way his arm felt. "I used to dream about living on the ocean."

"And now?"

"I don't know. I kind of like the traveling we do, seeing different places. People say I won't always like that, but it's still new to me."

"I don't mind the travel either," he said. "I like hotel living. That might sound odd, but there's something cool about regular room service and expensive dinners ... especially when the Legacy Foundation is footing the bill."

"Definitely. Dinner was good tonight."

"Yeah. You went a little heavy on the garlic."

I pressed my lips together, mortified.

When he looked at me, I found him smiling. "I guess it's good that I ate a bunch of garlic, too. We'll cancel each other out."

I exhaled heavily and elbowed his side. "You enjoy messing with me far too much."

"You enjoy messing with me, too."

He wasn't wrong. "It's going to be okay, Jack." I felt the need to soothe him. "We're not going to be eaten by a Megalodon tomorrow. We'll be safe on the boat. Don't work yourself up over it."

"I am not worried about being eaten by a Megalodon."

"So ... what are you worried about?"

"I don't know." He tightened his grip on me. "I feel uneasy. Even before you almost splattered your brains all over the medical examiner's floor, I couldn't shake the feeling that something bad was going to happen."

I often had feelings something terrible was going to happen, so I understood. "What do you think is going to happen?"

"I have no idea."

"Maybe you're just worked up because you don't want anyone to find out about us," I suggested. "Maybe you're feeling one thing and think you're feeling something else."

"I guess." He dragged a hand through his hair and smiled at me. "I feel better right now than I have since we got here. I know that's true."

"I'm glad. I feel better, too."

"Yeah, well, I was thinking."

Uh-oh. I hated it when he started sentences with that phrase.

"I was thinking we could spend a few more minutes here, then get some drinks at the tiki bar to eradicate the garlic breath and then take a long walk back to the condo before heading to bed."

That was so not what I was expecting. "Really?"

"Yup."

"Sounds good to me."

"This day is definitely looking up."

SEVEN

*J*ack held my hand until we drew near the tiki bar. He seemed reluctant to release it, but the job came first. I was torn. I liked being alone with him, getting to know him, the way his eyebrows drew together when he laughed. I got giddy and lightheaded occasionally when he leaned close, which was pathetic to admit.

On the flip side, when I got giddy I got giggly, and most people mistook me for a middle-school girl. Jack didn't seem to mind — at least he didn't comment on it — but the last thing I wanted when we were supposed to be learning information about a dead woman was for people to think I was acting like an idiot. I liked to retain the "stop acting like a moron" comments for those who knew me best.

I wasn't sure what to expect at the tiki bar. I visited with Millie during the day and there were a handful of people milling about, having a good time, and day drinking to their hearts' content. Now that the sun had gone down it was an entirely different atmosphere.

"Wow!" My mouth dropped open as I openly gaped. "Just ... wow!"

Jack absently ran his hand over my back as he surveyed the crowd. The beach was full of people, at least fifteen different large tables with gas fires burning at the center of them spread out around the sandy expanse. There were another thirty smaller tables on the pavement, people laughing and drinking as they bent their heads together and talked.

There was a lot of raucous laughter.

There was a lot of swearing.

Oh, and in one corner that was mostly shrouded in the dark, there was a lot of groping.

"What do you think is going on over there?" I asked, my eyes instantly darting to the groping corner.

"Nothing that I want to see," Jack replied, prodding me with his hand toward the bar. "Whatever it is, it's private and not likely to cool my blood."

I wasn't entirely sure what that meant. "Why do you need your blood cooled?"

Jack slid me a sidelong look, his gaze searching. Finally, he merely shook his head. "You don't get your appeal sometimes. It's maddening."

"Wait ... so this is my fault?"

"No one is at fault." He held his hands up in a capitulating manner. "We're here to work. Almost all of these people are wearing the lanyards from the conference, which means they're either writers or married to writers I would guess. Pick a table, I'll get us drinks and we'll start feeling them out."

It was a simple suggestion, but it raised alarm bells in the back of my brain. "Um ... I get goofy when I drink."

His eyes were curious when they latched with mine. "Define goofy."

"I say stupid things."

"Baby, you do that when you're sober."

I scowled. "I say even dumber things when alcohol is involved."

"Do you want to give me an example?"

I certainly didn't. "I'm not dumb enough to answer that while sober."

He barked out a laugh. "I think we'll give it a try anyway. One drink won't hurt you."

He was about to find out exactly how untrue that statement was.

"DID YOU KNOW SHAYNE RIVERS?"

Jack went right to work once he bought drinks and led us to a group of authors sitting around one of the fires. They looked to be having a great time, cackling like maniacs as they told stories and teased one another. I was uncomfortable interrupting their conversations and inviting myself to the party, but Jack didn't have that problem.

"Sorry to interrupt, but everywhere else is full," Jack said as he gestured for me to sit on the padded bench. "Just keep talking as if we're not here ... although, if you want to answer my questions that would be great, too."

"How could we pretend you're not here?" one of the women purred, her eyes moving over Jack as if he were a porterhouse steak and she'd been stuck with butt shanks for most of her life. "Who are you? Are you with one of the authors?"

"No." Jack shook his head. "We were called in to investigate the death of Shayne Rivers."

"Really?" The woman arched an eyebrow, her interest clearly piqued. "Are you with the police?"

"We're with a private group," Jack replied, seemingly calm and at ease. "Because sharks were involved, they needed experts. That's why they called us."

"And are you an expert on sharks?" This time the speaker was someone else, a relaxed-looking blonde to my right who shared a bench with a brunette. They'd been cackling like witches a second before, clearly enjoying themselves, but now the blonde was completely focused on us. Her name tag read "Lily Harper Hart," and that name sparked something in my head, although three sips of my drink were already futzing things up.

"I'm not an expert on sharks," Jack replied. "I'm head of security. The rest of the group is handling the shark business."

"So that means her?" Lily's eyes shifted to me. "Are you an expert on sharks?"

I took another sip of the extremely strong rum runner to buy time. "Um ... ."

"She's new," Jack answered for me. She's basically an intern."

The statement stung. "I'm not an intern," I grumbled, offended.

"Fine. You're not an intern," Jack conceded. "You're new, though. She's still learning the ropes."

"Is that why you have her at the tiki bar, just the two of you?" Lily's blue eyes were full of intrigue, as if she knew something the others didn't and wanted confirmation.

"We're just not ready to call it a night," Jack replied smoothly, his charm on full display as he winked at her. "We thought we would have a drink or two to settle our nerves. We flew all day. It's hard for me to sleep on travel days."

Lily didn't look convinced. "Well then, by all means." She gestured toward the small group. "Have some drinks and get to know everyone. I think it will be a marvelous exercise for your young intern."

"Thanks." Tension radiated off Jack's body, but he kept his smile in place. "I appreciate that. So ... what do you all write?"

IN TRUTH, MEETING THE AUTHORS was fascinating. I managed to slow my drinking to the point I took only a sip every five minutes or so and listened with slack-jawed excitement as Lily introduced us to everyone in her group.

There was Carter Reagan Yates, a prepper writer from Michigan who fathered a boatload of kids and built hobbit holes in his backyard in case of a zombie apocalypse. No joke. He was prepared for when the zombies arrived and had no intention of being munched on.

"I'm completely ready for the end of the world," he said with a straight face as he clutched what I could only describe as an adult sippy cup in his hand. "I've got enough rations put away to get us through five years of trouble. After that, I have the seeds and machinery necessary to start humanity over again ... right in my backyard."

"In Michigan?" I was dumbfounded. He seemed like a nice enough guy — the adult sippy cup notwithstanding — but the idea that he built hobbit holes in the hills behind his house freaked me out. And that was before he told me he'd stored more than one-hundred guns in those holes as well. "I've been to Michigan twice in the last few months."

It was a lame thing to say, but I couldn't think of anything else to ease the moment.

"Michigan is awesome," Carter agreed. His hair was long on the top and he had a beard straight out of *Duck Dynasty* reruns. If I hadn't already talked to him I would've assumed he was a serial killer before he even opened his mouth. "Michigan is one of the few places people will survive after the end of the world. Do you want to know why?"

"Because you're in Michigan," I answered perfunctorily.

"No, because of the Great Lakes ... although that was a very good answer."

"Thank you." I waited until Carter lost interest in talking to me before asking Jack the obvious question. "What's prepper fiction?"

"It's kind of like post-apocalyptic stuff," Jack replied, keeping his voice low. His thigh was stuck to mine because the bench we shared was narrow. He didn't seem to mind, which made me even giddier than before. "You know ... zombies, the grid fails, nuclear attack, etc. Only a small portion of the population survives and they're tasked with rebuilding the world."

Hmm. "Like *The Walking Dead*?"

"Basically."

"And *Revolution*."

Jack made a face. "Except most authors don't make their heroes and villains fight with swords."

"Okay. I get it. He has an adult sippy cup. That can't be normal, can it?"

Jack laughed so hard I had to smack his back to clear his airways. "That's not an adult sippy cup."

"It has a straw and a lid."

"It's just a cup," Jack explained. "They offer drink deals with the cup. It's more expensive to fill the first time, but saves money on refills."

"Oh." That actually made sense. "You're basically saying the guy waiting for the end of the world likes to drink."

"Pretty much."

THE NEXT AUTHOR OF note was Priscilla Jennings. She looked to be in her late fifties or early sixties, with short-cropped brown hair that resulted in extremely tight curls, reminding me of bad eighties perms I saw in various movies while flipping through channels on the weekends.

She talked in full sentences, kept her back ramrod straight, and said a lot of things I didn't understand.

"Hooky," she barked. "You have to write hooky if you expect to survive in this business."

I had no idea what that meant, but she was dead serious.

"What's hooky?" I asked Lily, leaning closer.

Lily smirked as her eyes shifted across the table. There was something about her I liked — she was snarky to a fault and said whatever came to her mind, which I could relate to — and I'd taken to asking her questions about the others in the group whenever I needed answers.

"That's her one-word mantra," Lily explained. "She just keeps saying it and people assume she knows something because she refuses to say anything else. She makes decent money and the assumption is that she knows her stuff, but she honestly doesn't know anything."

That was interesting. Lily didn't like her. She didn't come right out and say it, but it was clear she preferred avoiding conversation regarding Priscilla and her "hooky" prose. "Did she have a relationship with Shayne Rivers?"

Lily tilted her head to the side, considering. "Is that why you're here? To see if any of us had motive to kill Shayne? If so, you're in the right place. Pretty much everyone here hated her."

"Really? Why?"

Lily opened her mouth to answer and then clearly thought better of it. "It's a lot of drama, stuff that you won't understand and probably isn't important. I doubt it's worth killing over."

"She was killed by sharks." I was almost positive that was true. Jack's niggling voice that Megalodons were extinct occasionally filled me with doubt, though. "I'm simply curious."

Lily heaved out a sigh. "Okay, here's the thing: Authors are theatrical. We like our drama. It goes along with being creative. We can't seem to help ourselves. Shayne was at the center of a lot of that drama."

"How?"

"Well, at first she was simply an annoying woman who wrote UF."

"What's UF?"

"Urban fantasy."

"And that is?"

"Magical people with swords. They're usually running around a city. That's different from what I write, which is magical cozy mysteries, because my characters usually don't have swords, have sex off screen and hang out in small towns. There are rules for every genre you write. If you don't follow the rules, you don't sell."

"Huh." I found all this fascinating. "So Shayne wrote urban fantasy," I prodded.

"Right." Lily nodded as she returned to her story. "The author community seems big at times, but it's not. You would be surprised how many people write one book and think they're going to hit it rich and live like kings and queens off that one book for the rest of their lives."

"Not so, huh?"

"Nope. The key is regular releases. If you want to do this for a living, you must have regular releases. The problem is, not everyone can write fast enough to deliver them. I'm lucky and can remain focused, so I do okay. It takes others much longer to write a book, and they're the ones struggling."

I racked my brain to think of authors I read. "Most authors publish a few books a year, right?"

"It depends. Some can put out more than that. Those are the lucky people. A lot of authors try to say that you can only write two books a year because to do otherwise means you're producing substandard work. I don't find that true, but I overlap everything. A lot of people don't do that ... and that's why they need day jobs. No wonder they can only write two books a year if they have day jobs, right?"

"Uh-huh." I was starting to glaze over. "Did Shayne have trouble writing more than two books a year?"

"She did," Lily confirmed. "She had moderate success with her first series, some young adult paranormal crap that combined urban fiction with romance. It had a limited audience because her readers were destined to grow out of it, but she didn't look that far ahead to see what was happening.

"She invited several people to be co-writers," she continued. "Basically, that means she put together the outline and the other writers did all the work of penning the story. They got paid fifty percent royalties — and so did she — and got their names out there. She retained ownership of the property."

"That sounds like a good deal for her," I noted.

"It was," Lily agreed. "She made money without doing much of the work. That freed her up to do author services."

"Which are?"

"It's hard to explain." Lily shifted on her chair. "She offered list-building services — we're talking mailing lists — and advertising through her mailing list. She taught people how to make runs for lists, like the New York Times and USA Today. It started out pretty much above board ... and then she started skirting ethical lines."

"Really? Did she steal from people?"

"I guess that depends on who you ask," Lily replied, uncomfortable. "There were a lot of accusations being flung. I tried to stay out of that. I only grew interested in the situation when the trademark fiasco happened."

"What was the trademark fiasco?" Jack asked, sliding closer to me. It was only then that I realized he was listening ... and he appeared fascinated.

"She tried to trademark the word lusty."

"Why lusty?" I asked, confused. "Are the magical creatures with the swords lusty?" I realized what I said too late to take it back. "Wait ... that might've come out wrong."

Lily chuckled, genuinely amused. "Most authors write more than one thing. Shayne also wrote romance under the name Farrah Serendipity — and before you say anything, it was definitely a stupid name — and she created the Lustrous Brothers. They had lusty sex.

"Instead of trademarking Lustrous Brothers, she went after lusty and managed to secure a trademark," she continued. "That infuriated everyone because that wasn't the name of the series and she was sending nasty letters to others to get them to stop using the word. It turned into a whole big thing.

"There were lusty lumberjacks ... and lusty lab technicians ... and lusty male librarians who wanted to help you read porn," she said. "It took over the writing community for months."

"So what happened?" Jack asked.

Lily shrugged. "While all the mean stuff was going on over the internet — and it was mean and scary — a woman took Shayne to court and fought the trademark," Lily replied. "The case was eventually thrown out and she lost, but she did a lot of damage before then."

"What kind of damage?"

"You have to understand, this goes back to the authors being drama queens," she hedged. "She made a video that was three hours long stating her case. People mocked the video, then there was a Twitter campaign ... and online Facebook parties to bash her ... and then she wrote an open letter and referred to herself in the third person. It was basically a series of ridiculous stuff that had real-world consequences."

"And this was on top of the things she was doing with the mailing lists and stuff, right?" I pressed.

"That stuff ended up in court, too," Lily explained. "People sued her for stealing from them and not delivering on her promises. That got ugly."

There was so much ugliness in the story I couldn't keep up. "So ... what's the bottom line?"

"The bottom line is, if you're looking for someone who wanted to kill Shayne Rivers, you need look no further than this beach," she answered, gesturing to the open area around us. "Almost everyone here has had a run-in with her. Almost everyone here hates her. She had only a small group of friends, and everyone hates them as much as they hate her."

"Is the hate warranted?" Jack asked.

Lily shrugged. "It depends on who you ask. There's a lot of black hat stuff going on in the publishing world right now. I'm not sure that any side is completely without guilt. I know I said I a few horrible things to Shayne. And, before you ask, I'm not sorry. I think she was a certifiable nut and definitely a narcissist. And, when I say 'narcissist,' I mean she was diagnosable."

"I get what you're saying." Jack rubbed his chin and glanced around at the other authors, who were seemingly relaxed and having a good time. "I don't suppose you could give us a rundown on the people who hated her?"

"I could, but that would take all night."

"Just give us the highlights."

Lily let loose a sigh. "Okay, but you're going to wish you hadn't asked."

I was starting to believe she was right.

EIGHT

*I*n the end, the cadre of authors Lily introduced us to was seemingly never-ending.

There was Clark Savage, a militant prepper writer who wore a shirt that read "Due to price increases on ammo, do not expect a warning shot." He was in the make-out corner, a woman with pants so tight you could see absolutely everything south of the border as if someone had drawn the details there was plastered against him. She didn't wear a lanyard, and Lily swore up and down she was a prostitute. I wasn't so sure, but Jack refused to let me wander over to the darkened area close to the bushes to ask questions.

Then there was J.D. Wells, a science fiction and fantasy writer who seemed a little full of himself. His response when Lily introduced us was to say, "Now you can tell your friends you've met me and impress them." He wasn't overtly mean, but he was egotistical. His poor wife sat on the bench next to him, knitting in the dark — no joke — and merely nodded whenever he said something he thought was genius.

There was a JAFF writer, Abigail James, who talked numbers so fast that I worried I was trapped in a nightmare. Math was never my favorite subject. And, after the third time asking, she explained JAFF was Jane Austen fan fiction. I had no idea that was a thing, but she seemed to know her stuff. When she offered a book, I politely declined. I liked my fiction teeming with witches and murder mysteries. Endless streams of corsets and prideful men didn't exactly blow up my skirt.

There were quite a few more faces and names, but they all blurred. Finally, close to midnight, Jack insisted we had to retire because we had an early morning. Lily waved us off and returned to her drinking, leaving Jack and me to walk back to the condominium in relative silence.

"That was interesting," I said as we moved toward the front door. "I don't know that I'll be able to remember all those names."

"You're not the only one." Jack slowed his pace and dragged a hand through his hair. "The one thing we've learned is that Shayne Rivers had a lot of enemies. I mean ... a lot. I'm going to try to track down that video everyone was talking about, the one where she lost her mind on YouTube. That might give us some ideas."

"You think she was murdered and not eaten by a huge shark."

"I think that she might've been injured and thrown in the water and sharks finished her off," Jack clarified. "Even if she was dead when she hit the water, the culprit might've assumed the sharks would do all the dirty work and leave nothing behind."

That was an interesting hunch. "So ... what do we do?"

He shrugged. "Tomorrow morning we head out on a boat and look for a Megalodon. After that, we research these writers to see if we can come up with a viable suspect."

"I think that's easier said than done. Most of them are operating under pen names."

"I hadn't considered that."

"Some of them, like the creepy gun guy, are using variations of their real names. He kept his first name and changed the last. The guy with the adult sippy cup used his real name."

"Yes, well ... ." Jack trailed off as he ran his hands up and down my arms. "We'll figure it out." When he turned his face to me his eyes were lit with romance. "So ... I did enjoy the conversation about lusty lumberjacks."

I chuckled, genuinely amused. "Are you going to be a lusty security chief?"

"Not tonight." He was rueful. "I'll probably give you another kiss, though."

"Are you sure that's a good idea?"

"I think I've had just enough to drink that my inhibitions are compromised."

"Oh, darn."

He grinned. "Oh, darn, indeed." He leaned down and offered me a lingering kiss. It was sweet, simple and without pressure. It was a simple goodnight kiss, even though we were going to sleep in the same condominium and spend the better portion of the next day acting as co-workers and nothing more. "That wasn't so bad," he said when we separated.

My cheeks were on fire and I had to resist fanning myself. "Not bad at all," I agreed. "I ... um ... ."

"Oh, you're speechless." Jack was delighted. "That's kind of cute. At least now I know how to get you to shut your mouth."

"I am not speechless."

"Whatever." He grabbed my hand and gave it a squeeze as he dragged me toward the condo. "We need to get some sleep. The boat ride is going to take up the better part of our day. You don't get seasick, do you?"

"I don't think so."

Jack pulled up short. "You've never been on a boat?"

"No."

"Geez. I hope you don't get motion sickness. That'll make everything even worse, which is hard to believe since we're going to be looking for a Megalodon."

"I'm sure I'll be fine." I meant it. "How bad could it be?"

Jack made a face. "You might not want to ask that." He opened the condo door and waited for me to enter first. My attention drifted to the neighboring condo, and I was almost certain I saw the curtains shift before falling still. "Come on," he prodded, dragging my attention away from the window. "We need some sleep."

"I'm coming."

He gave me another kiss, this one quick as I crossed the threshold.

"Sweet dreams," he whispered, causing me to scowl.

I was certain my dreams would be anything but sweet.

IT SOUNDS AS IF YOU guys met quite the crowd last night," Millie said, a doughnut in her hand as she relaxed on the cutter as we headed out to sea the next morning. She didn't look worried in the least that we would cross paths with a giant shark. "I'm sorry I missed it."

The only thing I was sorry about was that she snored like an industrial saw and I'd managed only about an hour of sleep the previous night. When you coupled that with the two drinks I'd had at the tiki bar — and Jack's rather impressive kisses — my stomach refused to settle. When Bernard offered me a doughnut I quickly waved him off. "I'm good. Thank you."

Jack, who sat next to Chris a few seats down the row, cocked an eyebrow. "Are you sick?"

There was no way I was copping to that. "I'm fine."

"You heard her, Jack," Laura drawled from the spot to his right. "She's fine. She's a big girl — even bigger than we all thought — and she can take care of herself."

Jack slid her an annoyed look. "I didn't say she couldn't take care of herself."

"Then why are you so worried?"

It was a pointed question and I couldn't help thinking back to the curtain I was convinced I saw move as we headed into the condominium the previous evening. I'd managed to convince myself I imagined it, but I wasn't entirely sure that was true.

"Tell us about the authors," Millie suggested, lobbing a quelling look in Laura's direction before focusing on me. "Did anyone dislike Shayne Rivers?"

"Everyone hated her." I related what Lily had told me, hoping I didn't leave anything out, and when I was done, Millie was as confused as I was.

"That is ... weird," she said finally. "I had no idea authors were such dramatic souls."

"I learned a lot about authors last night."

"We learned more than I think either of us needed to know," Jack corrected. "There were things I learned that I can never forget ... like lusty lumberjacks."

"They're for people who love wood," I teased. "Lusty lumberjacks love wood. Get it?"

Millie giggled, as I intended. Jack merely rolled his eyes.

"Yes, we learned all about trademarks ... and predatory newsletter providers ... and Jane Austen fan fiction." He made a face. "I didn't even know Jane Austen fan fiction was a thing."

"I love Jane Austen fan fiction," Laura enthused, her eyes lighting. "There's something romantic about the idea of being dirt poor and having all your dreams come true because you stumble across the right man."

"You mean have all your dreams come true by moving into a mansion, right?" Millie challenged.

"Who doesn't want to live in a mansion?" Laura snapped.

I raised my hand. "I would rather live in one of those log cabins by the river," I offered. "I mean ... I don't want it to be tiny or anything. Nothing too big, though. Vaulted ceilings, a dock on the river so I can sit out there at night and watch the water. A place for bonfires. I think that sounds amazing."

"And I think that sounds like something losers would do," Laura fired back.

"I've always wanted to live on a river, too," Jack admitted, catching my eye. "I like the idea of quiet."

"Cities are better," Laura persisted. "You either need a big penthouse that takes the top floor of an entire building or a huge mansion. If I ever get the mansion, I want a driver so I don't have to deal with New York City traffic on my own."

I wrinkled my nose. "Why would you want to live in New York City?"

"It's the best place in the world."

72

I could think of better places, but I was a country girl at heart. "If you say so." I was determined to steer the conversation in a more productive direction. "As for the authors, they're simply too different to get a handle on. I mean ... the obvious suspects would be the two prepper guys because they have access to weapons and talked about being willing to kill to ensure their survival in a post-apocalyptic world, but that seems kind of prejudicial so I'm trying to refrain from rushing to judgment."

Jack's lips curved as he briefly shut his eyes and collected himself. "I was interested in the guy who has his own van, the one with his books advertised on a very colorful wrap. He showed us photos, so I know it's true."

"Yeah, I kind of want to see that van in person," I admitted. "Whenever I think of vans I think of pedophiles."

"That is a lovely thought," Jack intoned, shaking his head. "I was merely thinking about the van because it would be big enough to transport a body. Most of these authors flew into town, which means they had shuttle services transport them to the hotel. That guy has his own van, which is convenient."

I thought back to the guy in question. "He was full of himself," I said after a bit. "He wore a hat that said, 'I'm kind of a big deal,' and his wife sat in the dark knitting for hours."

Hannah, who had been looking at maps of the Gulf, finally joined the conversation. "She was knitting at a bar?"

"It wasn't a normal bar," Jack explained. "It was a tiki bar on the beach."

Hannah's smooth forehead wrinkled. "I don't think that makes it better. Why would she be knitting? Even I'm not uncomfortable enough in crowds to knit."

Hmm. That was an interesting statement. "You think she was knitting because she doesn't like crowds?"

Hannah shrugged. "I don't know. Was she a writer?"

"She wasn't wearing a lanyard."

"That means she was simply there with her husband," she pointed out. "She doesn't have anything in common with the people her husband is hanging around with. He sounds like a jerk of epic proportions. Maybe the knitting is a way for her to put up a fence in social situations."

I hadn't considered that. "I don't think her husband is evil or anything," I said after a beat. "It seemed more like insecurity to me, like he wanted to be a big deal because he was trying to impress some of the other authors who were legitimately big deals. I don't know ... does that make sense?"

"No," Laura answered automatically.

"Yes." Jack bobbed his head. "I felt that way, too. I didn't get an evil vibe off him or anything. He could simply be a good actor. We met so many people in such a short amount of time that it was hard to get a read on any of them."

"I got a read on the guy who had his tongue down the prostitute's throat," I argued.

"I really want to meet this guy," Millie enthused. "I love a man who isn't afraid to bring a professional to an amateur festival."

I cast her a sidelong look. "He was rubbing her ... you know ... a few feet from where people were sitting around a fire. It was extremely disturbing. Her pants were so tight you could see everything."

"She means *everything*," Jack stressed, causing me to frown.

"How hard were you staring at her?"

Suddenly innocent, he shrugged. "I was listening to your conversation with Lily but didn't want her to think I was butting in so I spent all my time watching the other authors. It was purely professional curiosity."

That was the biggest load of crap I'd ever heard. "Right. Anyway, as for the authors, we really don't know anything about any of them. They could all have joined together to murder Shayne Rivers for all we know."

"So we need information," Millie mused. "I'm kind of looking forward to finding out the truth about these people. I think it might be entertaining."

She wasn't the only one.

. . .

THE BOAT RIDE WAS NOWHERE near as much fun as I'd expected. After the initial rush, the thrill died. Once you've seen one expanse of water, you've basically seen them all.

We did see several pods of dolphins, some playfully matching the cutter's pace, and I couldn't help but smile as I watched them cavort. I'd never spent much time on the ocean, and even though the wind was wreaking havoc with my hair I found I was having a great time.

The feeling didn't last long. Once the water turned choppy and the cutter started bouncing, my stomach transitioned to mush and all enjoyment abandoned ship. I spent the entire afternoon hanging close to the railing, waving off anybody who tried to join me because I didn't want witnesses if I suddenly had to vomit.

Concern etched Jack's face when he braved my presence shortly before noon. I could practically read the "I told you so" slant of his shoulders.

"Don't give me crap," I muttered, resting my cheek against the railing as I sat at an awkward angle. "I'm not seasick. I'm hungover."

"You only had two drinks last night," he reminded me, carefully pushing my hair away from my face to study my eyes. He looked so concerned it tugged on my heartstrings even as I fought the urge to punch him. "You drank them over three hours. You're not hungover, Charlie."

"Well, I'm not seasick. I refuse to be the loser who gets seasick while we're looking for a Megalodon. I must have contracted the flu or something."

Jack's lips curved. "Only you would prefer having an illness that threatens to put you in bed for a week over a weakness that will pass once you're off this boat."

"I don't get seasick," I repeated. "I'm fine. I'm ready to take on the Megalodon."

"There is no Megalodon."

"There could be a Megalodon."

He smiled at my resentful expression. "You're going to be okay.

After we finish lunch, there's a specific area Chris wants to hit. After that, I'm insisting we return to shore."

"You'd better not use me as an excuse. I'm fine."

"I will find a different way to get him to shore to save your prized reputation. Don't worry about that."

"Well, it's up to you." I briefly pressed my eyes shut. I couldn't see him but knew he was still there. "You don't have to hover. I'm perfectly capable of taking care of myself."

"We're about to have lunch."

"I'm not hungry. I'm watching my figure."

"Your figure is fine, but I know you're not eating ... and I know why. I'm going to suggest cutting the ship's engines while we eat. That will give you a little break ... not that you're seasick or anything."

"That sounds delightful."

He looked as if he wanted to kiss me, but ultimately he dropped my hair and got to his feet. "This will be nothing but a memory in a few hours. I promise."

"Not if it's the flu and I die."

"Oh, I miss happy-go-lucky Charlie. I'd much rather have you babbling about a Megalodon than acting like this."

"I'll try to do that later."

"Okay."

Jack left me to wallow with my nausea. I pointed my eyes to the sea, closed them and willed myself to feel better. It wasn't exactly going well when another visitor came by, although this one was altogether unwelcome.

"Maybe you should jump and swim back to shore," Laura suggested, her smile bright. "That would help the seasickness."

"I'm not seasick."

"You could've fooled me."

"Yes, well ... why are you even over here? Jack says they're serving lunch below deck. You should head that way. I bet there are a lot of crewmen for you to hit on and none of them will care that you probably have an STD."

"That was a lame insult," Laura offered. "I expect better from you."

"I'll save my strength and try again later."

"Yes, well, maybe you would have more strength if you weren't out so late with Jack," she said. "You probably wouldn't have gotten sick if you'd had a good night's sleep."

Suspicion joined unease in my gut. I knew I'd seen a curtain move. That meant she was probably watching us from the window. "Or you could just mind your own business," I snapped back.

"Perhaps I think I am minding my own business. Have you ever considered that?"

"Why would I consider that?"

"Because we need to have another talk. It seems you didn't listen to me last time and I need to clear things up again."

I was in no mood for this. I got to shaky legs, leaning my hip against the railing, and shook my head. "I'm not dealing with this right now."

"And I'm not letting you walk away." Laura grabbed my arm. "I'm not done talking to you."

"Well, you're going to have to wait. I don't have the energy to talk to you."

"You'd better get the energy." She gave my arm a good shake. "I'm not joking. We're going to talk.."

"I don't want to talk."

"Well, we're going to." She shook me again, causing my stomach to lurch.

The reason I picked this part of the ship was because the railing was lower and I could sit and throw up (without getting to my feet) if it became necessary. Now, when I swiveled to lose the little I had in my stomach — which was practically nothing because I hadn't eaten since the previous evening — I had to bend over to make sure the vomit wouldn't blow back and hit me in the face.

"Leave me alone," I complained when she jostled me again, my eyes focusing on the silver backs of the dolphins playing in the ocean as the cutter slowed. "We'll fight later if you want. I can't deal with it now."

"Well, I want to deal with it now." Laura refused to back down. "I know what you've been doing, what you've been trying to do. You're not going to get Jack."

"Oh, geez. I ... ." I quickly lost interest in the conversation with Laura when I focused harder on the dolphins and realized they didn't look quite right. In fact, they looked completely wrong. "Those aren't dolphins."

Laura, uninterested in wildlife, kept her focus on me. "Stay away from him. I mean it." She gave me a hard enough shake that I fell forward. I was already leaning that way to get a better look at the creatures in the water beneath us and the forward momentum was enough to cause me to lose my footing.

I was already halfway over the railing before I realized I was too far gone to pull myself back. "Laura!" I desperately tried to grab her hand, hoping she could save me. She realized too late what was happening. To her credit, she did try to grab my arm.

It was far too late. I cleared the railing, my face pointed directly at the water as I dropped.

"Son of a ... !"

NINE

"*C*harlie!"

I heard my name the second before I plunged beneath the water. I hit hard enough that I lost my bearings, diving deep. I kept my wits enough that I didn't immediately kick — I didn't want to drive myself deeper, after all — and let my natural buoyancy come into play. When I was certain I was heading up, I kicked hard ... and surfaced in the middle of a hell storm.

I recognized right away that the creature circling me was not a dolphin. The telltale fin slicing through the water told me it was a shark. I wasn't an expert, but it seemed pretty big to me ... like a good forty or fifty feet long. Of course, that could've been my imagination kicking into overdrive.

My heart pounded as I treaded water and immediately looked back to the cutter for an escape. Unfortunately, even though the engines had been cut, the ship drifted quite a distance in the few seconds it took me to recover.

"Charlie!"

I jerked my eyes to the railing where I'd been standing moments before and found a panicked Jack standing next to Laura. Her lips were moving, her hands waving back and forth, but I couldn't hear what she was saying. Jack clearly wasn't interested.

"Shut up, Laura!" he bellowed, his eyes finding mine over the distance. "Hold on, Charlie! We'll get you out!"

He was trying to be reassuring, but when I felt something brush against my leg underwater I couldn't stop myself from screaming. "Omigod!"

"What is it?" Jack looked as if he was ready to vault over the side of the ship.

"Sharks." I pressed my eyes shut. "It's sharks."

"Is it a Megalodon?" Millie asked, joining the others at the railing. She had a sandwich in her hand and didn't look particularly worried. That only served to ratchet my temper up a notch.

"It's sharks," I hissed, glaring as another beast — perhaps it was the same shark, I couldn't say because it wasn't as if they were wearing nametags — circled in front of me. "Oh, geez. I'm going to be eaten by sharks. This is not the way I thought I would go."

"You're not going to be eaten by sharks," Jack barked. "I need you to swim in this direction. I'll get a rope ladder and throw it over the side. We'll have you out of the water in a few minutes."

That sounded great. There was only one problem. "If I swim, the sharks will eat me!"

"Then you should definitely do that," Laura suggested.

I could feel Jack's fury from one-hundred feet away when he glared at her. "Go away, Laura!" He sucked in a calming breath when she shrank back and focused on me. "You have to swim. It will take us too long to launch a lifeboat. You have to do it. I'm sorry."

I still wasn't keen on the idea. "But ... I don't think I can."

"You can do anything." He was firm. "I have faith. I will have a rope ladder waiting for you. I need you to swim for me!"

He looked so pained, so terrified, I could do nothing but acquiesce. "Okay, but if I die I want Laura prosecuted for my murder."

"Why should I be prosecuted?" Laura groused as I started to stroke in the water, my eyes peeled for movement on either side of me. "I'm not the idiot who fell in."

"You pushed me!"

A fin cut through the water, reacting to my raised voice, and causing my heart to skip what felt like a hundred beats.

"I did not. You fell. You're a klutz."

"Laura, if you don't get away from here I'll push you in," Jack threatened. "I mean it. Go away!"

"I think you should push her in," I offered, doing my best to ignore the onyx eyes watching me from ten feet away. "If she draws the attention of the sharks, I can get away."

"I'll keep that in mind." Jack disappeared from view, causing my heart to roll. I forced myself to keep swimming even when I felt something against my leg.

By the time Jack returned, he had several members of the crew with him and a rope ladder. They helped him secure the ladder, which seemed to take forever, but I was just approaching the side of the ship (which thankfully had stopped drifting) when he tossed it over the side.

"Can you get to it?" Jack peered down as I reached for the ladder. My fingertips brushed the braided line, but I missed. "I'll come down and help you." He already had a leg over the railing when one of the crew members stopped him. I couldn't hear what the man said, but Jack's angry curse told me it wasn't something good.

I reached again, and failed. This time when I hit the water there was a terrific splash. It was big enough to draw the attention of one of the sharks that had been monitoring my progress, and shifted its path so I was directly in front of it.

I didn't think, instead reacting out of instinct and lashing out with my magic before considering my options.

"Go away," I hissed, unleashing a potent blast with my mind. The pulse hit the shark square in the face and caused it to veer to the side at the last second, giving me a wide berth. I sucked up my courage, focused to the best of my ability and stretched again. This time I managed to grab the lowest rope rung. Unfortunately, I had zero upper body strength and couldn't pull myself up.

Jack, recognizing the problem, made up his mind on the spot.

"Hold on, Charlie. We're going to pull you to us. You can't let go. If you fall into the water a second time ... ."

He didn't finish the sentence. He didn't have to. I could figure the ramifications myself. If I splashed again, the shark would return. Even though I frightened it the first go-around, the odds of me being able to do it a second time weren't great.

"I'll hold on," I promised.

"Hold tight."

The ride back up to the deck was the stuff of dreams. Nightmares, to be more precise. I gripped the rope ladder so tightly my hands were raw and I thought I might fall because of the pain.

I managed to hold on as the crew members dragged me toward the deck. When I finally reached the top of the railing, Jack's hands were on me before I could grasp the metal bar, and he pulled me over the top, both of us tumbling to the deck because of my klutziness.

"Ow." I rubbed my knee as he wrapped his arms around me. "That hurt."

He didn't immediately answer, instead running his hands over every part of my body (although not in a sexy way). It took me a moment to realize he was looking for bite marks.

"I'm okay." My voice was raspy. "I'm okay."

"I'll be the judge of that." His fingers were gentle as they brushed over my bare legs. When he was finished, certain I wasn't missing any huge chunks, he pulled me in for a second hug. "You scared the life out of me, Charlie. What were you thinking?"

I wasn't so far gone I would accept blame for this mishap. "I didn't fall over ... or jump. Ask your little buddy why I went over." I wasn't big on tattling, but in this particular instance, I felt Laura deserved it.

Jack's eyes were hot embers of hate fire when he turned them to Laura. "What did you do?"

Instead of apologizing and taking blame, Laura feigned innocence. "She did it to herself. She shouldn't be so clumsy."

"I'm going to kill you," he muttered under his breath as he ran his hands over my shoulders. "Seriously, it's going to hurt."

Laura clearly wasn't concerned about Jack carrying through on the threat. "It's her fault."

"It doesn't matter whose fault it is," Millie said, appearing with a huge towel. "Charlie is safe. That's the most important thing."

"To you, maybe," Laura sniffed.

Millie ignored her as she wrapped the towel around my shoulders. "I'm more confused about where all those sharks came from." She turned to one of the crew members. "Why would so many sharks be in one place?"

"I only saw two," I offered through chattering teeth. "I mean ... I think."

Jack's eyes filled with something I couldn't identify. "You should probably look again, Charlie," he said quietly.

I followed his suggestion, making sure to keep a safe distance from the railing, and when I looked at the water it teemed with sharks. There had to be at least thirty of them, and they were all circling the same area. "I don't understand." My voice cracked. Had I known that many sharks were in the water I would've frozen. Fear would've claimed me, and getting out of the water would've been impossible. "Why are they all here?"

"There's a whale carcass over there." A crew member pointed to the east. "It's huge. They're feeding off it."

A whale carcass? I craned my neck, adjusting my eyes until I saw the huge mass floating on the water. My stomach rolled again, this time for another reason. "What killed the whale?"

Jack shrugged and hugged me again, clearly not caring that we had an audience. "I don't know. But you're okay and that's the most important thing."

BY THE TIME CHRIS, HANNAH and Bernard joined us on the deck, Jack had me tucked into a chair (seatbelt fastened), and he'd wrapped three towels around me to ward off the cold. It was a sunny day, hot and humid, but I couldn't stop shaking.

"She's in shock," he explained to Chris. "We need to head back right now."

"I can hear you," I pointed out, forcing a smile for his benefit. "I don't think I'm in shock."

"Of course you're in shock," he countered. "You fell into shark-infested waters and survived."

"They're bull sharks," Hannah said as she leaned over the railing to take photographs with her phone. "They don't play well with humans. You're very lucky, Charlie."

I knew she didn't mean it in a demeaning way, but the statement grated all the same. "Yes, that's me. Lucky Charlie. I think I might play the lottery tonight."

Jack shot me a dark look. "You need to rest. Close your eyes and ... leave that seatbelt on. I'm not kidding. I don't want you near that railing. Do you understand?"

Under different circumstances, I might've argued with him. I didn't have the energy. I was too tired ... and maybe a little shaky, although I would die before admitting that. "I have no intention of going near the railing."

Jack held my gaze for a moment, turning back only when he appeared satisfied I meant what I'd said. He was in no mood to play games with Chris, though, and stood toe-to-toe with our boss. "I want her back on land."

Chris, never one for confrontation, adopted a placating tone. "I know you're upset. I'm honestly glad I was below deck when she fell into the water because I would've totally freaked out. You did what you had to do as the chief of security. You saved her. I don't see what the problem is."

"The problem is that she's wet and cold."

"It's ninety-five degrees with ninety-seven percent humidity."

Jack scowled. "She's in shock!"

I was starting to think Jack was the one in shock. "I'm okay," I repeated, his gaze softening when it landed on me. "I really am fine. Chris wants to get closer to that whale, get some photographs. We both know why. We might lose this chance if we leave now. I'm fine."

"You could've died."

I understood that. I still felt it. In the grand scheme of things, though, I'd been in worse situations. "I didn't die. It won't take long to check out the whale. I can make it."

He licked his lips, uncertain. This time when he swiveled, it was toward Millie, which took me by surprise. "Tell her she needs to go back to shore."

Millie chuckled, catching me off guard. This wasn't exactly a funny situation. "I can see why I would be your best bet on that front," she acknowledged. "I'm like a mother hen at times. Charlie is safe. You thought quick and got her out of the water. The bull sharks were more interested in her than the carcass, but they didn't have time to attack. We got lucky."

I thought about the nudges I felt against my legs. I definitely got lucky. Now probably wasn't the time to mention that to Jack.

"Charlie says she's fine to explore the whale," Millie said. "I think she's old enough — and brave enough — to make her own decisions."

"Oh, geez!" Laura rolled her eyes. "She's going to be the queen of the group by the end of the day at this rate. I can't tell you what joy that fills me with."

"You'll be living in her dungeon if you're not careful," Jack seethed, his hands forming into fists at his sides before he slid his gaze back to me. "Are you sure you're okay with this? There's no shame in going back to shore to collect yourself."

"I'm fine." I meant it. "I want a closer look at the whale carcass, too."

IN THE END, THE CUTTER got us as close as we dared to the whale carcass. Jim Bedford, the chief marine biologist on the ship, joined us on deck to study the find. As we got closer, more sharks appeared, drawn by the blood and other sharks. I even noticed a black fin or two, which threw me for a loop.

"Is that an Orca?" I was beyond confused.

Jack, who refused to let me out of his sight, kept me behind him as he stared in the direction I looked. "I think it is. That's weird, right?"

"Not as weird as you'd think," Bedford countered, a camera gripped in his hand as he snapped photographs. "There are about five-hundred killer whales in the Gulf. This one was obviously drawn by the carcass."

"I thought they were strictly cold-water whales," I admitted.

"No."

"What kind of whale is it?" Millie asked, her excitement growing as we got a better look at the dead animal. "It looks pretty big."

"It's a Fin whale," Bedford supplied, narrowing his eyes. "They can grow to be almost ninety feet, although this one looks more like seventy-five."

I did the math in my head ... and then double-checked it because I wasn't lying about being bad at arithmetic. "That would make it bigger than any predators you should have in the water, right?"

Bedford nodded. "Yes. I know you guys are looking for a Mega-lodon, which I had my doubts about, but this whale would be bigger than that shark."

"Maybe that's why not all of it is eaten," Chris suggested. "It was too big for the Megalodon to eat in one feeding."

"I don't think so." Bedford tilted his head to the side. "It's hard to see any injuries. This whale could've died of natural causes, or been attacked by a pod of killer whales. I don't see any evidence that a big predator took it down. More likely it was multiple little predators or natural causes."

The response clearly wasn't what Chris wanted. "But you can't know that for certain, right?"

"I can't, but do you see any wounds large enough to suggest a Megalodon took this animal out?"

"No, but I'm not an expert." Chris looked to Hannah for help. "What do you think?"

"I know what you want me to say, but I have to agree with Mr. Bedford on this one," Hannah replied, cringing when Chris frowned.

"I'm sorry. I have to tell the truth. I don't think a big predator took down this whale."

"I'm not angry," Chris said hurriedly.

"Just disappointed." Hannah patted his hand. "I don't know what to tell you. I don't think this is what you're looking for."

"I think it's interesting to see multiple species feeding off the same animal," Bedford noted. "That over there is a Tiger shark. The bull sharks might get territorial in a few minutes if more tigers show up."

He slowly tracked his eyes to me. "You're darned lucky, Miss. The bull sharks probably wouldn't have eaten you because they prefer the whale carcass, but they would've gladly torn you apart for fun if they'd been feeling more aggressive."

My mouth went dry. "Well, that's a lovely thought."

Jack slipped his arm around my shoulders, clearly not caring that our co-workers were watching. "She's safe. Things could've been worse. Take your photos of the whale as quickly as you can, because then we're heading back to shore. I've had enough of this for one day."

He wasn't the only one.

TEN

*J*ack was manic until the cutter docked. After that, he practically dragged me toward one of the vehicles in the lot. He barked something at Millie and Bernard to get them to pick up the pace, but when Laura appeared near the vehicle as he was opening the passenger door for me, he glared so hard I thought his eyes might pop out of his head.

"You're not riding with us," he said firmly, his tone practically daring her to argue with him.

"Why not?" Laura adopted an innocent expression that I'm sure garnered her all sorts of free passes growing up. "It's not my fault she fell in."

"You were messing with her right before it happened," Jack gritted out. "She wouldn't have gone in if you hadn't been there. It's definitely your fault."

Laura refused to back down. "She's perfectly fine. I don't know why you're getting all worked up."

"I know you don't." Jack gestured toward the back seat when Millie and Bernard arrived. "Strap in. We're heading back to the hotel right now."

Millie looked as if she was going to offer up an argument — or at least tease him about being a bossy bully — but ultimately she thought better of it and climbed into the rental without complaint. Jack was more gentle with me.

"Do you need help?" He tried to give me an additional lift when I reached for the seat.

"I'm pretty sure I can manage to sit in a vehicle all by myself," I offered, looking at Laura and cringing at the way she scowled. The look on her face told me this was nowhere near finished. "I'm honestly okay."

"You need to change and rest." Jack's tone was clipped. "Put your seatbelt on."

I risked a glance at Millie and found her shoulders shaking with silent laughter. I didn't find this situation nearly as funny as she did. As for Laura, her meltdown was bound to be something else entirely.

"You're riding with Chris and Hannah," Jack said. "In fact, everything you do is going to be with Chris and Hannah for the next few days because they're the only ones who can tolerate you."

Laura balked. "I don't need to take this abuse. It's not my fault she fell in the water."

"Then whose fault is it?"

"She's klutzy."

"That did it." Jack double-checked my seatbelt to make sure it was fastened, as if I was a child, and then slammed the door. The rest of his words were muffled, but he was so loud and ornery I had no trouble making them out. "You had better stay away from her, Laura. I mean it. I'm not joking around. I'll have you fired if you're not careful!"

Laura turned haughty. "And what makes you think you have the power to do that?"

"Well, let's see," Jack drawled, annoyance practically dripping from his tongue. "There's the fact that I have hiring and firing power. When I took this job, I made sure that Myron was aware that I wouldn't be working with any loose cannons. That's exactly what you are."

Laura made a face. "You're overreacting."

"I'm not done," he hissed, leaning closer. "You've been nothing but mean and nasty to Charlie since she got here. You've harassed her, threatened her and sexually harassed me. Those are all firing offenses."

I watched Laura's face closely for a reaction. I wasn't disappointed. She realized quickly Jack meant business, and she turned from an innocent woman trying to manipulate a man into a hissing snake. "I'll go above your head if I have to."

"You can try." Jack didn't appear worried in the least. "Just remember, Millie is on my side."

"And she's divorced from Myron."

"But still has his ear."

"If you want to make this a war, Jack, I'm more than willing to declare it," Laura offered. "Is that what you want?"

"I don't care what you do. You're going to stay away from Charlie. You're also going to stay away from me. I've had it with you. I'm so angry I could ... ," he broke off, refusing to finish the sentence. I was glad. If he'd finished, Laura would have ammunition against him. "Stay away from Charlie. If you don't, you won't like what happens. That's all there is to it."

I SHOWERED WHEN at the condo, changing into comfortable khaki shorts and a T-shirt. When I exited the bedroom I shared with Millie I found Jack sitting on the couch watching a baseball game. He smiled when he looked up, much calmer than he had been on the ship ... and in the parking lot ... and in the rental.

"How are you feeling?"

"I'm fine," I said hurriedly, glancing around to make sure we were alone. "Where are Bernard and Millie?"

"Millie said she didn't want to be around me when I was in Hulk mode. I think she wanted to give us some time alone. You're right about her knowing. It's obvious."

He didn't look upset about that. "I think, after today, everyone will know."

"Chris and Hannah won't. They're in their own little world.

Besides that, no one will say anything so it's like nobody knows. That's how I prefer it for the next few weeks."

"Okay." I felt awkward as I sat next to him on the couch. "You're okay, though, right? You're not going to freak out or anything?"

He arched an eyebrow, amused. "Why are you worried about me? You're the one who swam with sharks."

That was true. I knew the memory would probably cause a few nightmares. "Yeah, but I was okay once I got back in the boat. You continued to freak out. It was weird."

"Weird?" He slid me a sidelong glance. "I think it was a little weird myself. I couldn't seem to stop myself. All I could think about was getting you out of the water. Once that happened, I had a lot of excess energy to burn. It came out a little differently than I expected."

I was amused despite myself. "You mean general bossiness? You have that even when you don't have excess energy to burn."

"Thank you."

"You're welcome."

We stared at each other for a long moment.

"You're really okay?" he asked finally, his fingers gentle as they brushed a strand of my hair away from my face.

"I'm fine. I was freaked out when it happened and thought for sure I was about to be eaten by a Megalodon, but I'm perfectly fine now." I didn't mention that I was convinced I would have nightmares. He needed to settle.

"Those were bull sharks. They were nowhere near the size of a Megalodon."

"They seemed bigger in the water."

"Yeah. I thought you were going to get bitten by the one that charged you toward the end, but it turned away at the last second. I swear my heart stopped beating there for a bit."

That was the shark I turned away with my magic. "Well ... maybe he decided I didn't look tasty."

"His loss." Jack gave me a quick kiss and then stood. "Come on." He extended his hand. "I didn't get lunch and you haven't eaten in eighteen hours. We should get something."

I took his hand. "Are you going to be a mother hen all day?"

"Yes. Get used to it."

"Just checking."

WE PICKED A SIMPLE restaurant for lunch, a place with outdoor seating and away from the hustle of the resort. It was late in the afternoon for lunch, so most of the patrons inside were drinking rather than eating.

"I think they spend their entire days drinking," I noted as I sipped my iced tea and waited for the waitress to deliver our wraps. "They're all wearing lanyards, which means they're with the conference. How are they learning anything if they're always drunk?"

"Isn't that the myth of the writer?" Jack challenged. "Write drunk, edit sober. That's a saying. In fact, three of the guys at the tiki bar last night were wearing shirts that said that."

He'd obviously been paying closer attention than me. "It reminds me of college. People there started drinking at noon, too."

"I think there's a difference. These people are on vacation. I doubt this is something they do day in and day out. It's a break for them, a chance to hang with their peers. It's not a regular thing."

"I guess." I took a long swig of my iced tea, my eyes drifting toward the door when it opened. I almost crawled under the table when I realized the pimento cheese woman was standing there. "Oh, no."

"What's wrong?" Jack was instantly alert. "Are you okay? Are you going to be sick?"

I scowled. "It's the pimento cheese woman."

He furrowed his brow. "The what?"

"The pimento cheese woman," I repeated, covering my face with one hand and pointing with the other. "The one who keeps trying to get me to go to her room and eat cheese."

Instead of being worried, or offended, Jack merely smiled. The expression erased many of the worry lines he'd been carrying for hours. "Ah. Your new girlfriend. I'm generally against sharing when it comes to romantic entanglements, but she's pretty cute. You can sample her cheese if you want."

If I could've reached over the table and strangled him without garnering attention I would have. Instead, I tried to remain still so she wouldn't notice me. It was a wasted effort.

"Hey." She sat at our table without invitation, gracing Jack with a pleasant smile before fixing her full attention on me. "They have crab salad wraps here that are to die for. Did you get one of those?"

The question caught me off guard as I slowly lowered my hand. "You're kind of obsessed with food, aren't you?"

"I totally am," she agreed, extending her hand to Jack. "I'm Sarah Hilton. I write urban fantasy. Do you like pimento cheese?"

I frowned. Was she offering Jack pimento cheese, too? How did that work?

"I don't know that I've ever had pimento cheese," Jack hedged, licking his lips. "If I ever get a chance, I'll definitely give it a whirl."

"You should." Sarah flicked her eyes back to me. "I hear you've been asking questions about people who have motive to want to kill Shayne Rivers."

"How did you hear that?" I was genuinely curious.

"It's a small community. Gossip spreads fast. Carter told anyone who would listen that you guys were questioning those who fought with Shayne, trying to find a murderer and all that. You know he's very suspicious of 'The Man,' right?"

I searched my memory. "Carter Reagan Yates? The guy who writes zombie fiction?"

"It's not just zombie fiction. It's post-apocalyptic fiction."

"Only serial killers go by three names," Jack supplied. "I think he might be a little off."

Sarah snorted. "He's actually a cool guy. He's a little crazy about the end of the world — and if he offers to let you visit his hobbit hole, the answer is always no — but he's taken care of a bunch of foster children and he donates his time to the community."

I was mildly ashamed of myself for jumping to certain conclusions. "He was carrying around an adult sippy cup last night."

"He likes his rum runners," Sarah agreed. "He only goes by three names because the letters spell out cry — you know, C, R, Y. He uses it as a marketing gimmick."

"Oh." Being an author was apparently more work than I realized. "Well, I promise not to give him too hard a time about the hobbit holes he's built into the hills behind his house to survive the apocalypse."

"That's my motto." Sarah bobbed her head and grabbed a breadstick from the basket at the center of the table. "You're going to have a hard time narrowing your field of suspects because everyone hated Shayne. She wasn't exactly popular."

"That's what we've been told," Jack said, leaning back in his chair and stretching his long legs out in front of him. "Did you have words with her?"

"Oh, definitely." Sarah wasn't shy in the least to admit it. I couldn't help but notice she had on another cat shirt today. This one featured a grumpy-looking feline and an admonishment about Mondays. "We crossed paths when I started my career. She blasted one of my books to her mailing list. I hadn't heard the stories about her at that point, so I didn't know any better."

"What stories are you referring to?" Jack asked.

"She's a narcissist," Sarah answered without hesitation. "I'm not just throwing that word around either. She definitely has narcissistic personality disorder. She thinks the world revolves around her.

"She's great at building people up at the start because she wants to make them loyal to her," she continued. "She'll turn on you fast, though, if you don't do exactly what she wants on her timetable. When she turns on you, she incites all the other people she's charmed to attack. We call them her flying monkeys."

Huh. Sarah may have been obsessed with cheese, but she was a fount of useful information. "If everyone hated her, where did she get these flying monkeys?"

"I guess I should've phrased that better. Most of the people who have been around for a bit recognized her for what she was ... a predator. She cons the newbies who are desperate and need visibility.

Those newbies stand by her out of a mixture of loyalty and fear. They've seen what she does to other people and they're afraid she'll turn on them. So they stick up for her in the hope she has no reason to turn on them."

"That sounds fairly terrible," Jack said. "Although ... we are talking about adults. What can she really do to them?"

"It depends. She could motivate her followers to one-star books. If the rating isn't good enough, advertising it is impossible, so she can basically kill an author's momentum by being evil."

"Has she done that?"

"She denies it, but yeah. She crippled a few authors. She also makes up stories and always plays the victim. She would attack authors she didn't like, and when those people retaliated she would say they were jealous and wanted to hurt her family, even going so far as to say someone issued a death threat."

"Did anyone issue a death threat?" Jack was intrigued. "I mean ... did anyone come right out and say they wanted to kill her?"

"No one is that stupid," Sarah answered. "One woman, a JAFF writer, did get into some trouble. Her sister made an offhand comment that she knew where to hide a body, and Shayne called it a death threat."

"I don't think that's how death threats work," I said.

"Definitely not," Sarah agreed. "That's why she was a master manipulator. She twisted things."

"Can you give us an example?" Jack pressed.

"Sure. Penelope Waters is a paranormal romance author. She used Shayne's services for a book blast and claimed she didn't get any downloads. She wanted a refund. Shayne refused to give the refund and Penelope had a meltdown about Shayne stealing from her. Instead of ignoring it or fighting back in a normal way, Shayne told everyone that Penelope had been bitten by an opossum and had rabies."

My mouth dropped open. "But ... why?"

"That's an absurd story," Jack noted. "Who would believe that?"

"Only people who fall for lies, but those were the kinds of people

Shayne surrounded herself with," Sarah explained. "Shayne told her followers they weren't to attack Penelope because she was clearly suffering from rabies and that was the only reason she would say the things she said. She was adamant that poor Penelope was a victim in all this and she didn't mind being Penelope's whipping post, even though it hurt her feelings. Do you know what Shayne's followers did?"

As a matter of fact, that wasn't hard to figure out. "They attacked Penelope on Shayne's behalf," I answered.

Sarah nodded. "Bingo."

"How did you know that?" Jack asked, impressed.

"It's basic pack mentality when dealing with teenage girls," I replied, my mind busy. "It's a manipulation thing. It happened to me a lot when I was in middle and high school."

"Someone accused you of having rabies?"

"No, but that absurd story is probably only one instance of what this woman was doing," I said. "My guess is that she was masterful when it came to dividing people, making others feel sorry for her. She was always the victim, right?"

"Definitely. Once she burned someone, she lost them. The group of people who hated her was much bigger than the group who liked her. That's why your suspect pool will be seemingly endless."

"What about you?" Jack asked. "Do you think you should be in our suspect pool?"

Sarah's smile was easy. "Of course. I'm the weird girl constantly talking about food during a murder investigation. I should be your main suspect."

Jack returned her smile, bemused. "I'll put you at the top of our list."

"There are a lot of people who should be at the top of your list with me. Shayne was truly hated."

"Who would you put as a close second?"

"Start with Clark Savage," Sarah answered without hesitation. "He believes women should be barefoot and pregnant — unless he's hiring a professional to get him off in the shadows. And he has issues with anyone who doesn't follow his politics. He's got a bad temper and has been known to snap."

Jack steepled his fingers, thoughtful. "Would he have the constitution to throw a woman in the water and let her be eaten by sharks?"

"I think he's capable of almost anything."

"Then I guess he's a good place to start."

ELEVEN

*J*ack managed to unwind after Sarah departed — although it was incrementally — and he was almost back to his normal self by the time we'd finished eating. Our lunch setting was much more low key than the fancy restaurant the previous evening, which seemed to help the cause.

He simply appeared to need time to decompress, which I gave him. I was more interested in watching the authors interact with one another. I found the entire group fascinating.

"What are you staring at, Charlie?" Jack asked finally, breaking the silence he instigated.

I shrugged as I munched on a potato chip. "That guy over there. Do you remember his name?"

Jack followed my gaze toward the militant gun nut who ended up in the bushes with what could only be described as a professional the previous night.

Jack nodded, his gaze darkening. "Clark Savage. I ran his name this morning before we left on the cutter. He's the guy your pimento-cheese-loving friend was talking about."

"You ran him?" I was surprised. Jack didn't show specific interest in the man while we were hanging out at the tiki bar. "Why?"

"Because there was something about him I didn't like," Jack answered honestly. "He was rude, crude and ready to pick a fight."

That was interesting. "You didn't fight with him. I watched you, even when we were separated."

Jack's lips quirked. "Why were you watching me? I'm guessing it's because you're hot for me."

My cheeks burned as I forced myself to hold his gaze. I recognized what he was trying to do — tease me into relaxing and make me feel better at the same time — and I appreciated the effort. That didn't mean I wasn't mildly embarrassed. "I wanted to make sure none of those randy romance writers took advantage of you."

"Lusty," Jack corrected. "That's the word they kept throwing around. They're all upset about the word lusty being trademarked."

"Yeah. I picked up on that." I sobered as I rubbed the back of my neck. "Doesn't that seem like a weird word to be able to trademark? I mean ... it's a single word. I don't know a lot about trademark law, but that seems like it runs counter to everything I've heard."

Jack was silent for a beat, and then his lips curved. "As a parapsychologist, did you do much research on trademark law in college?"

I frowned. "I had other classes. One of them was a basic law class. I actually found it intriguing."

"You get more interesting every single day, Charlie." His eyes were light and full of life. "I don't know much about trademark law. I think Millie does, so you might want to talk to her about it."

"Maybe I will."

Jack's smile remained fixed. "As for what you said, I tend to agree with you. I'm not sure I understand all the hoopla about this. That's why I Googled that court case this morning, too."

"It seems you were busy on the internet while the rest of us were sleeping."

"Yes, well, I didn't sleep well." He pursed his lips, as if he were lost in deep thought for a moment, and then shook his head. "Anyway, the trademark thing seems to be a big deal. Our victim managed to trademark the word because nobody expected her to try something so brazen. And she actually got the trademark through before anyone realized what was going on.

"The issue is that she's been going after anyone who uses that word in a title or series name. And before you ask, I only know this because people on the internet laid it out for me as if I was twelve," he continued. "So, while I think it's funny that things like Lusty Literary Novelists — seriously, what is that? — and Lusty Labor Day seem to have the writer world up in arms, I do understand where some of the anger comes from. She was filing nasty cease-and-desist letters and causing other authors to lose their livelihood."

"Oh." I hadn't really thought about it at that level. "I think money is often a motivating factor in murder. But I want to go on the record and say I still think it was a Megalodon. I don't happen to believe it was murder."

Jack leaned back in his chair and rested his linked fingers on his stomach. "There is no Megalodon."

"You don't know that."

"Charlie ... ." He looked pained as he collected himself and worked hard to keep from snapping at me.

"Something clearly ate Shayne Rivers," I persisted. "It was a shark ... a big one."

"Or someone killed her and threw her body in the ocean and multiple smaller sharks munched on her after the fact," he countered, his temper getting the better of him as his eyes filled with irritation. I wasn't a fan of arguing, but I liked seeing him get his anger groove back in this particular instance. That meant he was putting the events of the day behind him. "We have no idea how she died. Her body was in terrible shape. You saw it."

I thought to the small misshapen hunk of woman I saw in the morgue. "I did." I felt sick to my stomach and pushed my empty plate away. "It was awful."

Jack's expression softened. "I'm sorry for bringing that up. I forgot you got queasy when you saw the body. After everything you went through today, that doesn't exactly seem fair."

My annoyance ratcheted up a notch. He thought I was a weak female because of what happened in the medical examiner's office. I couldn't tell him the truth — at least not yet — and I had to play my role as fainter extraordinaire.

"I'm not delicate or anything." I chose my words carefully. "I simply wasn't expecting to see what I did. It was ... brutal."

"I know you're not delicate." Jack's hand was big and warm as it covered mine. "You're strong. It's just ... ."

"What?"

"You went through a lot today." He lowered his voice. "I didn't want to allow the fear in when I was trying to get you out of the water because I thought it would be debilitating, but you could've easily died, Charlie. It's not just the sharks — although they were a concern — but you hit the water hard. I heard it. You could've struck your head going down and we might never have been able to find you if you'd lost consciousness."

"Then the sharks definitely would've gotten me."

"I would like to say that's not a possibility, but you saw what happened to Shayne Rivers' body. You got really lucky today."

"And what does that have to do with the fact that I believe a Megalodon killed everyone's least favorite author?"

"I'm choosing to believe your nerves aren't allowing you to see straight."

"That's kind of insulting."

"Yeah, well, I don't want to argue with you about Megalodons, because it's the absolute worst thing to do given what you've gone through."

"I'm fine."

"That doesn't stop me from wanting to take care of you." He squeezed my hand, earnest. "You drive me crazy. I'm not going to lie. There are times I want to shake some sense into you."

"That's lovely," I drawled, causing him to smile.

"There are other times I want to wrap you in bubble wrap because you're so freaking cute it makes my head spin," he added.

And my cheeks were burning again. "Um ... ."

"Those two emotions often wage a tug of war in my chest," he said. "But no matter how cute I find you, I'll never believe a Megalodon killed Shayne Rivers. That's ... ridiculous."

"I'm sure that's how Martin Brody felt when people on Amity Island started losing limbs in the water."

Jack's face was blank for so long I realized he'd lost track of the conversation.

"Martin Brody is the chief of police in *Jaws*," I offered helpfully.

"I know who he is." Jack's expression was hard to read. "I happen to love that movie."

I brightened considerably. "Me, too!"

"I don't love that you're using *Jaws* logic as an actual argument."

"Well ... would you prefer I use *Sharknado* logic?"

"There is no logic in *Sharknado*."

"We can agree on that." I pretended to study my fingernails so I wouldn't have to make eye contact. "I'm not ready to give up the idea that there's a huge predator out there. It might not be a Megalodon, but that doesn't mean it's not something else."

Jack took me by surprise when he answered. "Fair enough. You're allowed to believe what you want. I simply want you to promise you'll be careful around the authors."

"I'm not afraid of the authors."

"No, but you are attracting them for some reason," he noted. "You've made friends with several of them, including the pimento cheese girl and that mystery author you were talking to last night."

"Lily Harper Hart."

"Right. Another serial killer name."

I snorted, genuinely amused. "I don't think it's fair to say I've made friends with them. I'm simply interested in what they do, so I ask the appropriate questions. Like anybody else, they're eager to talk about themselves."

"I still want you to be careful." Jack was firm. "If one of them is a murderer, you might make a likely target to elicit information from.

You've had enough trouble for this trip. Additional danger will probably drive me insane."

He was sweet when he wanted to be, which tugged on my heartstrings, even though his overbearing attitude grated. "I'll be careful, Jack. I always am."

"Ugh. The sad thing is you believe that's true. Just ... keep your eyes open. Your safety is important to me."

"I promise I'll take care. You have my word on it."

"That will have to be good enough."

JACK HAD WORK TO FINISH after lunch. He suggested I nap while he did it — something that made me laugh, which annoyed him — but instead Millie suggested an outing to the resort spa. I'd never been to a spa, so I was intrigued enough to agree. Jack wasn't keen on me being out of his sight, but Millie put her foot down and he ultimately acquiesced. The resort was on land, and well lit, which meant no potential shark attacks. He had nothing to worry about, which is exactly what Millie told him before dragging me out of the condo.

Once we arrived at the spa, Millie took over and arranged for hot stone massages, facials and pedicures. Since this was a new experience, so I wasn't sure what to expect. I was still flummoxed when I exited the massage room and found Millie soaking her feet in a tub of hot water.

"I was just rubbed down with burning stones," I announced.

Millie arched an amused eyebrow. "Hot stones, and it's good for you. It gets out all the tension and rubs away dead skin cells. You're fine."

How could she possibly know that? She wasn't there. "Listen ... ."

"No, you listen." Millie turned serious. "You could've easily died today. I know you're putting on a brave front for Jack — and that's kind — but you need to take care of yourself now. That means you enjoy the massage and pedicure and shut up."

I was taken aback by her tone. "See if I almost get eaten by sharks again when you're around to make me feel better," I grumbled as I climbed in the chair to her left and watched a woman — she was entirely too smiley — fill a churning basin with steaming water. "I have sensitive feet."

"You'll survive. Pick a nice color for Jack."

I slid her a sidelong look. "You need to watch what you say about that in front of him. He's dealing with a lot right now and I don't want him worrying that you're going to let something slip."

Millie made an exaggerated face. "Oh, please. The only ones who don't know are Chris and Hannah, and that's because they're wrapped up in each other."

"Are you sure Laura knows?" I was on the fence on that one. I couldn't help but feel Laura would be angrier if she truly grasped the situation.

"I think Laura *suspects*," Millie corrected. "She doesn't want to believe what her intuition is telling her. She'll figure it out for certain pretty quickly, though. Jack's reaction to you going into the water was a dead giveaway."

"That's not fair. He thought I was going to be chomped on."

"Do you think he would've reacted the same way if I went into the water?"

I shrugged. "I don't know. He's very fond of you."

Millie snorted. "The boy almost fell apart. He managed to keep his head, which was good because it was a tense situation, but there were a few minutes when I didn't think he'd be able to hold it together. I don't care what you say, he wouldn't have sat on the deck and petted me for twenty minutes after the fact."

"He was upset," I said lamely.

"Oh, you're cute, too." She poked my side. "You guys are good for each other. Er, well, you will be once you calm down a bit. You're getting there, but still have a ways to go."

"Thank you," I said dryly, forcing my eyes forward.

"You're welcome."

I lost interest in the conversation quickly when I recognized three women from the tiki bar sitting in chairs across the aisle. They were all deep in conversation, their heads bent together as they whispered.

They had their toes stuffed under what looked to be dryers and were either oblivious to our presence or simply didn't care that they had an audience.

"Who is that?" Millie asked, lowering her voice as she followed my gaze. "Do you know them?"

I nodded, thoughtful. I didn't remember the three women hanging around together the previous evening, so seeing them together now seemed somehow odd. "Leslie Downs," I supplied, pointing at the woman who had helmet hair. "She writes thrillers with James Sanderson. I think she might have stalked him, too."

Millie widened her eyes, amused. "I know James. I can give him a call if you want."

I was dumbfounded. "You know James Sanderson?"

"You'd be surprised at the number of rich people who travel in the same circles as Myron," she replied. "I've met James quite a few times. I can get in touch with him if you want."

It couldn't hurt. "If you can, that would be great. I'm dying to know the truth about what went down with him and her. I'm pretty sure she stalked him."

"I'll call him." Millie switched her gaze to the woman in the middle of the group. "Who is the one with the red hair?"

"That would be Abigail James. She writes JAFF."

"What's JAFF?"

"Jane Austen fan fiction."

"I didn't realize that was a thing."

"Join the club. She seems nice enough, if a little high strung. She talks with her eyes closed when she's drunk. I thought that was weird until another writer explained she does it because she dictates her writing and it's a reflex or something. I'm not sure I understand."

"Talking to someone when they have their eyes closed is disconcerting."

"Yeah, well, it was definitely weird."

"And the third woman?" Millie prodded. "Do you know who she is?"

"Priscilla Jennings. She's a romance writer who has nothing nice to say about Shayne Rivers."

"From what I can tell, nobody had anything nice to say about Shayne Rivers," Millie noted. "She was essentially the most hated woman in publishing."

"Yeah, she seems like one of those people who keep doing everything wrong even though she knows she's going down a dark path. From everything I've heard she was positively diabolical on some levels."

"Which simply means there were a lot of people who wanted her dead."

"I guess."

We lapsed into amiable silence as the nail technician ran what looked to be a huge cheese grater over the bottom of my feet and made me squirm. Millie found my reaction funny and burst out laughing while I scowled and stared at the ceiling to keep from kicking the poor woman — who was only doing her job, mind you — in the face.

"Who is that?" Millie asked finally, inclining her chin toward the last pedicure chair in our row, to where a lone woman sat with knitting needles and a skein of blue yarn. "Is she one of the writers?"

I stared at the woman for an extended period as I tried to remember her name. I came up empty. "I can't quite remember. I know she's married to one of the other authors. She had those knitting needles at the bar last night."

"She knit at the bar?" Millie was clearly amused. "That doesn't scream 'party person,' does it?"

"I kind of feel sorry for her. Her husband spends all his time boasting with the others — I mean, I have never heard a guy talk about himself as much as he does — but she's always kind of quiet and isolated in the corner. I think she might be lonely."

"You could try talking to her," Millie suggested. "The ones on the periphery are usually the ones with the best gossip."

That was an idea. "I'll consider it ... after I'm done with this tickle torture."

Millie's snicker was easy and relaxed. "You'll have to let go of some of your pre-conceived notions about money and wealth. A pedicure is one of life's little joys. You should learn to enjoy it."

"I'll keep that in mind. Ow! Don't clip off my entire toe or anything ... and I don't want pink nails. I will die of embarrassment if my toenails are pink. I want something strong ... like a blue or a green. Oh, but ... what's that unicorn color over there?"

TWELVE

*E*avesdropping is one of those skills some people master without much effort and others will always struggle with. I fall into the latter category.

Pretending I wasn't listening to what Priscilla, Leslie and Abigail had to say wasn't as easy as I hoped. Thankfully I was distracted by my newly-painted toenails. To be fair, I'd painted my own toenails before. They never looked as nice as they did now.

"Why are you staring at your feet?"

Jack found me leaning against a wall in the lobby shortly before dinner. I'd texted him my location — and he was determined the two of us would get away on our own this evening — so he made a stealthy getaway and tracked me down. I missed his entrance because I was focused on my jazzy blue toenails.

"What?"

He wrinkled his forehead, confused. "Do you feel okay? Do you want to go back to the condo and lie down?"

"Not even remotely." That was true. "Millie snores like a buzz saw. I hate sharing a room with her. She also kicks like a mule. This is the one and only trip I will undergo this particular sleeping arrangement."

Instead of being sympathetic, he snorted. "She says you're the one who snores. I heard both of you through the walls, so I don't know who either of you are trying to fool."

I balked. "I don't snore."

"You're asleep when it happens. How would you know?"

"I know."

"Fine. I'm sure you're a dainty sleeper. I ... why do you keep looking at your feet?"

I wiggled my toes for his benefit. "What do you think?"

He stared for a beat. "I like the blue. It's cute."

"What about this?" I grabbed his hand and pressed it to the side of my face.

His expression caught somewhere between a smile and a scowl, Jack merely shook his head. "Should I take this to mean you enjoyed your trip to the spa?"

"I have nothing to compare it to — this was my first time — but it was mildly interesting. I got rubbed with hot stones by a hot guy."

He stilled. "You got rubbed by a guy?"

I nodded. "My masseuse was male. Millie insisted. She says men have stronger hands."

"Were you naked?"

I sensed trouble. "I was covered by a sheet. Millie was right about his hands. They were magical. I feel like a new woman."

Jack grumbled something under his breath that I couldn't quite make out. It sounded like a curse ... or perhaps a threat. Once he regained control of himself he flashed me a tight smile. "What do you want to eat for dinner?"

"I'm fine with anything."

"That's what all women say and it's never true. Trust me. I've been on enough bad dates to prove there's no woman who will eat everything."

"How many bad dates are we talking?"

"I'm not answering that question." He flicked his eyes to the restaurant offerings. "We had Italian last night. There's a steak place. Or, there's a seafood place at the sister resort. It's not a long walk and it supposedly has one of those huge aquariums that take up an entire wall."

I brightened considerably. "Oh, do you even have to ask?"

He snickered. "Seafood it is." He held out his hand. "Come on. Let's get out of here before the others track us down. I told Chris we should all break up for dinner tonight because spending too much time together is detrimental to the group's mental health, but I wouldn't put it past Laura to try to finagle another big dinner."

"Let's definitely not allow Laura to get her way."

THE WALK TO THE OTHER resort wasn't bad, other than the heat. I wasn't used to humidity this brutal, and I was wet with perspiration when we arrived. Jack, of course, looked fresh and dry.

"It's not fair," I muttered when I looked him over, taking an extra moment to stand under an air conditioning vent in the gift shop in the lobby.

"What's not fair?" Jack's eyes danced over the souvenir offerings. "Do you see something you want?"

I shook my head. "Never mind."

"If you want something, I'll buy it for you."

I sighed. His moods were hard to gauge. He'd spent most of the day barking orders because my shark ordeal terrified him to the point he could focus on nothing else. Now he was more relaxed, but his attentiveness showed no signs of waning.

"I don't need anything. That's not what I was referring to."

"Then tell me what you were talking about."

"We walked five-hundred feet in oppressive heat and you look better than when we left, but I feel as if I'm melting. I'm sweaty, my hair has started curling and I'm pretty sure I'm going to have pit stains on my shirt. You look perfect. That's what isn't fair."

"Oh." His lips curved, lightening his features. "Do you want me to buy one of those fans with the turtles on it to cool you off?"

"I think I'll somehow survive."

"Good. Come on." He gave my hand a tug. "We'll get a table right next to the glass so you can stare at the fish. That will give us something to talk about besides how nice the restaurant is."

I blushed at mention of our nearly disastrous first date. "That turned out okay in the end."

"Yeah, it did."

Once we were settled, drinks and entrees ordered, Jack turned to business. "I started running a bunch of the writers, but only half of them publish under their legal names."

"That actually makes sense," I said. "I mean ... think about it. There are some weird people out there who might stalk them under the right set of circumstances. That has to be freaky.

"Plus, well, some of the romance authors are writing colorful scenes that might set off a pervert," I continued. "I don't blame them for not wanting their real names out there. I bet a bunch of them haven't even told their families what they write because it's too embarrassing."

Jack shrugged, noncommittal. "I don't know. I don't think there's anything embarrassing about it."

"I don't either. I think *some* people — probably fathers and mothers — might be mortified to read something like that from their offspring, though."

"Good point." He leaned back in his chair and extended his legs, placing his feet on either side of mine, mimicking his actions from our first date. "How are you feeling after your ordeal earlier? And before you rattle off the word 'fine,' you should be aware that I expect more than that. I want a real answer. Otherwise I won't let it go."

I couldn't swallow my sigh. "I'm okay. I was scared boneless when I was in the water — I'm still not sure how I managed to swim under those circumstances — but things happened so fast I couldn't really think about them. I'm probably lucky I didn't have a heart attack."

"The sharks really didn't want to hurt you."

"I know."

"I'm glad you weren't hurt."

"I know that, too."

He rubbed his foot against my ankle. "You got lucky. I tried telling

Chris that all of us going out on that cutter was a bad idea. He refused to listen."

"It would've been fine if I hadn't gone over the side. The thing we were truly lucky about was the fact that the Megalodon wasn't in the area."

"Do you have to ruin the night?" His face twisted. "I can't deal with talking about an extinct shark that is most certainly not hunting the waters of the Gulf of Mexico. The bull sharks are dangerous enough, don't you think?"

I took pity on him. "Okay. It's not a Megalodon."

"Thank you."

"Maybe it's the Megalodon's cousin, Slightly-smaller-lodon."

"Is that your scientific name for it?"

"Yes."

"Well, great."

I pressed my lips together as I watched him. He was doing his best to be pleasant, but the Megalodon talk had him walking a very fine line. I decided to change the subject. "On a different note, Leslie Downs, Abigail James and Priscilla Jennings were all in the spa together and they wouldn't stop talking about how much they hated Shayne Rivers and how they were glad she was dead."

Jack perked up. "Really? Did they say anything that would indicate they were legitimate suspects in her death?"

"No, but they seem to think her trademark thing is going to fall by the wayside now that she's dead and some court case she was involved in with one of her former clients will be dismissed. They mentioned her kids — who are apparently home with the husband. He's not bothering to travel to claim the body — and they said that half of them weren't even living with her."

"If they weren't living with her, who were they living with?"

"Her mother. Apparently Shayne couldn't handle her own offspring. She kept only three of the five."

"Huh. I'll look into that. Anything else?"

I searched my memory. "No. I think that's it."

"Good. Let's focus on us for the rest of the night and leave the possibly murderous authors as a worry for tomorrow. How does that sound?"

"I've had worse offers."

"There you go."

I WAS STUFFED AFTER dinner, a meal of scallops and asparagus weighing me down. Jack insisted on ordering an expensive dessert for us to share, so I thought there was a chance I might burst — or at least have to unbutton my shorts — on the way back to the hotel.

Jack chose to walk along the beach rather than the sidewalk, claiming it was because of the view, but I knew he preferred the beach because it was quieter and we could be alone without risking running into our group.

In truth, I appreciated the walk. It was relaxing after a tense day.

"They have another tiki bar over here," I noted as we passed the satellite resort's pool. "It's quieter than the one at the main resort."

"I see that." He squinted as he studied the tables around the bar. "Isn't that the science fiction writer we met last night?"

I followed his gaze, taking a moment to search, and then nodded when I recognized the man in question. "J.D. Wells. He's the one who said he was a big deal. Told another author that perhaps one day she could own real estate, too — if her husband allowed it. And he shot up insulin at the fire."

"He shot up insulin at the fire?" Jack looked surprised. "I didn't notice that."

"He was trying to be discreet."

"Are you sure it was insulin?"

I nodded. "He didn't drink. He had water. I'm pretty sure he's diabetic. He didn't get high or anything off the injection. Does it matter?"

"No. You're simply more observant than I realized."

"Yes, I'm a regular Sherlock Holmes."

Jack released my hand and slung his arm around my shoulders, directing me toward the tiki bar and away from the beach. "How about we have a nightcap before heading back?"

"Are you sure?"

"As long as you don't get drunk and I have to carry you."

"That happened one time."

"Yes." He took on a far-off expression. "That's when I knew you were going to be trouble ... and I probably wouldn't be able to resist you."

"Really?" My heart did a little dance. "You didn't act like you were charmed that night."

"That's because I wanted to kill you for drinking with a murderer."

"Hey, we had no idea he was a murderer at the time ... and that was entirely Millie's fault. She's the only reason I even went to the bar that night."

"You're going to blame your lack of judgment on Millie?"

I nodded without hesitation. "Yes. I'm an angel."

"I thought Hannah was the angel."

"I'm a different sort of angel."

"A fallen angel?"

"Maybe."

"Well, my little devil girl, let's get a drink. While we're at it, we can question Mr. Big Deal. He might have some information, and it will be easier to get it out of him without an audience."

"Sure. I want something fruity with an umbrella. We are in paradise, after all."

"I think I can manage that."

IT TURNED OUT, J.D. WELLS was a fount of information. The problem was, his favorite topic was himself. He directed the conversation back to the wonder that was J.D. Wells whenever we tried to direct his attention toward some of his fellow writers.

"Basically, when it comes to publishing, I'm something of a miracle man," he explained, a huge glass of water clutched in his hand. He wasn't drunk, thankfully. If he was this bad about monopolizing the conversation without alcohol fueling him, I would've hated to see how he was when his blood was juiced with a few rum runners.

"A miracle man, huh?" I wasn't sure how I was supposed to respond. In the real world I would've called him on his attitude and walked away. But because he possessed information that might be of use to us, that wasn't an option. "You should have a shirt made up proclaiming your magical powers."

Wells blinked several times. "What makes you think I don't?"

"Oh, well ... um ... ."

"You're the one who owns that bright van in the parking lot, right?" Jack asked, wisely changing the subject. "The one with the hot chick holding a gun and her boobs hanging out?"

I'd seen that van. Oddly enough, I hadn't noticed the boobs. I'd been more interested in the magical cats winding their way around the vehicle. "Oh, right. The pedo van."

Jack stiffened, making me realize I said the last part out loud. "What she means is ... ." He stalled, clearly at a loss to explain my words.

"All vans remind me of pedophiles," I offered quickly.

"That doesn't sound better," Jack hissed.

I held my hands palms out and shrugged. "It's all I have."

"Oh, you are absolutely adorable," Wells' wife offered from a chair a few feet away. I hadn't even noticed that she'd joined us. Christine Wells was quiet like a cat. Perhaps she was the inspiration for the cats on the van. In typical fashion, just like the previous two times I'd seen her, she had a skein of yarn in her lap and busy knitting needles in her hands. "Seriously, I don't think anyone could be cuter than you."

I looked to Jack, debating if it was an insult.

"Hey, I already thought you were cute."

Clearly fed up with the conversation wandering away from his favorite subject, Wells insisted on dragging us back. "Did I tell you about my new book?"

Jack feigned politeness. "I don't believe you have."

"It's about a mutant shark that's combing the Florida coast." Wells' eyes lit with excitement. "The shark is prehistoric — I mean absolutely huge — and it was trapped in a deep trench for centuries and only freed because of global warming."

I worked my jaw. "Wow," I said finally. "That's ... wow. What do you think about that, Jack?"

His shrewd eyes told me exactly what he thought about it. "That's kind of interesting," he hedged, clearly searching for the right words. "That's kind of what happened to Shayne Rivers, isn't it? The police aren't looking for one big shark, but she was killed in the shallows and there was definitely shark activity."

"I know." Wells didn't even fake sadness. "Could the timing be better or what? I have the book finished, but it still needs to be edited. I'm getting on that the second I get home because this book will be huge. I'm even going to dedicate it to Shayne. That will get more attention."

I was horrified. "Don't you think that's a little ... unsympathetic?"

Wells shrugged, unbothered. "Why should I care about that? She was a horrible woman. I can't think of anyone who liked her. At least she'll be benefitting me in death. She certainly didn't help me in life."

I glanced at his wife to gauge her response, but her focus was on her knitting, though she did bob her head and echo his sentiment. "She was a mean woman. She always picked on my husband, called him names and tried to hold him back. I don't know anyone who will miss her.

"I mean ... I don't think anyone wanted her to die or anything, but sometimes the good Lord sends out a fitting burst of karma and rights a terrible wrong," she continued. "In this case, she's dead and she's going to help J.D. sell a lot of books. That's karma."

I could think of a few other ways to describe it. "Well, at least she got what was coming to her," I said finally, ignoring the sidelong look Jack shot me.

"Definitely," Christine agreed, holding up her project and smiling. In the limited light, it took me a moment realize she was making some sort of square with a shark fin in the center of it. "Do you like it?" She was enthusiastic and amiable ... and just a little bit creepy. "I'm making a shark afghan for J.D.'s office. Isn't it to die for?"

"It's definitely ... something."

"Definitely," Jack echoed, moving his hand to my back and slowly rubbing up and down. "So, tell me more about this shark book. I'm a huge fan of stuff like that. What's the plot?"

I had no idea what Jack was digging for, but I figured he knew what he was doing. I settled in next to him, letting him lead the way, and allowed my mind to wander. Surely the shark bit was too similar to be a coincidence, right?

Right?

THIRTEEN

*W*e made our escape from the tiki bar as soon as we could pull it off without looking suspicious. Jack's reaction to Wells was almost funny, especially the way he insisted on keeping himself between us. Ultimately, the shark writer was so busy talking about himself and his magical power of book launching that he barely noticed when Jack and I slipped away.

The wind picked up during our walk back to the condo. It was so warm I felt as if I were trapped in an oven.

"Wow." I fanned my face as we slowed our pace to stare out at the water. "It's hot. You're even sweating."

He smiled as he attempted to smooth my hair, his fingers getting snagged in the process. "I kind of like how wild you look, like an island girl who hasn't brushed her hair in years," he teased. "I didn't know hair could get that big without hairspray."

I frowned. "That is not the way to make me feel attractive."

"You don't need help feeling attractive. Even with ridiculous hair you're the cutest one out here."

I took an exaggerated look up and down the beach. "I'm pretty sure I'm the only woman out here. I don't know where the rest of the writers are, but I'm guessing they're not dipping their toes into the surf."

"Their cute blue toes."

I rolled my eyes. "Fine. I got a little overenthusiastic at the spa."

"I think that is cute, too," he said. "You had a rough day. If you find some joy getting your toenails painted, what's not to like about that?"

"You're being awfully easy to get along with."

"That's me. Mr. Amiable."

I rolled my eyes. "I can think of a few other words for you when you get a bug up your butt."

"I thought those were ass crabs."

I smiled at the memory. "You're feeling extremely charming tonight, aren't you?"

"I really am." He lightly tugged my hand and pulled me close, wrapping his arms around my back and staring hard into my eyes. "You scared me today," he admitted, not for the first time. "I was going to jump in that water and get you. That's all I could think to do."

"That probably would've been a bad idea. I was fine with you pushing Laura in to serve as a distraction, though."

He chuckled. "I don't often panic, but I was pretty close to that today. I had no idea how to get you away from those sharks."

"And yet you held it together and figured out a way to get me out of the water. I wasn't even nibbled on. But I have to admit, the few times the sharks brushed against my legs was terrifying. I seriously thought I was going to have a heart attack."

"I bet." He blew out a sigh. "You're okay. That's all that matters." He took me by surprise when he leaned forward and kissed my forehead rather than my lips. "You're okay and after a good night's sleep you'll be even better." He wrapped himself around me and rocked back and forth while staring at the water.

"I think you might need a good night's sleep, too," I said after a beat, amused by his reaction. He kept it together for most of the afternoon and our date, but he couldn't maintain through the walk home. It was kind of cute. "I'm not sure how well I'll sleep with Millie snoring. Plus ... I'll have nightmares. I know it. There's nothing I can do about it."

Jack pulled back long enough to stare into my eyes. "Do you have nightmares often?"

I shrugged, unsure how to answer. Some of my nightmares were tied to my abilities. It was too soon to talk about that. "Sometimes. It's going to happen tonight. There's nothing you can do about it."

"We'll see." He stroked his hand down the back of my hair, his body going tense at some point and causing me to draw back. The obvious question was on my lips but I never got a chance to utter it because Jack was focused on the beach trail that led to the resort. "Who are you?"

I had to squint to make out the approaching figure in the darkness. When I did, I relaxed much quicker than Jack and offered Lily Harper Hart, the cozy mystery author with the sarcastic tongue who made me laugh around the tiki bar the previous evening, a friendly wave.

"What are you doing out here?" I asked, resting a hand on Jack's forearm to still him. "I would think you'd be drinking with your buddies."

"They're closing the tiki bar," Lily replied, her gaze busy as it bounced between us. She looked amused. "I came out here to make sure there were no stragglers. Apparently a big storm is set to roll through in the next twenty minutes or so."

"Why would anyone be out here?" Jack asked, legitimately curious. "I thought you guys were congregating closer to the resort so you didn't have to travel great distances for cocktails."

"Oh, you're kind of funny." Instead of being offended by Jack's tone, Lily snorted. "You're kind of crabby, though, aren't you? Given the way you two were looking at each other, I'm guessing it's sexual tension fueling you."

My mouth dropped open. "What? I ... what?"

"Ignore her," Jack said. "She doesn't know what she's talking about."

Lily snickered, her eyes lighting with mirth. "I don't, eh? So you two have progressed beyond kissing and groping? I guess I was wrong about the sexual tension."

"We don't grope." I looked to Jack for confirmation. "Right? We haven't gotten to groping yet, have we? I don't want to miss that."

My statement was the only confirmation Lily needed. "That's what I thought."

Jack scowled. "I'm starting to dislike both of you now."

"No, you're embarrassed and annoyed," Lily countered. "Embarrassed because you're wondering if you should be progressing to groping – and probably beyond – and annoyed because I interrupted a private moment. I don't mean to distract you or anything, but I wanted to make sure no one passed out in this area before the storm rolls in. That almost happened the first night we were here."

Intrigued, Jack slipped his arm around my waist and focused his full attention on Lily. "What do you mean? The first night was the night Shayne Rivers died, right?"

"Yeah." Lily's expression twisted as she shook her head, taking on a far-off expression. "We didn't know she was out here. We thought she'd gone back to her room. Everyone was relieved about that because we didn't want to talk to her anyway. She made everyone uncomfortable."

"Because she was a narcissist?" I asked.

"She was definitely a narcissist," Lily agreed. "I think she had at least three diagnosable personality disorders, narcissism being one of them."

"What were the others?" I didn't really expect an answer, but I was the curious sort.

"She was histrionic, paranoid, dependent and possibly borderline."

I was expecting her to say Shayne was crazy and call it a day, so I was understandably surprised by her clinical take on things. "That's quite a clinical diagnosis."

"She was a lot of trouble," Lily said. "She was definitely paranoid. She didn't trust anyone. That was probably a good idea because none of us liked her and weren't even remotely trustworthy where she was concerned. She was also definitely histrionic. She craved attention, wanted to be at the center of everything, and was insincere and superficial.

"The narcissism goes without saying," she continued. "She lacked empathy and lied every chance she got. The borderline personality disorder is more up in the air. She definitely threatened to harm herself, but I very much doubt she would've carried it out."

"Wait ... she threatened to kill herself?" Jack's interest in the conversation deepened. "Has anyone considered that she threw herself off the pier that night and the sharks coming along was merely a coincidence?"

"You'll have to talk to the cops about that," Lily replied. "She didn't try to kill herself. That wasn't in her nature. She threatened to kill herself for the attention. Whenever someone got angry with her, brought up the things she'd done, she talked about suicidal thoughts taking over. That was calculated. She knew what she was doing."

"I've known people like that," Jack murmured, shaking his head. "I had an aunt who threatened to put her head in the oven if people didn't take her more seriously. No one ever worried she would do it."

"That's how we were with Shayne," Lily said. "She was never going to kill herself. She just wanted the attention and thought she was fooling people."

"Well, that's something to think about," Jack noted, sliding his eyes to me when I jolted at a flash of lightning. "We should probably get under cover. The rain will hit soon. I think you were right about this storm being a doozy."

"They're all doozies," she said. "The heat and humidity build up, cause a burst, and then they pass. It will be hot and clear again by tomorrow morning."

"Just out of curiosity, who were you looking for out here?" Jack asked as he began to prod me toward the condo. "I mean ... you said people were out here the first night. Who was that?"

"Clark and his little friend." Lily's derision was clear as she wrinkled her nose. "He calls some service and arranges for a different woman each night, as if we're going to believe he somehow picked up a pretty twenty-something and she actually wanted to spend time with him."

"He's the one who wears the aggressive shirts, right?" Jack asked.

Lily nodded. "He has a few diagnosable personality disorders, too. He wants to be part of the group but is only accepted because people like Carter. They write the same genre, but one of them is way more popular than the other. I'm sure you can guess why."

"Personality," Jack concluded.

Lily nodded. "Carter says ridiculous stuff sometimes and stirs the political pot, but he's likable while he does it. Politics are part of the prepper genre, so that's simply something we have to put up with. Most of us try to avoid politics because it turns off readers. Prepper writers are the exact opposite."

"Huh." I hadn't really considered that. "So Carter is liked and Clark isn't?"

"Basically," Lily agreed. "Carter manages to charm people despite holding some rather extreme beliefs and putting forth outrageous conspiracy theories. Everyone dislikes Clark."

"And yet you're out here looking for him," Jack pointed out.

Lily shrugged. "I'm a sap. What can I say? He was caught out here during a big storm that first night and had to hunker down in one of the mini cabanas. He said it was so dark and nasty he couldn't see the pier, even though it was well lit and right in front of him."

Jack shifted his gaze to the pier and nodded, another bolt of lightning splitting the sky, causing the hair on my arms to stand on end. "Well, thanks for the mental health breakdown. You should probably get back to the hotel. No one is out here."

"I'm on it." She offered a wave as she trudged through the sand toward the resort. "Save the groping for when you get inside. The storm is almost here."

Jack scowled as I grinned.

"I think she's kind of funny," I said before he could disparage her. "She reminds me of Millie."

"She kind of reminds me of Millie, too," he groused as he pulled me away from the water and angled us toward the condos. He clearly didn't want to dally with a storm barreling down.

"You like Millie."

"I do, but one Millie is more than enough."

I wasn't sure I agreed. Two sounded like it could be all kinds of fun.

WE MADE IT BACK TO THE condo with seconds to spare. We were barely through the door when the sky illuminated, flashing against the sterile white walls of the living room, and the downpour began. I jumped at the sound of thunder, and Jack hugged me from behind as I watched the torrent of rain.

"It's okay," he whispered. "It's just a storm."

I nodded as I watched. "I generally like storms. I find them soothing."

"Me, too."

"Not today, though."

He tugged my hair away from my face to study my profile. "Because of the nightmares?"

"Yeah."

"I don't know what to do about them," he admitted, helpless. "I can't stop them."

"I don't expect you to stop them." That was true. "I just have to get through them." I cast a look to the bedroom I shared with Millie. "I should probably head in there. It's late and I'm sure we'll have another full day tomorrow."

"Yeah." Jack didn't release me, instead resting his head on my shoulder. "If you need me during the night I'll be on the couch."

"You can't save me from my nightmares."

"It would be nice if I could."

We shared a quick kiss, one much lighter than the one on the beach. Both of us clearly didn't want to risk anything heavy with Bernard and Millie sleeping under the same roof. I bade him goodnight and walked into the room, the sound of Millie's echoing snores causing me to cringe. They were louder than the storm.

I stared at her a moment, unsure what to do, and then made up my mind. I changed into a comfortable T-shirt and knit shorts, grabbed the extra blanket and pillow from the end of the bed, and headed back to the living room. Jack was already stripped to his boxers and on the couch when I returned.

"What are you doing?"

"I can't sleep with Millie snoring like that. It will make things worse. I'm going to sleep on the floor."

"No, you're not. You won't get any sleep if you're uncomfortable."

"I think that's my only option."

"You can sleep on the couch and I'll take the floor."

"Then you won't get any sleep," I pointed out.

"I wasn't the one who went through an ordeal today."

I wasn't sure about that. He seemed more upset about me falling into the ocean than almost anybody, including me. "You need your sleep. It's important."

"Well, you're no less important." He studied me for a long moment, his features illuminated thanks to the light on the front walk and the quick flashes of lightning. "We'll share the couch."

My heart stuttered. "W-what?"

"We'll share the couch," he repeated, sliding under the blanket and gesturing for me to join him. "Maybe we'll both sleep that way, without nightmares."

I remained unsure. "What if you get ideas and grope me?"

Instead of dismissing the idea outright, he grinned. "You'll have to wait to find out if that happens. I can't make any promises. My hands have a mind of their own."

I sighed, resigned. His offer was better than anything else on the table. I plopped my pillow on top of his and dropped the extra blanket on the floor before rolling in next to him.

"Wandering hands will be grounds for amputation," I warned as he spooned behind me, making sure he had me tucked in and I was comfortable before resting his head on the pillow.

"I'll try to refrain." He sounded tired as I closed my eyes, my mind already drifting.

"The storm makes it nice for sleeping," I murmured. "I hope I don't dream badly."

"Me, too." He lightly kissed my cheek. "Go to sleep. If your dreams are bad, remember that I'm here. It's going to be okay."

"Yeah. Probably. I hope I don't have any embarrassing sex dreams while we're sleeping like this. Actually, I'm more worried about you having those dreams than me. I hope you can contain yourself."

Jack's lips curved against my ear. "No promises. Go to sleep."

"Watch your hands," I repeated.

"Charlie?"

"Yeah?"

"Go to sleep."

There was nothing else to do, so I did as he asked. The day caught up with me hard and fast. Surprisingly, when I slipped into dreamland, there were no sharks in sight. There were, however, a few murderous writers to contend with.

They weren't nearly as scary.

FOURTEEN

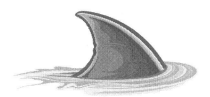

I woke warm and comfortable despite the fact that Jack and I were on top of each other. My dreams, while not trouble-free, hadn't been nearly as disastrous as I envisioned. Unfortunately, I didn't get a chance to bask in our proximity upon waking because we weren't alone.

Ahem.

Millie didn't even try to play coy as she cleared her throat, and when I snapped open my eyes, I found her standing in the middle of the living room, hands on her hips as she stared.

"What's going on?" Jack asked, his voice sleepy.

"I was just about to ask you that," Millie replied. Bernard was with her, still in his pajamas, and he looked amused at the turn of events. "You guys aren't naked under that blanket, are you? I'll be scarred for life if you are."

Jack scowled. "We're not naked. Don't give me grief."

"I believe that's part of my job description," she said lightly. "If I don't give you grief, who will?"

"I think Laura has taken on the mantle of commander in grief."

"True enough." Millie's gaze was speculative and I could feel my cheeks burning. "Did I miss something important last night? You guys disappeared right before dinner, which wasn't lost on Laura, by the way. Where did you go?"

Jack made no move to release his arm from my waist. "We went to dinner and then a walk on the beach. Why do you care?"

"Because I'm a busybody."

"Well, at least you admit it." Jack shifted to study my face. "How did you sleep?"

"Fine." I wanted to play it cool, so I kept my smile pleasant rather than flirty. Of course, I was terrible at flirting. For all I knew, my version of a flirtatious smile could've resembled a velociraptor. "No nightmares, but I did dream about that shark book guy chasing me around while screaming he was kind of a big deal and trying to lure me into his van."

Jack snorted. "He's definitely weird ... and on top of the list of people I'm going to research today." He briefly focused on Millie. "Why are you still here? Get cleaned up. We're supposed to meet for breakfast as a group to plan our day."

"Yeah, yeah." Millie waved off the order. "I have a question before that happens."

Jack was calm. "What question is that?"

"Are you guys going public with this relationship? I mean ... can I openly terrorize Laura with what I found this morning? That would make my day better."

"No, you cannot." He vehemently shook his head. "You already knew, which means Bernard already knew. I was going to drag the revelation out with you guys, but given the storm last night and what happened to Charlie, I didn't want her sleeping alone on the floor."

"She could've slept with me," Millie pointed out.

"You snore loud enough to wake the dead," Jack challenged. "She needed sleep. She got it out here. Do you have a problem with that?"

"No." Millie looked uncertain as she pursed her lips. "If you want, starting tonight, you guys can have the second bedroom."

"How will that work?" I asked, confused. "Where will Bernard sleep? You can't put him on the couch. He's old ... er, older. That's rude."

Bernard's eyes twinkled. He often found me funny, which was a blessing. My personality was something of an acquired taste.

"He'll be with me, numbnuts," Millie snapped, catching me off guard. "If you guys are going to sleep together, I don't see any reason Bernard and I can't do the same."

I'd often wondered if Millie and Bernard had something going on the side. She was careful not to show her hand, but they were unbelievably tight. "I knew it!"

Jack snickered as he rolled to his back. "I don't care if you guys share a bedroom, Millie. I won't tell Chris. I know you worry that he'll get his nose out of joint because of Myron, but he won't hear it from me."

I was taken aback. "Haven't Millie and Myron been divorced for a long time?"

"Yes, but Chris is a bit weird about it," Millie replied. "He still thinks of me as his aunt, which I encourage. Plus, Myron occasionally gets weird about things. Bernard and I agreed when we started dating to keep it quiet. Jack has always known, though."

I cast him a sidelong look. "I asked and you wouldn't confirm it for me."

"It was none of your business." He was firm. "I still maintain that we're all up in each other's business too much. I don't care if you guys share a room. Your snoring is louder than anything else you could possibly do."

Millie turned haughty. "Oh, don't get too full of yourself. I'm loud no matter what I do."

"I can vouch for that," Bernard said dryly. "Still, I appreciate the offer. That will give you guys some privacy, too."

My cheeks were back to burning and the look on Jack's face told me he didn't miss the color that was obviously flooding my features.

"We might not be there yet, but thank you for the invitation," he said, choosing his words carefully. "We'll move things around later tonight. I think we should head to breakfast as soon as possible — and keep all the sleeping arrangements quiet — because Chris supposedly has assignments for everybody today."

"We can handle that," Millie said. "I'm great at keeping secrets."

Jack was understandably dubious. "We'll have to see about that."

IT TURNED OUT, MY ASSIGNMENT was the best. Chris sent me to the local aquarium to meet with a shark expert named Ty Crocker. He was expecting me, and open to answering anything I might ask. Jack arranged to go with me, pointing out he would ask harder questions that might ultimately be necessary, and Chris agreed without argument.

Laura, on the other hand, was suspicious. She gave Jack and me the evil eye throughout breakfast, occasionally asking what Jack did for dinner the previous night, but he smoothly sidestepped every question she lobbed. He knew better than to get caught up in her web, and I was thankful she focused her attention on him rather than me.

Jack drove, which was fine. I wasn't familiar with the roads or traffic in the area. I spent all my time staring at the ocean and marveling at how bright the sun was following such an intense storm.

"How did you sleep?" I asked as he followed the signs to the aquarium. "I never got the chance to ask."

"I slept hard. I was out right away. I worried when I woke that I somehow slept through your nightmares, but you seem pretty together. I take it you slept okay, too."

"Oh, yeah. I didn't even realize how tired I was until my head was on the pillow. After that, there was no holding me back. I was gone."

"You didn't move all night."

"Neither did you."

"I was comfortable."

Speaking of that ... . I chewed on my bottom lip as I turned to study his profile. He was focused on the traffic, but the tension he carried in his shoulders the previous day seemed to have evaporated. I had a question, but I wasn't sure I should ask it.

Instead, I internally hemmed and hawed as he drove, waiting until we were in the aquarium parking lot to blurt it out. "Why don't you have a problem with Millie and Bernard knowing about us?"

If he was surprised at the way I asked the question, Jack didn't show it. Instead, he picked a spot, put the rental in park, and turned to face me. "Because Millie already knew. You told me that. She shares everything with Bernard. That means he knew, too. There was no reason to keep it a secret."

"Yeah, but ... we both agreed it was probably best to keep things on the down low until we were sure."

"Honestly, I was more worried about Laura," Jack admitted, smoothing his hair. "She's unpredictable. Chris and Hannah are lost in their own little world. I don't think they'll care. It will take them forever to notice on their own. I'm fine with that."

"Do you think there's something Laura could do to us?"

"No, not necessarily."

He looked uncomfortable at the question, which meant I needed to push harder. "You're hiding something. I want to know what it is."

He heaved a sigh. "It's just ... we're not supposed to fraternize with co-workers. It's company policy."

"Oh." Realization dawned. "So ... we could get fired for dating."

"We could," he agreed. "Laura is the type to report us, which is funny because she would be the first to break the rules if I agreed to go out with her."

"Right." My mind was busy. "Do you think we'll get fired?"

"I don't know," he shrugged. "I won't have an issue finding another job if it comes to that. You, on the other hand, managed to beat out a lot of eager people for this position. There isn't as much out there for you if things fall apart."

He wasn't wrong.

"If you're worried about losing your job, I understand." He sounded stretched, tense. "You should probably tell me now. I'm already attached to you, but I'll understand if you need to put the job first."

The statement threw me for a loop. "I don't have any intention of choosing the job over you. I get now why you wanted to keep it quiet, though. It's ... a little scary. This is my first real job that doesn't involve being an intern or asking someone if they want fries with their burger."

Jack chuckled as he collected my hand and gave it a squeeze. "Bernard and Millie have been doing this for years and they're fine. I do believe Laura is going to become an issue at some point. She's suspicious right now, but she doesn't have proof. Eventually she'll trip over that proof and she'll want to make things difficult for you when she does."

"She already tries to make things difficult for me whenever she can swing it. I can handle that."

"Is there anything you can't handle?" Jack's eyes were plaintive. "Tell me. I would rather we deal with stuff together than hide our feelings or fears."

That was a nice sentiment. "I just don't want Laura to make things hard for us. I haven't learned everything I need to learn from this place yet." I didn't mean to say the second part out loud, but the words were already out of my mouth before I could pull them back. "I mean ... I've only been on a few assignments. I want to see more of the world before I lose the chance."

"You're not going to lose the chance." Jack was calm as he squeezed my fingers. "If it comes to it, I'll quit my job. That way you'll be safe."

I balked "You can't quit your job. That's not fair."

"There are hundreds of jobs I'm qualified for," he pointed out. "You're just starting. You need this job for a bit longer."

"I don't want you to quit. Part of the reason I like this job so much is because of you."

He smiled, his eyes filling with delight. "That's very sweet, but we don't have to worry about this right now. Laura doesn't know. She doesn't have proof. We have time. We just need to play it safe in front of her for the time being. I think we're both capable of that."

I swallowed hard and nodded. "Okay. I'll do my best to keep from groping you."

He chuckled. "You're obsessed with that word now, aren't you?"

"A little bit."

· · ·

TY CROCKER DIDN'T LOOK like a normal scientist. He was young — in his early thirties — with long blond hair pulled back into a pony-tail. He had one of those trendy beards that was well-groomed and (thankfully) devoid of food, and he was all smiles when he welcomed Jack and me into his office.

"Welcome. I hear you're with the Legacy Foundation. I've heard great things about the group."

"We've heard great things about you," Jack said perfunctorily. He was good at getting information, even though he wasn't always the easiest guy to get along with. "You've been with the aquarium for a few years, right?"

"I consider this my home." Crocker bobbed his head and smiled at me, his eyes lingering to the point I felt mildly uncomfortable. "You look familiar. Have we ever met?"

"I doubt it," I replied. "I'm not local."

"Yes, but there's something about you." He tapped his bottom lip, thoughtful. "Wait ... you're the woman who fell in the Gulf near the whale yesterday. I have photos. That's where I know you from."

Jack scowled as I fought to tamp down my embarrassment.

"That would be me," I conceded. "I swam with bull sharks and lived to tell the tale."

"You're extremely lucky," Crocker noted. "The whale carcass was enough to make the bull sharks territorial. They're known to fight over food, go into frenzies. The more sharks that appeared in the area, the more likely they were to rip one another — and any interlopers — into pieces."

I swallowed hard at the unfortunate visual. "Oh, well ... ."

"She's fine," Jack interjected, his eyes flashing. "She doesn't need to be reminded of what happened. We got lucky and fished her out. She was a little shaky, but she's back to her normal self now."

"I'm glad for that." Crocker seemed sincere. "Things could've taken a tragic turn, but they didn't. That's good for all of us. The last thing we need is another shark attack right on the heels of that author dying. People are already irrationally afraid of sharks. An incident so close to the first would've unnecessarily added to a panic that could've resulted in sharks being slaughtered for no good reason. It's happened before."

"Well, we don't want that." Jack shifted in his chair, clearly uncomfortable. "We do want to talk to you about the whale, though. It was big. I understand you were sent out to take a look. Do you have any idea how it died?"

Crocker hedged. "I wasn't aware you were here to investigate whales."

"We're not," Jack said. "We're trying to figure out how Shayne Rivers ended up in the water. There's no way of telling if she was dead before or after the sharks got to her. My boss is convinced there's a large predator in the Gulf — something bigger than bull sharks — and we're trying to figure out if a predator took down that whale or if it was something else."

"I see." Crocker steepled his fingers, his expression grave. "I can't say with any certainty what happened to the whale. Creatures die in the wild all the time. It's rare that we can see a feeding frenzy like the one that occurred where Ms. Rhodes had her incident yesterday, but it's not unheard of. It was a nice scientific find.

"That said, I don't know how the whale died," he continued. "It was missing large portions of its anatomy. That could've happened from accidentally running into a ship ... or predators ripping apart the carcass after it died. As for a big predator taking it down, I think that's unlikely. The Fin whale is the largest animal in the Gulf. There are no predators that could take it down."

"What about a Megalodon?" I asked automatically, earning a groan from Jack, which I opted to ignore. "A Megalodon is big enough to take it down, right?"

Crocker worked his jaw, clearly trying to decide if I was serious. "Um ... ."

"Ignore her," Jack offered. "She's just being Charlie."

"No, I want an answer," I persisted. "Could a Megalodon have taken down that whale?"

"Megalodons are extinct," Crocker said finally. "They don't live in the Gulf of Mexico."

"I understand, but let's say a Megalodon somehow survived and was roaming around," I said. "Could a Megalodon have taken out the whale?"

"Not likely." Crocker licked his lips, all traces of flirtatious energy disappearing. "A Megalodon would've eaten the whale. There would've been nothing to study after the fact. It wouldn't have left a huge carcass behind."

"What if it couldn't eat all of the remains? What if it was full?"

"Sharks are almost never full," Crocker replied. "Their entire existence consists of eating and then hunting for their next meal. They're killing machines."

"So ... you're saying it's impossible that a bigger predator killed the whale and left the carcass behind," I mused. "That's kind of a bummer."

"Yes, a bummer." I didn't miss the look Crocker shot Jack. He clearly thought I was off my rocker. "Did you have any other questions? I should probably get back to work otherwise. As much as I love the idea of talking about Megalodons, I was under the impression you had legitimate questions about this area."

"We have a few," Jack said. "I don't want to take up much of your time, but I just want to clarify a few things regarding bull shark activity close to the shore. Most importantly, in regard to the author who died, would bull sharks have gone after her even if she was already dead?"

Clearly more comfortable with Jack's line of questioning than mine, Crocker relaxed a bit. "Absolutely. Bull sharks are scavengers, too. Is there a possibility she was already dead when she hit the water?"

"There is. We're trying to prove things either way."

"Well, I would love to be of help. I hate it when the locals panic about shark activity. The odds of being attacked by a shark are slim. I'll help however I can. What do you need to know?"

FIFTEEN

*J*ack was quiet on the way back to the resort.

I was a big ball of annoyance.

"I don't like it when people talk down to me," I announced.

Jack arched an eyebrow. "I wasn't talking down to you."

"Not you. I'm talking about the aquarium guy. Ty. Who names their kid Ty?"

"It's probably short for Tyler."

"I don't like nicknames."

"Really, Charlotte?"

I stilled, my agitation ramping up a notch. "That's different. I never should've been named Charlotte in the first place. That name doesn't fit me."

"I agree Charlie fits your personality better," Jack said. "Maybe Ty fits his personality better."

"I still don't like him." I folded my arms over my chest and stared out the window. "He acts as if I don't know that Megalodons are extinct. I know that. I watch *Shark Week*. I'm not a total idiot."

Instead of agreeing, Jack sighed. "I don't think he was calling you an idiot. I believe he merely thought you were enthusiastic over something that couldn't possibly be true."

"How is that different?"

"Idiots aren't cute. You happen to be adorable, something I think he believed from the moment he saw you ... until you started droning on and on about Megalodons."

Oh, well, that was just ridiculous. "All I said was that I didn't think it was impossible for a large predator to be wandering around the Gulf munching on people. I hardly think that's cause to nominate me for the Doofus Hall of Fame."

"I'll keep that in mind." Jack pulled into the parking lot. The only open spot close to the front door happened to be next to J.D. Wells' creepy van. "This thing really is garish."

I couldn't argue with that. "I'm telling you, the only people who buy vans like this want to kidnap children and do detestable things to them – or dress like clowns."

Jack pocketed the keys and pushed open his door. "Clowns?"

"They're creepy."

He shook his head. "Come on, I have a plan for the rest of our afternoon."

"Does it include telling me I'm a moron for believing Megalodons could've survived?"

"We'll see how the afternoon goes."

IT TURNED OUT JACK'S IDEA wasn't entirely bad. He found an outdoor bar, with appropriate shade so I didn't melt, and we ordered iced tea and set up his laptop.

"So, what are we doing?" I asked after the caffeine perked me up a bit. "Are we researching Megalodon migratory patterns? I think Chris and Hannah already did that. They didn't find anything of use."

"Imagine that," he drawled, his attention on his screen. "They didn't find anything useful studying the migratory patterns of sharks when the land masses we call continents looked completely different. I'm shocked."

"Nobody needs your attitude."

"I'll work on it." He tapped a few keys. "As for what we're doing, I've been running searches on some of these authors. It hasn't been easy because tracking down real names is difficult. Luckily, I happen to know someone who could help."

"And who is that?"

"I have a friend in the IRS."

"No one has friends in the IRS."

"I do. We served together overseas. He managed to help me track down real names to go with the pen names. It's not exactly on the up-and-up, so I expect discretion if anyone asks where I got the information."

I was tickled he felt comfortable enough to confide in me. "Oh, well, I like learning things through nefarious means."

Jack grinned. "Somehow I knew that." He motioned for me to move my chair closer. "Let's see what we've got, shall we?"

We started with Wells. He seemed the obvious choice.

"His real name is John Smith," Jack announced. "His wife's maiden name is Christine Pratt. She's listed as Christine Wells on his incorporation documents, but she never legally changed her name."

"Smith is a boring name."

"Which is probably why he changed it for writing purposes."

"True. What does it say?"

"His background is clean, not as much as a parking ticket that I can find. Up until about a year ago he lived in a trailer park with his wife. They were living paycheck to paycheck, barely scraping by, and then he started making money with his books."

"Shark books?"

"I don't know. Haven't you looked up his books?"

"No."

"You have a phone."

I scowled. "And here I thought you were Mr. Information."

"I'm Mr. I Only Have So Much Patience and You're Wearing On It."

I could see that. "I'm looking." I scrolled through the information I found online. "It seems he started with a fantasy series, and it did pretty well. Then he wrote something called *Killer Aliens: A Space Opera*, and that has quite a few reviews, so that means it must have sold. I don't see the shark book listed."

"He said he hadn't published that yet, that he was hoping to rush the editing and get it out quickly," Jack noted. "Maybe that's a new genre for him."

I played with my bottom lip as I considered the logistics of Wells being a killer. "He's kind of big," I said. "I don't mean that in a derogatory way. It's just ... do you really think he could carry a body to the end of the pier and dump it over the side without help? That's quite a walk."

"I've been thinking about that, too," he admitted. "He has the van."

"You can't drive a van on the pier."

"No, but you can drive a van to that small parking lot right next to the pier," he pointed out.

"And then what? He'd still have to walk the rest of the way."

"Not if he took a golf cart."

I knit my eyebrows. "What golf cart?"

"The one the security guards keep handy at the base of the pier. I saw a few of them when we first arrived, and I checked. They leave them out there overnight."

"I bet they don't leave them out there with keys. That would be an accident waiting to happen with so many bars on the premises."

"That's a fair point, but it's not hard to hotwire a golf cart. I know from personal experience."

"You've hotwired a golf cart?" I was skeptical. He was far too straight-laced for that.

"Back in my younger days I liberated a golf cart from a local resort one evening."

I was learning more and more about him every day. "Did you get in trouble?"

"I was grounded and had to work at the resort for free for six weeks. My father insisted."

I was impressed ... and slightly amused. "Oh, well, that's terrible." I fought the urge to laugh. "Were you a caddy?"

"A cart kid."

"One of the guys who washes the carts?"

"Exactly."

"I bet you learned your lesson on that one."

"I did," he nodded. "Never stole another golf cart. That doesn't mean Wells wouldn't risk it to get rid of a body."

I sobered. "Okay, let's say I agree that he's a viable suspect, which I'm not sure I do. What's his motive?"

"Maybe Shayne Rivers was writing a shark book and was trying to steal his thunder. Didn't that pimento cheese chick tell you that she was threatening to steal that mystery lady's thunder by working with James Sanderson? Maybe she made a habit of stealing ideas from other writers."

It was an interesting thought. "The thing is ... there's really nothing new left. Everything is old and just approached in a different manner. I can't see stealing a shark attack book — of which there have been hundreds written — as a motive for murder."

Jack tilted his head, considering. "You're probably right. That doesn't seem like much of a motive. Maybe there's more we haven't discovered."

"Maybe, but he's hardly the only suspect."

"True." Jack moved on to Leslie Downs. "Okay, so I managed to pull police records. She writes under her real name. I don't know if that's smart or stupid."

"I would think most readers are normal and don't want to hurt anyone," I offered. "There's probably only one wacko for every one-thousand normal readers."

"It only takes one wacko to cause a problem," Jack noted. "That's exactly what she did to James Sanderson, by the way. The story she told you was missing a few key details."

I leaned back in my chair and smirked. "I can't wait to hear this. I knew she was off the minute I met her. Nobody has helmet hair these days ... unless they have severe mental problems."

"I'll have to trust you on the hair, but if this author photo is any indication, I get where you're coming from. So, Leslie Downs has been an author for several years. I don't know if she ever published under a different name, but under her name she's done some nutty stuff.

"First, the James Sanderson thing was a bigger deal than I realized," he continued. "Apparently it was all over the news."

"I don't remember hearing about it."

"I'm betting if he'd been a Hollywood star things would've been different," he said. "Anyway, according to the police report I managed to pull, Leslie Downs first tracked him down at some thriller conference in New York. He was signing books, and he did a question-and-answer session with readers. The first hint of trouble came when Leslie wanted to ask a question but wasn't selected. She melted down and had to be escorted out of the building by security."

"That doesn't sound freaky or anything."

Jack snickered. "That night, he was having dinner with his wife in the hotel dining room — an extremely ritzy establishment — and Leslie showed up at his table dressed as a waitress," he said. "She asked for his autograph, went so far as to take his order, and then invited herself to sit down at his table.

"Sanderson had dealt with enough crazy people that he knew not to push her too far, especially with sharp utensils nearby, so his wife alerted the desk while he pretended to be interested in her spiel," he continued. "Security eventually came and took her, but not before she stole his napkin and shoved it in her shirt."

I was legitimately puzzled. "Why would she want his napkin?"

"I have no idea. I'm sure it was for a freaky reason."

"I'll bet."

"Sanderson lived in Connecticut and returned home after that," Jack said. "He thought things were over, but then Downs started calling him at home. He had no idea how she got his number and she refused to tell law enforcement when questioned. Things got so bad with incessant calling they killed their landline.

"He never agreed to write a series with her," he continued. "He was

141

polite during the dinner fiasco and said her idea sounded intriguing. My guess is he said that because he didn't want to agitate her. She took it a different way and became obsessed."

"How long did he put up with her antics before the cabin thing happened in Minnesota?"

"Two years."

"Wow!"

"Yeah, she's all kinds of nutty."

"Why wasn't she arrested?"

"It's harder to get a restraining order than you think," Jack replied. "He probably tried but couldn't find a sympathetic judge. All of that changed when she showed up at the fishing cabin. He called the cops, she was dragged away, and she was forced into a forty-eight-hour psychiatric hold.

"When the hospital said it couldn't keep her, Sanderson decided to make her an offer," he continued. "She voluntarily signed the restraining order — which covered Sanderson and his immediate family — and he agreed to let her write in his world.

"There were certain stipulations, like no print or audio books, and she couldn't use his name in the blurb," he said. "Other than that, she could do whatever she wanted."

"Does she make money off the series?"

"Not much, according to the financial information I've been able to pull. She does okay. She probably makes more money than you. Compared to some of the other authors here, she's at the low end of the spectrum."

That was interesting. "Just out of curiosity, what do these other authors make? I mean ... do they make so much I might want to cry?"

"Actually, the median income appears to be about fifty grand a year," Jack replied. "There are obviously outliers, those who make more. There are also some who make far less. I can't see any rhyme or reason in the figures, and I'm not sure that's ultimately important."

"I always thought the most important questions asked when heading up an investigation regarded money. Other than love — or lust, I guess — money is the second-biggest motivating factor."

"I don't argue with that." Jack rubbed the back of his neck as he studied his screen. "I'm going to dig further on Downs. I find her worrisome enough, especially because Shayne Rivers was reportedly trying to steal her gig. I wouldn't put it past her to kill a woman and toss her in the Gulf for the sharks."

"Not to be the naysayer yet again, but she's not a very big woman," I offered. "How would she be able to drag the body all the way down the pier? I know you're going to say the golf carts, but not everyone knows how to hotwire a golf cart."

"Fair enough. Maybe she had help."

"Like who?"

Jack shrugged. "What did you say were the names of the women with her in the spa?"

"Oh, um ... Abigail James and Priscilla Jennings."

It didn't take Jack long to run both names. "Abigail James is a real name. She's a married mother of two who lives in New York. She graduated from college, has no priors, and makes a middle-of-the-road income."

"So ... not a suspect?"

"I'm not ruling anyone out, but she's not high on my list unless we learn something else about her."

"Okay. What about Priscilla Jennings?"

"That is not a real name," Jack replied after a few keystrokes. "Her real name is Margaret VanBuren. She's in her sixties, married, no children. She lives in Wyoming."

"Who voluntarily lives in Wyoming?"

"People who like space and hate neighbors."

"I see you've given it some thought."

Jack's smile was back and he looked from the screen long enough to wink at me. "You'd be surprised how many things I've given serious thought to. As for Priscilla, she doesn't have a record either. She had a dispute over taxes at one point, but nothing major. She's fairly quiet. She writes sports romances."

"Like the quarterback gets a touchdown and everyone gets naked?"

"Pretty much."

"I don't think that's my genre."

"You and me both."

"What about the guy with the prostitute?" I asked, my mind traveling to Clark Savage's antics on the beach. "What can you find about him?"

"Um ... ." Jack pursed his lips as he studied his screen. "Well, Savage isn't his last name, but Clark is his first name."

"What's his real last name?"

"Lickenfelt."

I pressed my lips together, momentarily embarrassed that my first reaction had been to laugh out loud. That was a high school reaction. I couldn't stop myself from giggling. "Seriously?"

"Yup."

"I see why he changed his name."

"Right? He's got a heavy online presence, proudly owns more than seventy guns, which I have no problem with in theory, unless he's a complete nutball – which is starting to look possible. He runs a weekly podcast on how to survive the end of the world, and is eagerly awaiting the Rapture because he's convinced only the righteous will be left behind."

"I thought those left behind in the Rapture were supposed to be the bad people?"

"Apparently not in his world."

"What about Shayne Rivers?" I asked. "Did he have anything to do with her?"

"I'm not sure. It appears he's gotten into it with numerous different writers on the internet. It's a small community and there are a lot of fights. Since Rivers was prominent on the internet and liked to draw attention to herself, and Savage is the same way, it's entirely possible they butted heads."

"An internet fight isn't usually enough to kill someone over."

"No, but we don't know if Rivers pushed his buttons another way. We'll have to tap into the gossip vein if we want to know the answer to that question. I don't suppose one of your new friends would be able to help us?"

"What new friends?"

"That cozy mystery writer you like and the pimento cheese chick would be my top choices. They seem the most normal ones here."

"You think the pimento cheese chick is normal?"

"More normal than some of the others we've met."

I heaved out a sigh. "Fine. We can ask them. If that pimento cheese question is code for something I don't recognize, though, I expect you to step in and save my virtue."

"I can manage that."

I could only hope that was true.

SIXTEEN

*S*arah Hilton was easy to find. I left Jack to continue digging on the other authors — something he seemed leery about because he said I was a trouble magnet when unsupervised — and found her at the coffee bar. That seemed to be her favorite hangout. She probably didn't need the extra caffeine, but it wasn't my business to say.

She was sitting at a table with Lily Harper Hart. Both of my information sources together. I couldn't get much luckier.

"There she is." Lily beamed and leaned back in her chair as I approached. "It's our intrepid investigator. How are things going on your end?"

"I have a few questions." I felt uncomfortable asking but it was part of the job, so I sucked it up. "I'm going to grab something to drink. I'll be right back."

"We'll be waiting," Sarah sang out.

She was odd. I happened to like odd. If she'd stop offering me pimento cheese she would be practically perfect.

By the time I rejoined them, they were deep in conversation. They seemed to be talking publishing business strategy, and both knew what they were talking about.

"I prefer trilogies, but I get what you're saying about longer series in mysteries," Sarah offered. "In fantasy, trilogies are the preferred method of reading. Mystery readers like long series, though. I think it's a smart plan."

I felt out of place as I sat with them, clutching my green tea and glancing between faces. They appeared friendly and relaxed. I was the one worked up.

"You look as if you're about to pop a vein in your forehead," Lily noted, her lips curving. She always seemed to be in a good mood ... unless she was about to blow up at someone. Then she lost her temper for a few minutes and was right back to being in a good mood. It was an interesting phenomenon. "Just tell us what you want to know. We'll either answer or we won't."

"I'll probably answer no matter what," Sarah admitted. "I have a big mouth."

Lily snickered. "I believe that's an ailment I suffer from, too. Foot-in-Mouth Disease. Untreatable and sometimes deadly."

I laughed. They were good at putting me at ease. "I need information about some of your fellow authors."

"You mean gossip."

"Well ... kind of."

"You're in luck," Lily said. "I love gossip. Who do you want dirt on?"

"Well, for starters, what can you tell me about Leslie Downs and her relationship with Shayne Rivers?"

"It was ugly," Sarah answered without hesitation. "If there was a national hair-pulling contest, they would've both medaled."

"Did they actually pull each other's hair?"

"Not that I know of. You would lose your hand in that nest of snakes Leslie has going," Lily said. "Someone needs to tell her the eighties are over and that much hairspray is never a good idea."

"It's also a fire hazard," Sarah offered sagely.

"I know a little about her relationship with James Sanderson," I started. "I know about what happened at the restaurant ... and the fishing cabin. What I'm interested in is how Shayne's partnership with James would've affected her."

Lily shrugged, noncommittal. "It's hard to say," she said. "Um ... it's a difficult situation. I've never understood the appeal of writing in someone else's world. I prefer making up my own characters. Other people have trouble plotting and creating, so they jump at the chance."

That didn't make much sense. "Writers have trouble plotting?"

She chuckled. "You'd be surprised how many authors hire someone else to do their plotting. Like Jezebel Walters over there." She pointed to a woman who looked of Indian descent, pretty skin offset by glossy black hair that made me envious. She sat at a table by herself, a look of fury on her face as she scanned the lobby.

"What's her problem?" I asked. "She doesn't look happy. Also ... Jezebel isn't her real name, right? No one would name their kid that."

"I'm sure there's some idiot out there who thought it was a good idea, but her real name is Jessica Walton," Sarah replied. "She writes urban fantasy, like me."

"Are you friends?"

"There are times I wish I had a truck so I could run her over, back up, run her over, back up, run her over ... ."

Lily held up a hand to still Sarah. "We get it. Jezebel is the Devil. Think about pimento cheese and not running over people. It's better for your blood pressure."

Sarah grinned. "I'm always thinking about pimento cheese."

"I've noticed." Lily cleared her throat and shifted her eyes to me. "Jezebel is ... a unique individual."

"Is that code for something?"

Sarah bobbed her head. "It's code for being the Devil."

Lily snickered. "She's a solid writer. Not spectacular, but solid. When she first burst on the scene everyone was impressed because she was selling a lot right out of the gate. She managed to find readers through Shayne's newsletter services, and they were positioning themselves as a power publishing couple. But it all fell apart."

I was hooked. "How did it fall apart?"

"Well, for starters, it turns out that Jezebel can't plot. Not at all. A

Dick and Jane book is too difficult for her to plot. She paid Shayne to plot for her."

I shook my head. "I'm not going to pretend to get the publishing world," I said after a beat. "That seems counterintuitive to doing this for a living."

"I'd agree, but that's not how Jezebel sees it," Lily explained. "She makes decent money, but she spends a lot, too. She's a heavy advertiser, and that cuts into her bottom line. When she had her falling out with Shayne she also lost her most popular series."

"I need more information than that."

Lily happily launched into her tale. "So, Jezebel and Shayne were tight for years, both coming up in the publishing world at the same time and writing similar books," she started. "They were a fearsome twosome, and Jezebel was knee-deep in a lot of the gaslighting Shayne was doing. She was simply smarter about it than Shayne and publicly kept her hands clean."

"She was kind of behind the scenes," I mused. "That means she was probably even more manipulative."

"Bingo. Anyway, things got rough when the writing community turned on Shayne. Jezebel — and you're right, the more I say it, the more I realize it's a stupid name — started feeling blowback. People didn't want to associate with her because of her partnership with Shayne. She was almost as hated in the writing community, which is saying something, because we never agree on anything."

I rubbed my hand over my knee, considering. "I'm guessing Shayne didn't take that well."

"Not even a little. She's prone to meltdowns on the internet and she had a big one, although she didn't name names. She learned a lesson when she got dragged into multiple lawsuits with other authors and stopped publicly shaming, instead resorting to vague postings."

"I think someone else mentioned those lawsuits. It seems Shayne had multiple fights going with a lot of different groups."

"Oh, you have no idea," Sarah intoned. "The only people who stood by her were those who were new and couldn't understand what was going on. That forced her to turn more manipulative, which made people angry because she was trying to paint herself as a victim."

"Go back to Jezebel," I prodded. "What happened with her and Shayne?"

"Eventually Jezebel tried to end their working relationship," Lily replied. "She'd been warned multiple times but didn't care. Without Shayne to outline her series, she was forced to end it because she can't plot."

"I don't even know what to make of that."

"The series made a lot of money," Sarah said. "Like ... a lot. She spent a lot of money to promote it. Without new books, it basically withered and died on the vine. Jezebel wouldn't admit that she needed someone else to plot her books, so she lied to her readers and said she wanted to end it.

"Then she partnered with several other authors to write series, but basically she was relying on them to plot," she continued. "Her bitterness about the series she had to end grew. There was a conference in San Antonio a few months ago that ended with them screaming at each other in front of other people."

"Yes, that was lovely," Lily drawled, her smile mischievous. "I love a good public meltdown when I'm not in the middle of it."

Sarah snickered. "Your meltdowns are always entertaining. The one in San Antonio was just sad. They tossed accusations at one another, Shayne faked tears and pretended to be a victim of bullying. That was always her go-to excuse, by the way. *Bullying.* Everyone was jealous and she was the most bullied writer in the world."

"Meanwhile, she was gathering her followers to attack other authors with fake one-stars," Lily said. "Those one-stars ended a few pen names before the authors even had a chance to get a foothold. I know a few authors quit because of it. Others went undercover to protect themselves and started new pen names."

"And one-stars are?" I prodded.

"Reviews," Sarah replied. "I know it sounds ridiculous, but the reviews are important. It's not just for ego. You need them for advertising."

"Okay, but there's no way bad reviews would be enough to kill over."

"Probably not," Sarah agreed. "Losing your livelihood might be, though. I know Jezebel, for example, is making a third of what she was when she was working with Shayne. That's probably still okay money, but she bought an expensive house and her husband doesn't work. Money is a great motivator for hate."

This whole thing kept getting more and more convoluted. "So why is Jezebel here? And why is she sitting alone?"

"Oh, that's both sad and funny," Sarah replied. "She posted a notice on a community message board that she would be in the lobby and available for questions from new authors for an hour. She expected to be inundated and told authors to hurry before she was swarmed. This is that hour ... and no one cared enough to show up."

Sarah and Lily looked amused at the turn of events.

"You think it's funny because you don't like her," I surmised.

"We think it's hilarious," Lily conceded. "She's unpleasant ... and I can't tell you how tired I am of being referred to as jealous. I have no patience for grown women who use that word as a weapon. I'm too old to be jealous."

I waited because I was certain she wasn't finished.

"I'm not too old to laugh at that idiot believing people worship her, though," she added, causing me to smile.

"What about Leslie Downs?" I prodded. "Could Shayne's potential deal with James Sanderson have hurt her enough that she might've wanted to kill her?"

"Leslie is a nut. Like ... a total nut," Lily replied. "She's judgmental and casts aspersions on everyone else while trying to build herself up. She's easy to ignore and dismiss ... except when you remember what she did to James Sanderson.

"The thing is, we don't have any proof that Shayne was going to partner with Sanderson," she continued. "Shayne said that, but she was fighting with Leslie at the time and she's always looking for a reason to irritate people. It could've all been talk. We'll never know because Sanderson refuses to speak publicly about any of his writing partnerships."

"Leslie was deranged enough to frighten him, and he's been around a long time," Sarah added. "She makes me nervous. She irritates me, but I'm also leery. I think she's one insult away from going postal. I can only hope she doesn't have access to a gun."

Speaking of guns ... . "And what about Clark Savage?" I asked. "Did he ever cross paths with Shayne?"

"Oh, absolutely." Lily bobbed her blond head. "They fought about multiple things, including the fact that Clark believes women should be seen and not heard."

"As much as I hated Shayne — and I did hate her, make no mistake about that — the things Clark said to her on certain writing forums were ugly and unnecessary," Sarah said. "He called her husband names because he's a house husband who takes care of the kids while she handled the heavy lifting with their finances. Clark insisted she should stop writing and let some hard-working man have her space on the bestsellers lists."

I was horrified. "That seems like an antiquated belief."

"Yeah, well, he's a real douche," Lily offered. "No one likes him. The only reason he's allowed to hang around with us is because he's friends with Carter."

"Who everyone does like, right?"

"Yes. He puts on an act for his readers about being a tough guy, but he has a soft heart. He's a good guy."

I cracked my neck as I leaned back in my chair. "Let me ask you this; if you had to choose, who do you think would have the strongest motive for killing Shayne?"

"I have no idea," Lily replied. "The list is long. When I write my murder mysteries, I always have to consider a proper motive. The thing is, in the real world, motives aren't always as strong as you believe them to be."

"Good point. Still, someone had to want her dead."

"No one would come out and say that," Sarah said. "I mean ... not really. Someone might joke about it, or say it while drinking, but no one would be stupid enough to utter those words in front of an audience."

"What about her husband? What can you tell me about him?"

"Her husband is an issue all by himself," Lily answered. "I've never met him. He doesn't go to the conferences. He stays home and takes care of the kids while she represents her publishing business as a sole proprietor."

"That has to be emasculating."

"Maybe, but from his point of view he doesn't have it so bad," Sarah said. "He doesn't have to work. Her mother has two of the kids, the ones with special needs. She parades the others around Facebook while pretending to be a super mother. Then, when things don't go her way, she makes up stories about how the kids are sick or her husband has relapsed. She was a master at making people feel sorry for her even though she victimized people."

"Wait ... her husband relapsed?"

"He's a drunk," Lily supplied. "At least if you believe her. He drinks five days a week and sleeps in his own bedroom because she's always up late working in the master bedroom. She's a martyr and always paints herself as the hardest-working woman in the industry."

"Maybe her husband got fed up," I suggested. "Maybe he left the kids with someone else, traveled here, killed her and then turned around and headed home. If she really was so intolerable, he might've had a girlfriend and they could've worked together to carry it out."

"I guess that's possible," Lily hedged. "I actually like the notion for a book and I'm totally stealing the idea. But I'm not sure he could pull that off. There's a record when flying. You can't fly today without somebody knowing."

I hadn't thought about that. I was used to flying on private jets now, which meant I didn't have to go through security and the normal hoops other passengers were forced to jump through. "Maybe the girlfriend flew here and dispatched her. They could plan to keep their relationship secret until enough time has passed."

"That's not impossible, but I'm not sure why the husband would risk it," Lily said. "He had a lot of money to play with and didn't have to work. With Shayne dead, I'm betting there's going to be a fight over money ... especially because her mother has custody of the two kids. Shayne wasn't making nearly the money she was two years ago. They had a lot of bills, a fancy new house they built when the money was coming in. I'm not sure it would've benefitted him to kill her."

That was something to consider. "Most crimes are committed by people who know the victim, who have rage for the victim. I can't see someone being upset enough about bad reviews and even a few stolen dollars on promotions to kill someone."

"I agree," Lily said. "I think we're either looking for someone who is mentally unbalanced or an individual who had a much bigger fight going with Shayne, one we didn't know about. I'm not sure which of those options makes more sense."

"Or maybe it was neither of those things," I suggested. "Maybe she really was eaten by a gigantic shark. The medical examiner says the teeth marks on her torso were huge. Half of her was eaten."

"Oh, gross!" Sarah wrinkled her nose. "That sounds like that book J.D. Wells is writing. I don't even like stuff like that, but he's told me about that book so many times it's seared in my brain."

"He mentioned it to me last night, too," I admitted. "He said he's going to rush the publication to take advantage of Shayne's death. The fact that he openly admitted it makes me think he's probably not a suspect."

"Probably not," Lily agreed. "He's kind of annoying, but he has a genuinely good heart. He overcompensates. He's never been a success at anything, and he desperately needs accolades now that he is a success. The only way I can see him going after Shayne is if she threatened to take what he worked so hard to achieve."

"Did she do that?"

"Not that I'm aware of. They both write urban fantasy, but their genres aren't that close. His is more action to her romance. They didn't have much overlap."

"So ... you think the shark plot is just a coincidence?"

Lily shrugged. "Maybe. The thing is, J.D. has been talking about that book for almost a year. Everybody knew about it."

"Meaning that anybody could've stolen the plot for inspiration to hide a murder," I mused.

"Exactly."

I sighed. "We keep getting more suspects, but no answers. It's frustrating."

"Do you know what would help with that?" Sarah asked, her eyes sparkling.

"You're going to say pimento cheese, aren't you?"

"How did you know?"

"Just a wild guess."

SEVENTEEN

Tracking information on the authors who wanted to hurt Shayne Rivers wasn't easy. There were simply too many of them. That's exactly what I told Jack when I returned to the outdoor bar where I'd left him. He was elbow-deep in searches, and he was no longer alone. Laura and Millie sat with him, and the presence of one irritated me much more than the other.

"There she is," Laura called out, what looked to be a blue cocktail in her hand. "We wondered where you ran off to. You shouldn't leave the rest of us to do all the work."

I scowled. "I was talking to people."

"Ignore her," Jack ordered. "She's just being Laura. What did you find out?"

"Either a lot or a little." I took the open seat between him and Millie, laying out the information in a quick and concise manner. I didn't leave anything out, but when I stitched things together I wasn't sure it made sense. "The thing is, absolutely everyone hated her. While I think it's ridiculous to kill someone over reviews, the way Sarah and Lily explained it that actually costs authors money over the long haul."

"And money is always a motivation for murder," Jack mused, rolling his neck. "I've been running more names. Carter Reagan Yates

156

has an interesting background. He's been in a bit of trouble ... and apparently likes to grow pot in his backyard, but everything he's been involved in is relatively minor."

"He's not the prepper writer people dislike," I pointed out. "That distinction goes to Clark Savage."

"But you didn't find a motive for him to kill Shayne," Jack countered. "You found a reason she might want to kill him."

"Yeah. And I want to kill him for that nonsense, too," Millie said.

"I don't." Laura had already downed three-quarters of her drink. "I like the idea of staying at home and letting a man do all the work. It has to be a man who makes a lot of money, though. I'm not settling for peanuts."

"You are an absolute delight," Millie drawled. "Women everywhere should stand up and salute your attitude."

"I know, right?"

Millie made an exaggerated face and focused on Jack. "Who do you think has the strongest motive to kill her?"

"That's a good question. I think a lot of people might want her dead. I'm trying to track the husband's movements right now. I think it's odd that he's not coming to Florida to claim her body."

"I asked about that, too," I said. "Apparently he's a house husband and takes care of the three kids they have living with them. Lily and Sarah said there would be no motive for him to kill her because the grandmother with the other two kids will put up a fight for the money. Plus, without Shayne around to write and keep the royalties coming in, that money will dry up quickly."

"Maybe he didn't realize that," Laura suggested.

"Or maybe he simply was staying for the money and now he's in a bad spot," Jack countered. "Either way, it's interesting to think about. We need to get inside the minds of these people. There could be motives hidden under other motives."

"I'm not willing to give up on the idea of it being a Megalodon," I said. "Er, or maybe not a Megalodon but a big predator. The simplest answer is often the right one. Maybe she got drunk and fell into the water and was eaten by a shark."

"Or maybe she was killed and her body was tossed into the water as part of a cover-up," Jack argued. "We have no way of knowing which answer is correct right now. That's why we have to pursue all avenues."

"So, what do you suggest?" Millie asked. "Charlie has been digging in with these writers to get answers. She's been working hard. You must have an idea how you want to approach this?"

"I do," Jack confirmed, his expression serious. "I think we should try ruling people out one at a time. Attacking the group as a whole is getting us nowhere."

"And how do you suggest we do that?" Laura asked.

"I don't suggest *you* do anything," Jack replied. "You're not part of the group."

"I beg to differ."

"And yet you're not included in our plans." He was firm as his gaze landed on me. "You have good instincts. Who do you want to focus on?"

I wasn't sure how to answer. Luckily, Laura opened her big, fat mouth so I didn't have to.

"Oh, yes, Charlie is perfect," Laura muttered. "Charlie is smart ... and funny ... and everybody loves Charlie."

"You're just figuring that out?" Millie challenged. "I don't know what that says about your deduction skills."

Laura scowled. "Charlie is annoying, and not at all smart. She fell into shark-infested waters, for crying out loud."

"You do not want to get me going on that," Jack warned, extending a finger. "I'm serious. It will not end well if you if you force my hand. I could have you fired for what happened on that ship."

Laura balked. "I didn't do anything!"

I couldn't take another round of arguing. Instead, I decided to be proactive. "I want to focus on Abigail James and Priscilla Jennings."

Jack's eyebrows hopped up his forehead. "Why? They seem the least likely to be involved."

"Which means they're probably hanging with the group to gather information," I said. "The quiet ones know more. They're probably gossiping to themselves constantly."

"Actually, that's not a bad idea. Do you have an idea how you'll get them to talk?"

"No, but I figured I'd take Millie with me. She's good at being sneaky."

Millie beamed. "I am."

"Okay, well ... ." Jack slid a look at Laura and leaned forward, gesturing for me to do the same. When we were almost touching, he whispered. "You can't leave me alone with her."

I patted his arm. "You're a big boy. You can take care of yourself."

"I don't want to take care of myself. I think I should go with you."

"You have more background checks to run," I reminded him. "Millie and I will have a better chance of getting close to those women without you around. You're a distraction."

"Flattery will get you nowhere. Don't even think about leaving me."

"I have no choice. The job comes first." I couldn't hold back my grin as I stood. "I hope to see you again."

"Ha, ha. You're so funny." He glared at Laura as she brightened.

"I'll help you with your research," Laura offered. "We don't spend nearly enough time together."

"And yet it's ten times more time than is necessary," Jack grumbled.

"Oh, don't be like that. Give me an assignment."

I LEFT JACK TO DEAL with Laura on his own terms. He was a big boy, and if he had to get mean so much the better. Other women would've been leery about leaving their boyfriends with a sexually charged viper, but I never worried about Jack falling for Laura's machinations. That simply wasn't the way he operated.

"Where should we start looking?" Millie asked. She seemed eager to be part of the operation.

"I don't know. I ... ." I trailed off, narrowing my eyes when I saw movement on the manmade lake that surrounded the resort. I heard voices, and when the people who owned them finally drew close I realized it was two girls on a paddle boat. They were making the rounds of the entire resort, and given the way the foliage grew on both sides they weren't easily seen unless the people at the various bars and pools were looking directly at them. "Hmm."

"Oh, don't even think about it." Millie shook her head, firm. "I am not riding a paddle boat."

"I think it's a good idea." I kept my voice calm. "If we're quiet, no one will even see us. We can go-around the entire resort and eavesdrop without anyone noticing."

"Yes, but it's a paddle boat. I hate paddle boats."

"Have you ever been on a paddle boat?"

"Yes. They're stupid. Have you ever been on a paddle boat?"

"No, but they look comfortable and fun. How bad can it possibly be?"

"You're going to regret asking that question."

"UGH. MY CALVES HURT."

We'd been on the paddle boat only twenty minutes when I realized Millie was right. I waited another ten minutes to voice my disdain for the situation.

"I hate to be the one to tell you 'I told you so,' but I told you so." Millie made a face, her legs pumping in rhythm with mine. "People claim paddle boats are relaxing and fun, but they're stupid. My legs hurt ... and it's too hot, so I'm sweating ... and my butt hurts from this hard plastic."

I couldn't argue with that sentiment. My hindquarters ached a bit, too. "I don't understand why they don't include cushions. That would make this so much more comfortable."

"Perhaps you should ask management."

"Perhaps I will." I wasn't in the mood to listen to Millie gloat. "Just ... keep your eyes open for authors. We're looking for two specific women. I think they're going to be thick with gossip."

"Oh, well, I can't wait." Millie rolled her eyes. "What do they look like?"

"One has brown hair cut above her shoulders. And she wears a lot of LuLaRoe stuff."

"Great. Leggings in ninety-five percent humidity. That sounds ideal."

I ignored her tone. "The other has curly short hair that looks as if it's been permed to within an inch of its life. She runs around saying the word 'hooky' constantly. I have no idea what it means."

"Maybe she was saying hooker."

I pictured Priscilla and shook my head. "No. She doesn't seem the type to be writing about hookers. Someone said she writes sports romance."

"Like homeruns on and off the field?"

"Yes."

"Like aces on the court and in bed?"

I could sense where this was going. "Yes."

"Like putting the puck in the goal both on and off the ice?"

"How many of these are you going to throw out?"

"I don't know. Let's see. There's soccer, golf — I have great putting jokes — and rugby."

"No one plays rugby."

"I know people who play rugby."

"I'm done with this conversation." I held up my hand to let her know I meant business. "I don't think they're involved, but they might know information about the people who are."

"Why?"

"Because they're always hanging around ... and listening."

"Fair enough. Let's find them."

TWENTY MINUTES LATER I was ready to abandon ship and eat my deposit on the paddle boat. Millie had turned into a complaint machine, and even though I liked her under normal circumstances I was considering making her my arch nemesis for the day. I couldn't stand the sound of her voice.

"Not one more word," I snapped, grimacing as I tried to alleviate the weight on my tailbone. "I can't deal with you when I'm in pain."

"We're both in pain, Charlie," she drawled. "It's pain you caused. I told you this boat was a bad idea. In fact ... yeah. I'm done." She tilted to the side and rolled out of the boat, landing on her feet in the manmade lake and causing my eyes to go wide. "You're on your own. Sayonara. Adios. Arrivederci." She saluted as I continued drifting forward, a huge grin on her face.

"You can't just leave me," I complained, grabbing onto the nearest palm frond in an effort to stop my forward momentum. "We're supposed to be a team, working together for the greater good and all that."

"You never said we would be doing it in a paddle boat. I draw the line at paddle boats. I have standards."

I found that hard to believe because she was standing in thigh-deep water with her hands on her hips. "Get back in the boat."

"No."

"I mean it. I'll leave without you." That wasn't really a choice. The current, which seemed light and easy at first glance, was wreaking havoc on my almost nonexistent upper body strength.

"Go. This adventure isn't for me. I'm heading back to the tiki bar. You can find me there when you reclaim your mind."

"Ugh." I let loose the palm frond, groaning when it smacked me in the face. This was so not the way I saw this afternoon going.

BY THE TIME I RETURNED to the paddle boat rental dock my face was red from too much sun and my hair was wider than it was long thanks to the humidity. The man standing at the kiosk asked if I'd had a good time. I could only glower.

To give myself time to recover, I moved into a shady alcove under one of the footbridges and fanned myself. I caught a glimpse of my reflection in one of the nearby windows and scowled. I looked a total wreck.

"I hate this day," I muttered as I tried to comb my fingers through my hair. I was so lost in the task I almost didn't notice the two women wending through the shortcut that led toward the resort store. That would've been a mistake, because it happened to be the two women I was seeking.

"I like the ocean, but this weather is ridiculous," Priscilla complained as she patted her curls. "No one should have to deal with this much humidity."

"Things could be worse," Abigail said pragmatically. "You could be shark food."

Priscilla burst out laughing. "I know. Am I the only one who thinks it's poetic that she died that way? She had no problem eating people alive when she was running her business, and now she's dead because she was eaten alive."

While Abigail didn't appear to think it was as funny as her friend did, she didn't admonish her. "Do we know she was alive when she hit the water? I haven't heard anything since news spread that her body was discovered in the shark net. I mean ... I know those special investigators are here. Have they said anything?"

"I haven't talked to them. That young one, the chick who keeps running around with the really hot guy, has been poking her nose into things. I saw her talking to Sarah Hilton and Lily Harper Hart a few hours ago. She seemed to be digging for information, but I couldn't get close enough to hear what they were saying. You know how Lily is. The second she saw me, she wouldn't stop staring."

"She's definitely obnoxious," Abigail agreed. "She thinks she's better than everybody else because she writes mysteries and gets along with people. I could get along with people if I wanted. I just don't see the reason."

"I'm with you. People are overrated."

I shrank back when I realized Priscilla was looking at her reflection in the window. I didn't want her to see me — that would be uncomfortable as all get out — so I hunkered in the shadows to avoid detection.

"One thing I will say, those investigators seem to be looking at people instead of sharks," Priscilla continued. "I find that interesting.

That says they believe Shayne was killed before she went into the water ... or maybe was pushed into the water. They've been looking for suspects."

"There's no end to suspects," Abigail noted. "If I were them, I'd focus on Leslie. Everyone knows she's nuts."

"She's definitely nuts, but I think she's too obvious of a suspect. I'd focus on J.D. Wells. He's got that shark book coming out and the timing couldn't be more perfect. You just know he's going to try to book gigs on talk shows to make a big deal about his book and how Shayne's death fits with the story."

"Yeah, but there's no way he could've carried her out to the water," Abigail said. "He would've needed help, and that's too risky. Besides ... why would he kill her? Wouldn't it make more sense for him to kill that wife of his who spends all her time sitting around knitting? That would be a better story for his purposes."

"Maybe he likes his wife?"

"Who could like that woman? She's ridiculous ... and says stupid things. Do you know she came up to me the other day and asked if JAFF was about Jane Austen characters? I mean ... It's called Jane Austen fan fiction. What does she expect?"

"Maybe she was nervous and trying to make conversation. She bugs me, but I don't think she's evil or anything. Now, if we're talking about evil, look at Clark Savage. We all know he hates women."

"Oh, he *is* a good suspect." Abigail smiled. "I bet you're right. He killed her. We should start spreading that rumor to see if it sticks."

"I'm all for that. Let's get out of here. I could use a drink."

I waited until I was certain they were out of sight before straightening, ignoring the odd look the paddle boat guy gave me as I watched them disappear inside the building. I was hoping they would have information to help me narrow the field. Instead, they merely gave me ideas regarding multiple people who were already suspects.

There had to be a way to figure this out.

EIGHTEEN

*E*ven though Abigail and Priscilla said absolutely nothing of value, they gave me something to think about. When a woman is disliked by everyone, that means the person who decides to kill her must have an impressive motive. It has to be a motive beyond everyone else's motives.

With that in mind, I headed toward the front desk.

I had a plan, but it wasn't exactly easy to pull off. I had to wait for an opening when no one was loitering close to the clerk. Then, when I stepped forward, I instantly made eye contact and burrowed into her brain.

It's less invasive than it sounds.

No, seriously.

"What room was Shayne Rivers in?" I kept my voice low so as not to draw attention.

The clerk, a young woman with bright eyes my magic managed to dull, merely blinked. "Shayne Rivers?"

"She's an author. The one who died."

"Oh. She's not registered under that name."

Of course she wasn't. I searched my memory. I couldn't remember her real name. "What name is she registered under?"

"Elsie May Haymark."

Someone had to be messing with me. "Seriously?"

The clerk nodded, solemn.

"Okay, what room was Elsie May Haymark in?"

"Seven eighty-four."

"I need a keycard to get in that room."

"Of course." She didn't put up an argument. I pushed her hard enough that I knew she wouldn't. I didn't have time to waste. I learned I had the power to push people by accident when I was in high school and wanted to get out of gym class. At first I thought it was a fluke. Then I realized I could do it at will ... as long as the person I was trying to push didn't put up too much resistance. If that happened, no matter how I tried, I never got my way. Thankfully, this woman either didn't care or couldn't muster the strength to push me out of her head.

The young woman created a keycard quickly, handing it over without argument. "Have a nice day."

I accepted the card, a bit of guilt rolling through me. "I want you to have a nice day," I stressed. "No matter what happens, don't feel guilty about this."

"I never feel guilty." Her smile didn't waver. "That's why I keep dating married men. If I felt guilty, I'd stop doing that."

I frowned. I didn't have time to waste, but ... . "Why do you date married men?"

"They have money."

"They also have wives."

"You can't make a man cheat. That's on them."

I was keenly disappointed. Here I thought she was a mild-mannered soul, but she was something else entirely. "I want you to stop dating married men."

Instead of agreeing, she frowned. "Why would I do that?"

Hmm. That was interesting. She had no problem acquiescing when I was trying to break the law. When attempting to correct her morals, though, she put up a rather impressive resistance.

"Well, just keep in mind, the next married man you sleep with is going to give you herpes. You don't want herpes, do you? It'll limit your dating options."

She frowned. "That sucks."

"Yes." I bobbed my head. "Start dating men your own age. Single men."

"They might have herpes, too."

She had a point. "Invest in condoms ... and better taste in men."

"Whatever." She waved me off. "Have a nice night."

"I will." I was ready to leave, but I forgot to ask the most important question. "Has anyone been in Elsie May Haymark's room since her death? I mean ... other than the police?"

"No. It's supposed to be closed until the detectives release her room. They're not ready to do that yet."

"Well, that's good. I was never here. Make sure you remember that."

"I will."

"Make sure you remember the part about catching herpes, too."

"I'm on it."

I hoped that was true.

I FOUND SHAYNE'S ROOM without trouble and was happy to see there was no police tape barricading the room. Breaking in was one thing. Crossing police tape was another. I was a good girl at heart. Er, well, at least some of the time.

I knocked just to be on the safe side, but wasn't surprised no one answered. I let myself in, making sure to draw the curtains tightly to ensure nobody could see light from the hallway, and then proceeded to search the room.

It was a typical hotel room, double beds in the first room I entered. I thought it was weird the beds were so close to the door until I realized she had a beach view, and the living quarters were on that side of the suite. It made sense, even if it was a bit backward.

Most of Shayne's personal items were in the bedroom. I wished I'd had the forethought to bring gloves, but explaining that if caught would've been difficult. Instead, I grabbed a washcloth from the bathroom and clutched it between my fingers as I searched through her suitcase.

Clothes. Toiletries. Shoes. Socks. Nothing of interest. I even checked the zipped pockets to be sure. After that, I headed to the living room.

Shayne's computer was open on the table. I hit a key and the computer sprang to life, which meant it was idling rather than shut down. It didn't ask for a password, which I was thankful for. There were three windows open when I sat in the chair. I decided to approach them in order.

The first was a bibliography of sorts. It listed all of Shayne's published works and had sales figures beside the entries. I used the washcloth to hit a few keys and saw that she made an okay living, although I had no idea how she managed to raise a family of five on fifty grand a year, especially if her husband didn't work. She had Tieks in her suitcase. Those were expensive shoes. Obviously her book sales didn't allow her to purchase them.

The second window was a spreadsheet that listed her various sources of income. I found that much more interesting. Once I figured out exactly what I was looking at, it was easy enough to read. It seemed Shayne's income from books was the smallest pot she was dipping from. The funds she had listed were varied, and she was making a solid six figures a year from her newsletter services and another six figures from something she referred to as "coaching." I made a mental note to ask Lily what coaching might be and snapped a screenshot of the numbers with my phone so I could peruse them later before moving to the final window.

That's where I hit pay dirt. It was her email, and it seemed she had at least eight business addresses funneling to the same central address.

I was flabbergasted when I read some of the messages. The sheer bulk of them were from her clients, and after skimming a few I moved on to the emails that boasted the more interesting topic headings. For example, "I hope you die a horrible and flaming death" was an obvious curiosity.

That particular email came from a woman named Debra Wakefield. Shayne apparently took her money and then never came through on a promotion. After a good fifteen emails back and forth, Debra lost her temper and promised to file a lawsuit. Shayne responded by wishing her well and then mentioning that her child would probably need surgery soon, so a lawsuit wasn't exactly helpful. The tone was cold and condescending, and I could tell why people disliked her.

Another email was from a woman named Rory O'Sullivan. She started out by calling Shayne a "feckin' muppet" and promised to kick her in the pink bits should they ever cross paths. The woman was in Ireland, so I figured it was a long shot she was our killer. Still, I photographed the message and moved on.

I spent two hours going through Shayne's emails. She'd been bombarded with hate messages, which would've been enough to cause most people to shut down. Not Shayne. She answered each email with a hateful message. It was almost as if she fed on people's hate.

It was fascinating ... and perplexing.

The setting sun told me it was getting late, so I gave the room another cursory search before leaving. I took the washcloth with me so I had something to use on the door, and made sure to wipe down the handle when I exited. I left the washcloth in the vending area and then headed toward the elevator, my mind busy.

Part of me felt sorry for Shayne. Being hated by that many people couldn't have been easy. It had to take a toll mentally. Of course, the way she responded to people was equally hateful. I very much doubted people singled her out to go after simply because she was successful, something she continuously wrote back in her return emails.

"I'm sorry you're so jealous, but I can't change the fact that I'm more popular and famous than you." That was one of her favorite mantras ... and it grated. I didn't know the woman, but her attitude reminded me of every high school girl I'd ever hated.

The lobby was full of people when I entered, although none of them belonged to my group. I decided to text Jack to see what he was doing for dinner when a waving hand caught my attention.

Sarah, a bright smile on her face, gestured for me to join her. Even though I grew tired of talking about pimento cheese, I found her interesting. I wasn't sure when it happened, but I was convinced she was one of the few authors I could trust.

"What's up?" I asked when I approached. "Are you guys eating here?"

"We had a few afternoon meetings today," she replied. "They don't go late. I just wanted to make sure you're aware we're having karaoke at the bar with the big fiberglass shark in the middle of the resort once we're finished."

Karaoke? I gulped. "Um ... ."

"It's a lot of fun," she said hurriedly. "It's nowhere near as lame as it sounds."

"I don't think I'd be very good at karaoke," I hedged. "I mean ... I'm tone deaf."

"You don't have to sing."

That was true. Of course, listening to other tone-deaf people sing wasn't much better than struggling through nonsensical verses of old eighties tunes either. "I'm not sure what we're doing, but I'll keep it in mind."

"You definitely should. All your suspects will be there, and I've always thought you could learn a lot about people by the songs they sing for karaoke. You should give it a shot."

I wasn't sure how to answer. Thankfully, the decision was taken out of my hands when Jack appeared on my right and graced Sarah with a bright smile. "What should we give a shot?"

"Karaoke," Sarah replied without hesitation. "Charlie says she's tone deaf, but I bet she has a nice voice."

"I bet she does, too." Jack's grin was obscenely wide, which meant he was up to something. "I'll make sure she shows up for karaoke. When is it?"

"It starts at eight. It's at that bar that's smackdab in the center of the resort."

"We will be there with bells on."

Sarah snorted. "Yeah, I bet. You're going to do something mean and trick her into singing. That's written all over your face."

"Do I look like a mean guy?"

"You look like an angel," she replied. "A fallen one."

"I'll take that as a compliment."

"Take it however you want." Sarah gathered her items from the table. "I need to get going. I look forward to seeing you later. Make sure you pick a good song."

I finally found my voice. "I won't be singing."

"Never say never." She waved at me over her shoulder and then disappeared into the crowd.

I could feel Jack's eyes on me, and I was uncomfortable when I finally met his gaze. "So ... um ... how was your afternoon?"

"Fine. Once I got rid of Laura, it was fairly pleasant. How was your afternoon?"

"Oh, well ... it could've gone better. Millie didn't last long as my sidekick."

"I know. I ran into her at the tiki bar."

"Did she tell you what she did?"

Jack's lips curved. "She did. I think it's funny that she abandoned ship."

"It was a lot of work to take that paddle boat into port by myself."

"You're young and fit. You obviously survived."

I rolled my eyes. "I'm still going to make her beg for forgiveness."

"I look forward to seeing that." His expression was hard to read as he looked me over. "So, where did you go after she abandoned you?"

Uh-oh. I sensed trouble. He was fishing for information, and I had absolutely zero good answers. "Well, when I first got off the boat I was hot and sweaty and needed a break from the sun," I offered. "I stepped under one of those footbridges, you know the ones I'm talking about?"

He nodded.

"I needed a few minutes to collect myself because of the heat," I said, barreling forward. "While I was there, I caught sight of Abigail

171

and Priscilla. I didn't want them to see me, so I was forced to crouch down and hide."

"Did you hear anything good?"

I shrugged, noncommittal. "Not really. They seemed perplexed. They were spitballing names left and right, but they clearly don't have any information that we would find useful."

"Well, that's mildly disappointing. But not unexpected. If you were going to murder someone, would you confide in one of those women?"

"Absolutely not. I would confide in Millie if I needed help disposing of a body. She might abandon me on a paddle boat, but she would totally turn into a ride-or-die chick if I had a body to bury."

Jack's brow quirked. "Good to know. Where did you go after that?"

He was suspicious of my movements. Okay, maybe "suspicious" wasn't the right word. He was testing me, though, and I wasn't sure how I should answer. Breaking into Shayne's room was one thing. He wouldn't like it, but he would probably let it go because he was as curious as I was. Explaining how I got into the room was the problem.

"Um ... ." I chewed my bottom lip.

"Before you attempt to lie, you should know that Laura saw you going into the main hotel building earlier today," Jack offered. "I know you were there for a few hours. She made sure to tell me. By the way, I guarantee she knows something is going on between us. She hasn't come right out and said it, but she's getting more and more desperate."

Great. There was no easy lie to get out of this. That meant I had to tell a version of the truth. "You're probably not going to like it," I hedged.

"Try me." He folded his arms across his chest and waited.

"I broke into Shayne Rivers' room and went through her computer."

Whatever he was expecting, that wasn't it. Jack's mouth dropped open and a spread of emotions fluttered across his handsome features as he struggled to find words. Finally, when he did speak, he asked the obvious question. "How?"

"I conned the girl at the front desk into giving me a keycard."

"How?"

"I said I was with Shayne's family." That was a lie, but not a big one. Lying about where I'd spent my afternoon would've been a big one. This was a little one. At least that's what I told myself.

"And she just gave you a keycard?" He was incredulous.

I fished it out of my pocket for proof. "Yeah. Are you going to start yelling?"

"I haven't decided yet." His eyes flashed with something, but it didn't entirely look like anger. "Did you find anything?"

"She had a lot of hate mail."

"Anything good?"

"I took screenshots of the mail and her banking information."

Jack widened his eyes to comical proportions. "Charlie, you probably left fingerprints all around her room. What if the cops decide to dust after the fact?"

I told him about the washcloth.

"Seriously?" Instead of fury, I found respect waiting for me in the depths of his eyes. "That was smart."

"Wait ... are you saying you're not going to yell? I expected a big fight."

"I'm saying that you could've been dumber when breaking into the room."

"Oh, that's so sweet," I drawled.

He cracked a smile. "I want to see those screenshots."

"If you agree not to yell I'll show them to you."

"If you agree to sing karaoke I'll agree not to yell."

Crap! He had me over a whiskey barrel and he knew it. "Oh, I really am tone deaf."

"I honestly don't care. I just want to pick the song."

Now he was going too far. "I could've lied about what I was doing."

"No, you couldn't have done that." His voice softened. "You're inherently honest. I like that about you."

I swallowed hard. "So ... no yelling?"

"No yelling." He took the keycard from me. "No going to her room again without me either. We're a team. That means we break the law as a unit."

"That sounds fair."

"Now, come on. We'll get dinner, you can show me those screen-shots, and then we'll pick a song for your karaoke debut."

I scowled. "I'm starting to dislike you a great deal."

"You'll get over it. I'm too handsome for you to stay angry."

That was true.

NINETEEN

*J*ack was in the mood for steak, which was fine with me. After ordering, he spent a good twenty minutes going through my screenshots. When he was done, he took a minute to think before speaking.

I thought for sure he'd changed his mind and decided to yell.

"You could've gotten in trouble if you'd been caught, Charlie."

His voice didn't sound particularly accusatory, but I was on edge, so the admonishment grated all the same.

"I wasn't caught."

"You could've been caught."

"But I wasn't."

He sighed. "Fine. You weren't caught." He held up his hands in capitulation. "What do you think about the information you found?"

I chuckled at the shift in his demeanor. "Are you using this as a teaching moment?"

"Maybe."

"Well, in that case, I think Lily was right about her being a narcissist. She seemed to feed on the attention from angry emailers. Even though it was negative attention, she desperately needed it."

"That's an interesting observation." He sipped his lemonade. "What else do you see?"

"Is this a test?"

"No. I think you have strong instincts. You would've made a good cop ... if you could shake your tendency to run headlong into danger. Breaking into rooms would probably hold you back, too."

I smirked. "I don't look good in uniform."

"I'm betting that's not true. But I want to know what you think."

It could've been a trap. I was so convinced he would melt down about my break-in that I was still on edge waiting for it to happen. But he seemed earnest, so I decided to give it a whirl.

"I'm not an expert on psychological conditions," I said finally. "I took a psychology class when I was a freshman, but not much of it stuck."

"Fair enough. I don't need the right words. I simply want to hear your opinion."

"She was crazy."

Jack's lips twitched. "That seems ... clinical."

"She had issues," I clarified. "She thought she was the center of the universe, that people were trying to emulate her at the same time they were trying to tear her down. There was a divide in her thinking that didn't make sense. If people were jealous and wanted to be like her, why were they so upset about the things she was doing?

"I saw some of the instances of online bullying Lily and Sarah mentioned," I continued. "She was horrible ... and relentless. She worked her little group of flying monkeys — I think that's what they called them, and it fits — into a frenzy in those messages. She told them that her enemies were taking food out of the mouths of her children, made up a bunch of stories about her children being sick even though there were no medical bills in her email, and basically unleashed a group of people who were only operating on one side of a very ridiculous story based solely upon her rather dubious word. I can see why people were terrified to go against her, and why the flood gates essentially opened when one person was brave enough to take a stand."

Jack grabbed a breadstick from the basket at the center of the table. "I think that's a pretty apt judgment. Anything else?"

I felt emboldened. "She's a grifter."

Jack's eyebrows flew up his forehead. "Care to expound on that?"

"She doesn't care like the others," I explained. "She takes no pride in her work ... other than what it can get her. She's built a publishing persona — this Shayne Rivers person who is kind and cares about her fellow writers. Couldn't be further from the truth. She's not a writer so much as a con artist.

"I think, if we dig deep enough into Elsie May's background we'll find a laundry list of things she's done in other groups," I continued. "Being a writer wasn't the first scam she ran. She's too good at it. That means there are others in her past. Perhaps she was one of those eBay scammers who were on the news, or maybe she ran grifts in person and that's how her family survived for a bit."

Jack beamed. "That was very good. I think you're absolutely right. Before we head to karaoke, I'm starting a search on Elsie May and her husband. If she's run more scams than this — and I'm betting the trademark thing plays into her overall goals — then her list of enemies is probably even greater than we thought."

I tried not to bask in the glow of his grin. "How would the trademark thing be a scam?"

"They're referred to in some circles as 'trademark whores,'" he replied, rubbing his foot against mine under the table and causing me to grin like an idiot. "People file for trademarks they believe will be of value, and then it becomes their job to protect the trademark. Ultimately, the plan is to force someone else to pay to use the trademark.

"So, if it takes a couple of hundred dollars to file for the trademark, they'll sell it — or use of it — for thousands of dollars to make life difficult for other people," he continued. "This doesn't just happen in writing. It happens with other businesses, and people make real money doing it. I believe Shayne Rivers simply modified the concept."

"Huh." I rubbed my chin. "If she has something really bad in her past we might've been wasting time from the start. I mean ... maybe someone took advantage of her travel schedule and exacted revenge for a grudge from a long time ago."

"See, you're so smart." His smile was back as he tapped the side of his head for emphasis. "You do extremely idiotic things sometimes, but you're very smart. Has anyone ever told you that?"

I shrugged. "I'm smart enough to know that we shouldn't go to karaoke. You need to take my word for it."

"Oh, we're going to karaoke."

My smile slipped. "I'm not singing."

"You're singing."

"No, I'm not."

"Yes, you are."

I had news for him. I drew the line at singing in public. There was absolutely nothing he could say to talk me into it. I didn't care how handsome he was. "I'll sing if you sing," I said finally.

Jack straightened. "I don't sing."

"Then I don't sing."

"We'll just see about that."

We definitely would.

IT TURNED OUT KARAOKE was more fun than I envisioned. I didn't sing — which was a relief for everyone, even if they didn't know it — but Jack and I had a good time.

Lily and Sarah included us with their group, which happened to be the center of attention. Most of the people we'd been looking at as suspects were there, except for Clark. His absence didn't go unnoticed.

"Where is the guy with the obnoxious shirts?" I asked Lily as she delivered a tray of drinks to the table.

"You'll have to be more specific," she said, smiling. "Half the people here wear obnoxious shirts ... including Sarah."

She said the second part for Sarah's benefit, because the pimento-cheese-loving woman faked indignity.

"My shirts are awesome," Sarah countered, smoothing her T-shirt.

It featured a smiling kitten face and the phrase "show me your kitties." She didn't seem embarrassed to be wearing it in the least. "Lily just wishes she was cool enough to wear a shirt like this."

"Uh-huh." I wasn't convinced. "I was talking about the guy you said had a prostitute at the tiki bar the other night. Clark Savage. He's the only one in your group who isn't here. That other prepper guy is here, although he seems happiest sitting outside where it's cooler."

"Clark is ... an ass," Lily said after a beat, making me smile at her bluntness. "Be glad he's not here. He would bring everyone down if he was allowed to sit in a corner and rail against women ... and minorities ... and old people. I don't think he likes anyone but himself, but I've learned to keep my mouth shut where he's concerned."

I was officially intrigued. "He hates minorities, too? I mean ... I knew he hated women. I've heard stories about it. That's one of the reasons he fought with Shayne, right?"

Lily wasn't stupid. She recognized I was digging for information. Instead of immediately answering, she glanced around. I had no idea who she was looking for, but when her eyes landed on Abigail and Priscilla her expression darkened and she motioned for me to follow her outside.

I did without hesitation, carrying my drink to the patio. Jack was still inside — he'd made friends with a high fantasy author with an outgoing personality — but I wasn't worried about him assuming I'd left. He'd be able to see me through the bar's windows.

Lily selected a small table at the back of the patio. I had to admit, the breeze felt nice. Getting a reprieve from the singing was also nice.

"I had no idea there were so many enthusiastic singers in your group," I noted as Lily sipped a rum runner. They appeared to be the drink of choice at the resort.

"Karaoke is an acquired taste," she explained. "I never acquired it. My friends were more the 'let's get drunk in a field' variety, and I couldn't understand why the writers I made friends with were so excited to sing the first year we attended this conference. It certainly wasn't my thing."

"Obviously you got over your aversion."

"I did," Lily agreed, smirking. "I don't sing, but others do. They enjoy it. The line is long and not everyone will get to belt out a tune. You will find more people willing to give it a shot as the night progresses, mostly fueled by free alcohol. Even Jezebel, who wouldn't know a high note from a low blow, will give it a shot. She'll pick a song that makes you want to slit your wrists and everyone will laugh at her, but she likes attention so she'll try it."

I stared at her for an extended period of time and sipped my drink. She knew something. Or maybe she wanted to share something, but didn't want to volunteer it. She wanted me to drag it out of her. Perhaps that was her way of protecting herself.

"We found out some interesting information about Shayne Rivers today," I offered, watching her closely for a reaction. "It seems she has something of a past when it comes to ripping people off." Now, to be fair, that was an exaggeration. Jack and I theorized that was true, but we had no proof of it. Still, I wanted to feel out Lily for her opinion on the subject.

"Really?" Lily's eyes flashed with interest. "That doesn't surprise me. I wish I could say it did, but ... no. She was too good at manipulating people. She didn't stumble, led her followers straight to the trough of poisoned water, and convinced them to drink deeply. It makes sense that she's done this before."

"She had a lot of enemies," I noted. "A lot of people wanted her dead."

"Are you asking me if I wanted her dead?"

"I'm not sure." That was true. "You're blunt, but you don't seem the type to wish death on people. You're more the type to wish a raging case of ass crabs on someone."

Lily chuckled. "What are ass crabs?"

"I read this story about people who pass out on the beach and crabs creep into crevices," I replied. "Jack called them ass crabs. It kind of stuck."

Delighted, she belted out a laugh that echoed over the entire patio. "You're blunt, too. I think that's why I like you."

"Yeah, well, that doesn't always work in my favor," I said. "Sometimes I act before I think. Almost all the time I talk before I think."

"You'll find that as you get older it's okay to speak your mind," she offered. "The older you get, the less you care about what others think of you. I certainly don't care what others think of me. That doesn't mean I say everything that comes to my mind. In fact, I tend to curb my impulses a good fifty percent of the time."

If that were true, she probably had some wild things she was keeping to herself because she didn't seem the shy type. I found that funny. "Well, you can say whatever you want around me. I can't be offended."

"Everyone can be offended."

"Not me."

"Everyone can be offended," Lily repeated, sobering. "Even Shayne could be offended. She was doing most of the offending, mind you, but she wasn't all bad. She donated money and time to an autism foundation because one of her kids was autistic. She also spoke out regularly on behalf of battered women. I might have disliked her a great deal, but I was behind both those efforts."

That was interesting. "You're saying that Shayne was more than one thing."

"I'm saying that she was ninety-five percent crazy and five percent tolerable," she corrected, causing me to smile. "I worry that in the aftermath of her death everyone is spending time talking about the things she did wrong. They were numerous, don't get me wrong, but she did a few things right.

"Besides that, no one deserves to die like that," she continued. "To be eaten alive by sharks ... that's the most terrible death I can imagine."

I could imagine a few more, but my mind was a freaky place at times. I thought about telling Lily that we had no way of knowing how Shayne died, but I was quick enough to realize that would be a terrible idea. It was better to keep her cause of death murky.

"You still haven't answered my question regarding Clark Savage," I prodded. "Why isn't he attending this little shindig with you guys?"

"Because he's not welcome."

"He's welcome around the tiki bar with you."

She sighed, the sound long and pronounced. "He's technically not welcome there either, but he doesn't pick up on social cues. He's an obnoxious man who happens to be friends with a friend. We all like Carter despite some of his rather ridiculous beliefs. I mean ... the man purposely bought a camper from the seventies so it could survive an EMP attack. No running air conditioner and the cupboards look like disco threw up in them, but he's convinced he'll survive an EMP attack and makes his family go through drills because he loves them. That's all that counts, right?"

I had no idea what an EMP attack was. "Why isn't Clark here? Is he off with another prostitute? Now that you told me that first woman was a prostitute, that's all I can think about."

Lily snickered, shaking her head. "I know why you're asking about Clark. You don't have to hide it."

"What do you mean?"

"You found out about Shayne's past. That means you found out about Clark."

I did my best to hide my surprise. "I can't say either way if we found any ties between Clark and Shayne." I was purposely trying to be vague. "I'm sorry. I'm not allowed to talk about specific aspects of our investigation."

"Don't bother." Lily waved off my lie. "You found out that Clark and Shayne used to date in high school and they broke up under very bitter circumstances. I'm not surprised you stumbled over the truth. The only reason I didn't tell you was because Carter didn't want anyone to jump to conclusions and we promised to stay out of that aspect of the investigation."

I had to bite the inside of my cheek to keep from calling out to Jack. "I don't blame you. It's fine. We found out through our own methods."

"I'm glad. I felt bad lying."

"Yeah. Um ... ." I wasn't sure what to say. Thankfully, Jack picked that moment to track me down, and he was just tipsy enough to draw

Lily's full attention. "You didn't sing, did you?" I was horrified at the prospect.

Jack's chuckle was warm as he shook his head and extended his hand. "No. You conveniently got out of singing, too. But I am cutting myself off. I'll have a hangover if I'm not careful and I don't like hangovers when I'm on the job."

I wasn't a fan of hangovers at any time, but this seemed the perfect opening to make our escape. "Okay. We can head back to the condo." I took his hand and ignored the way Lily smirked. She found our relationship amusing, which was mildly embarrassing. "You're not so drunk you can't walk back, are you?"

He shook his head. "Just drunk enough to make sure our walk takes three times as long as it should."

I was confused. "Why?"

"Because he wants to spend time with you," Lily answered, laughing as she shook her head. "Geez! You're smart on some things and dumb on others. Ah, well. You'll learn." She gave me a half-wave. "If you want more information, I'll be around tomorrow. Just be warned, if you try to question Clark he won't take it well. Watch your step around him."

"I will." I waited until she was gone to speak again, turning to Jack with excitement. "I have big news."

"Great." Jack's smile was lazy. "You can tell me tomorrow. I don't want to focus on work right now."

"What do you want to focus on?"

"Well, I have you, a beach and the moon. I'm pretty sure I want to focus on that."

My belly warmed with pleasure. "I guess that's okay. I can tell you my news tomorrow."

"Good. Come on." He tugged on my hand. "The night awaits ... and I have grand beach plans running through my head."

I had no idea what he meant by that, but I was keen to find out.

TWENTY

I piled Jack into the spare bedroom when we got back to the condo. Bernard's things were missing, so I figured he followed through on the plan to move in with Millie. Jack wasn't drunk so much as happy, which was funny. I wasn't used to being the responsible one, but I poured him into bed, yanked off his shoes and then took a long shower to wash away the dried sweat and grime of the day.

When I returned to the bedroom he was fast asleep. He'd removed his shirt and jeans, and was resting on top of the comforter in nothing but boxer shorts. For a moment I considered heading to the living room to sleep on the couch. If I were a man and him a woman, that would be the considerate thing to do.

I knew nothing would happen — no hanky-panky, so to speak — so I slipped into a T-shirt and knit shorts, and slid in next to him. I was out within minutes, and unlike the previous evening, bad dreams didn't threaten to chase me.

When I woke, I found he'd shifted beneath the covers during the night and was spooned behind me. It was a nice feeling until I realized he was awake and waiting for me to join him in the real world.

"Do you have a hangover?" I murmured sleepily, stretching as I rolled to my back and faced him.

He shook his head, his morning stubble making him all the more attractive ... if that was even possible. Seriously, it was criminal how good he looked after a night of drinking. "I'm okay. I didn't get that drunk."

"You were kind of drunk."

"Not really, but I did have a good time."

"I did, too." I stared at him because he was too pretty to look away from. "I kind of wish you'd gotten drunk enough to sing."

"That will never happen." He tucked a strand of my hair behind my ear. "Having a room to ourselves is nice, huh? We don't have to worry about anyone barreling in on us."

"It is nice," I agreed. And awkward, I silently added. Everything was still new between us, so new we weren't quite comfortable in our surroundings. "So ... um ... Lily let something interesting slip last night."

I thought it was best to turn the conversation to our investigation.

"Oh, yeah?"

"Apparently Clark Savage and Shayne Rivers — or Elsie May Haymark, whatever you want to call her — dated when they were younger. They knew each other from the real world before they both joined the author world."

Romance vacated Jack's eyes, replaced by keen interest. "Well, that is interesting."

"She thought I already knew, which I let her believe, but she didn't say anything earlier because Carter asked her not to. He didn't want attention unfairly pointed in Clark's direction."

"Except it's fair attention." Jack dragged a hand through his morning-mussed hair. "Well, that is definitely interesting. We need to pull information from that time period."

"Can you do that?"

"Yeah. The thing is, we need to talk to someone who knew them back then. I doubt we'll find that person at this resort. We need to do some digging."

"Maybe we'll luck out and find they were locals."

"I don't think we're going to get that lucky. Although ... it does paint an interesting picture, doesn't it? I have to wonder if Shayne's husband was aware that she was hanging in the same location with an ex-boyfriend."

"Have you been able to confirm that he didn't get on a plane and head here?"

"Yeah. He's still in Louisiana."

"Is that where they live?"

"Yeah."

"That's not too far away to drive."

"No, but I've run checks on his credit cards. He didn't pay for gas in the days leading up to her death," he said. "It's not impossible that he paid cash, but with the price of gas that seems unlikely."

"What about Clark? Maybe he was irritated enough with Shayne that he killed her. Maybe that's why he had a prostitute the night we arrived. He was feeling guilty about what he did and needed someone to take away the pain."

Jack chuckled. "I guess that's possible. I find it interesting that Clark's entire persona is anti-women. He says women should stay at home and take care of kids while men go out and earn a living. In hindsight, that seems to be a direct response to Shayne's relationship with her husband.

"I mean, he stayed home, watched the kids and let Shayne fund their entire lifestyle," he continued. "That had to be hard for a guy like Clark, who wants to be in charge. Maybe they broke up because both of them wanted to be in charge and there was no compromise to be made."

"Or maybe high school came to an end and they came to the realization that their union wasn't sustainable."

Jack steepled his fingers on his abdomen and stared at the ceiling fan. "Clark and Shayne's shared past feels too important to be a coincidence. I think we definitely need to delve deeper there."

"Yeah. I didn't see any emails from him in her inbox. That would've stood out."

"We're still going to look." He rolled back to face me, amusement lining his face. "We have an hour before breakfast. What do you want to do?"

My cheeks burned as panic wrapped around my heart. "Oh, well ... ."

As if reading my mind, Jack's smile slipped. "Not *that*, you pervert. We're not there yet and I have no intention of going there until you're ready. Calm yourself."

I relaxed, but the embarrassment remained. "It's not that I'm opposed to that," I said hurriedly. "It's just ... we're sharing a condo with Bernard and Millie. It seems disrespectful."

He snorted. "That's a private thing," he agreed. "That's something that will come about when it's time. It's not time. Not yet."

I was secretly glad he was willing to wait. "Um ... if that's not what you were talking about, I'm kind of lost."

"I thought we could simply do this." He slipped his arm around my waist and tugged so that I was facing him, his mouth inches from mine. "I think we can spare ten minutes."

I remained confused. "For what?"

"This." He gave me a soft kiss and then pulled me close, wrapping his arms tightly around my back as he rested his cheek on my forehead. "See. Not scary at all."

Then why was my heart pounding so hard I thought it might burst through my chest? "Not scary at all," I agreed.

Jack could read the lie on my lips. He simply chuckled. "You'll get used to it."

We lapsed into silence, the two of us laying close but not moving. After a few minutes my heart rate returned to normal and I thought there was a chance I might drift off. Instead, I found myself scrambling when the bedroom door burst open to grant Laura entrance.

"Hah!" She strolled to the center of the room and pointed at us, her eyes filled with fire. "Hah!"

Jack barely shifted. "Why are you making that noise?" He ran his hand up and down my back in a reassuring manner. "By the way ... have you ever heard of knocking?"

"I shouldn't have to knock." Laura was full of anger, and it spilled forth like lava from her lips. "We're on the job. This is business. That means you shouldn't be doing something in here I can't see."

"Does it look like we're doing something nefarious?" Jack challenged.

"You're in bed together!"

"So what? We're not naked."

"But ... you're in bed together!" She was spitting mad, her cheeks so red I thought she might pass out. My cheeks were red, too, but for an entirely different reason. "You're together!"

"So what?" Jack released me and rolled to his feet, glaring at her as she stomped her foot. "You're not supposed to be in here, Laura. We didn't invite you. Get out."

"You can't kick me out."

"I just did."

"Well, I refuse," Laura snapped. "Do you have any idea what you're doing? You could get fired for this. Fraternization is frowned upon. In fact ... Charlie could get fired for this." The notion caused Laura's eyes to sparkle as she brightened. "Wait ... Charlie could get fired for this." She seemed thrilled at the prospect.

"Charlie isn't getting fired," Jack barked, his hands landing on his narrow hips. "It's not happening. Not now, not ever."

"You're not in control of that. All I have to do is make one little complaint. You're much more valuable to the team than she is."

Jack growled as I rubbed my cheeks. I couldn't believe this was happening. In an odd way it made sense, though. Laura was never going to give us a chance to get to know one another if she could wedge herself between us. It was inevitable she would find a way to end things.

"What's going on?" Millie asked, her eyes sleepy as she appeared in the doorway. Bernard, dressed in a T-shirt and shorts, shuffled behind her. He seemed more confused than anything else.

"I'll tell you what's going on," Laura snapped. "I came in here to rouse everyone for breakfast and I found these two ... in bed together."

She waved a derisive hand in my direction. "They were on top of each other."

"Really?" Millie's eyebrows migrated north as she focused on my face. "It's about time. Good for you. I was hoping a change of sleeping arrangements would cause that to happen."

Jack scowled. "We were not on top of each other. We were simply ... you know what?" He changed course quickly. "It's none of your business what we were doing, Laura. The door was closed. You knock on a closed bedroom door. You have no right being in here."

"I have every right," Laura hissed. "Fraternization isn't allowed. You know that. All I have to do is place one call and she's out of here."

My heart rolled. This was getting out of hand.

"You don't want to do that, Laura." Jack lowered his voice to a dangerous level, iciness washing over him so fast he reminded me of an iceberg. "If you push me on this you won't like the outcome."

"You're not in charge." Laura was haughty. "You're breaking the rules. It's ... disgusting. She's practically an intern."

"You're just jealous because Jack wants to be with Charlie and not you," Millie argued. "Don't bother denying it, you little guttersnipe. You've been after Jack since you joined the group. You're not bothered that two members of the team are involved. You're bothered that you're not one of them."

"Don't talk to me as if I'm ten," Laura snapped. "I am not jealous. I don't get jealous."

In general, I hated that term. Jealousy was one of those things that served absolutely no purpose. This one time, I had to agree with Millie, though. Laura was very clearly jealous ... and not taking it well.

"What do you want from us?" I asked, finding my voice. "What do you expect to happen here?"

"I expect you to lose your job and Jack to come to his senses," Laura replied. "And don't you worry, I'll make sure that happens." She turned on her heel and flounced from the bedroom, leaving me with a mountain of doubt on my shoulders.

"Am I going to get fired?" I asked, hating how pitiful I sounded.

"No," Jack answered. "That won't happen."

"Definitely not," Millie agreed, determination ticking in her set jaw. "Leave this to me. I've got everything under control."

BY THE TIME WE MET in the dining room for breakfast I'd managed to shower and dress. I wasn't exactly talkative for the walk to the main building and Jack's mood wasn't improved by my silence.

"And there they are," Laura crowed when we walked into the dining room. Hannah and Chris were already seated, but Millie and Bernard were absent. "The Legacy Foundation's newest super couple. Er, well, for at least the next five minutes. After that, we're going to have a super security chief and an opening for an intern."

"I'm not an intern," I reminded her, weariness threatening to overtake me as Jack pulled out a chair so I could sit. I didn't understand why Laura insisted on being the most annoying person in the room. She was horrible ... and seemed to derive power from it.

"You're not an intern," Jack agreed, taking his seat next to me. "You're pretty freaking far from an intern. In fact, you've contributed more in the few months you've been with us than Laura has in the years she's been part of the team."

Laura narrowed her eyes to dangerous slits. "I'll let that go because I recognize that you're upset about losing your little girlfriend. Don't dwell on it. You'll get over it faster than you realize."

"Laura, you should be aware of something," Jack noted as he grabbed two menus from the center of the table, handing me one as he glared holes into Laura's pretty but twisted face. "If it comes down to it, I will leave the group. Charlie will stay. We've already talked about it."

Laura's mouth dropped open. "What? You can't be serious."

"Oh, but I am."

"No one is leaving the group," Chris said hurriedly, taking control of the conversation. "The group is not changing ... unless you want to leave, that is, Laura."

The huffy woman made an exaggerated face. "Is that supposed to be a joke?"

"No." Chris was grave as he shook his head. "I've been on the phone with my uncle this morning. It seems Laura's complaint went straight to the top."

Instead of being embarrassed, Laura preened. "Well, when you break company rules you have to expect swift action."

"Definitely," Chris agreed, his voice taking on an edge. "My uncle and I had a long talk. He asked if Laura's charges were true. I responded that I didn't know because that's the truth. I explained that if Jack and Charlie were together — which was a private matter — that I had no idea because they were so adept at their jobs they didn't let on."

Sensing a change in the wind, Laura straightened her shoulders. "But ... ."

"I also pointed out that I was involved with Hannah, which was also against the rules," Chris continued, ignoring the worry flitting through Laura's eyes. "My uncle was curious as to why you would report Charlie and Jack, but not Hannah and me. You were aware of both relationships, after all."

"Because ... because you and Hannah are professionals," Laura sputtered. "Besides that, you're the boss. There are separate rules for you."

"My uncle said the same. He was annoyed, by the way, at being woken with such an inconsequential issue. For the record, he's lifted the fraternization rule from our group. It's still in place for the rest of the company, but given the way we travel and the inordinate amount of time we're forced to spend together, he thought that we should have different rules."

Laura's lips turned down. "What do you mean?"

"Fraternization is now fine as long as it doesn't infringe on our performance as a group," Chris replied, his eyes hard as he stared down Laura. "The final decision is now up to me if someone is going to get in trouble for fraternization, which I don't see happening."

"So ... they just get away with it?"

"Yes." Chris was firm. "You, however, will be facing an inquiry at the main office when we return. I didn't ask for it — so don't attack me — but it seems Millie and Uncle Myron had a chat this morning. She was angry and had a few things to talk to him about."

"They're divorced." Laura glanced around the table as if looking for backup. Finding none, she doubled down on her resolve. "Why would Millie get involved?"

"I think we all know the answer to that," Chris replied. "She's still on the phone with him now. She had some interesting ideas for your performance review."

Laura's face went slack. "You can't punish me for this."

"I'm not in charge of any of that. If you're upset, take it up with Uncle Myron. He'll be personally looking over your review."

I risked a glance at Jack and found him watching the scene with smug satisfaction. "Did you know it would go down this way?" I whispered.

He shook his head. "No, but I knew it would be all right." He slipped his arm around my back and met Chris's even gaze. "We won't shirk our duties."

"I know." Chris smiled at me. "I think it's kind of cute."

"It's new," Jack corrected. "We don't know where it's going yet. I promise that it won't infringe on our duties. We're dedicated to our jobs."

"If I had any doubts about that you wouldn't be here. As for you, Laura, I'd start thinking long and hard about how you're going to explain your actions to Uncle Myron. He does not like being bothered with trivialities."

Laura's eyes were filled with fury when they locked with mine. She was in trouble, but she was nowhere near done with me. I could read that with absolute clarity.

Ah, well. That was a problem for another day. I opened the menu with more zest than I felt only minutes before. "I'm thinking pancakes this morning. I worked up an appetite last night."

Jack chuckled at Laura's scowl. "Sounds good. I'm famished. Pancakes all around."

TWENTY-ONE

*L*aura made a big show of stalking into the lobby, standing on the other side of the restaurant window and talking on her phone. When she first started the conversation she was all smiles, as if she were about to win some big award. Within seconds of carrying out her conversation, that smile was gone. By the end, she was yelling, and whoever she was talking with appeared to be yelling back.

"What are you guys looking at?" Millie asked, appearing at the table.

"How did you get here without us noticing?" I glanced around, confused. "Are you a ninja or something? We've been watching the front door."

"I came in through the side door," Millie replied, her gaze traveling to Laura. "What is she doing?"

"Auditioning for her role as the Devil in *Rosemary's Baby*?" Jack replied dryly.

Millie's eyebrows migrated higher on her forehead. "Someone's in a mood."

"I am in a mood," Jack agreed, his temper coming out to play. "I don't understand why she can't simply be a decent person. She always takes it to a level where it's impossible to tolerate her."

"You're looking at it the wrong way," Millie said as she took the open chair to my left. "Laura believes the way to get ahead in life is to push others behind her. She doesn't understand that not everybody is in the same line."

"Oh, that was almost poetic," Jack drawled. "I still can't stand her."

"Well, none of us can stand her." Millie was blasé. "She's a terrible person. However, one look tells you all you need to know in this particular situation. She's not getting her way. Trust me. I talked to Myron. He wasn't happy with the early-morning call. He's handling the situation."

I was curious if he was handling the situation because of Millie and Bernard or Chris and Hannah. My money was on Chris and Hannah. I'd yet to see Myron and Millie interact for more than five minutes at a time — Jack swore up and down that longer interaction elicited fears of the end of the world — but they'd been polite and cordial during those instances. In fact, Myron seemed rather fond of Millie, as if he wasn't quite over her. I kept that observation to myself.

"So ... what are we doing otherwise?" I asked. I wanted to get the group back on track rather than dwell on Laura. If we spent all our time thinking about Laura, the conversation would ultimately turn to Jack and me. The relationship was too new for that.

"We're having breakfast," Jack replied. "I believe it was you who ordered that huge mound of pancakes."

"I'm talking about work. What are we doing for work after this?"

"Hannah and I are going out on the cutter again," Chris announced, causing Jack's head to snap in his direction. "We've set up a special consultation with Jim Bedford. He was the man we talked to briefly after Charlie's accident. We're heading back out with him."

Jack was flabbergasted. "Why am I only just hearing about this?"

"Because I'm your boss and I made the decision," Chris replied blandly. "I believe I'm allowed to schedule my own day."

"And I believe I haven't signed off on that trip," Jack countered, refusing to back down. "As head of security, I get to lodge an opinion on activities ... and I'm not a fan of that one."

"I'm still the boss." Chris was firm. "You don't believe we're dealing with a Megalodon."

"No sane person believes we have a Megalodon out there hunting," Jack argued.

"Well, if there's no Megalodon, you have absolutely no reason to believe I'm in any danger on the boat." Chris was smug as he folded his arms across his chest and met Jack's annoyed gaze. "Isn't that right?"

"I can see where you would think that," Jack supplied. "The thing is, I didn't believe we were dealing with a Megalodon a few days ago and Charlie almost died while out on the water. Do you see where I'm going with this?"

Chris's smile slipped. "I have no intention of getting in the water."

"I don't believe Charlie did either."

"Charlie is right here," I reminded them, waving in case I'd suddenly turned invisible without my knowledge. "I fell in because of Laura. I'm sure Chris will be fine as long as she's not there."

"You can come with us if you want," Chris offered.

The way Jack's body tensed told me he would absolutely lose his head if I agreed to that. "Thank you for the offer, but I've come to the conclusion that I'm not a boat person." I thought back to the way my stomach constantly somersaulted during the previous trip. "Apparently I'm prone to seasickness."

Jack immediately calmed. "I thought you weren't admitting you were sick."

"Yeah, well, Laura wouldn't have so easily been able to knock me over the edge if I hadn't been off my game. I don't want to head out on the cutter again. I much prefer drawing the Megalodon into shore so I can see it from the pier."

"Oh, geez." Jack slapped his hand to his forehead. "This is seriously the stupidest assignment we've ever been on."

"I think you're exaggerating." Chris leaned back in his chair. "I find this assignment exhilarating. We're on the beach, at a beautiful resort and we're looking for an animal that's supposed to be extinct. What's more exciting than that?"

"I don't even know how to respond to that," Jack muttered, shaking his head.

Chris ignored the security guru's pouty reaction and fixed me with a bright smile. If he was annoyed by the turn of events, worried that Jack and I would fall off the rails and disrupt the natural chemistry of the group, he didn't show it. "What do you have planned for the day?"

"Oh, well ... ." I shifted, uncertain. I hadn't gotten that far. Jack and I were still playing cuddle monsters in bed when our morning was upended.

"Bernard and I are spending the morning on the pier," Jack announced, taking me by surprise. "The shark net they put in the other day was temporary. I heard the maintenance crew talking. They had to order a permanent one. That's going up today."

"How do you know that?" I asked.

"I keep my ear to the ground. We're going to watch the installation. And, before anyone asks, we're not watching because we think a Megalodon is going to show up. We're watching because I have questions about that net — and how it managed to get destroyed in the manner we saw the first day we arrived. The people who can answer those questions will be on site today."

"That's a good idea," Chris enthused. "Make sure they give you measurements from the destroyed net so we know how big the Megalodon is."

There are times I think Chris is earnest to a fault, that he could never say anything that isn't true. There are other times I'm convinced he's a master at trolling people. This was one of those times. The look on Jack's face was absolutely priceless.

"I can guarantee the word 'Megalodon' isn't going to escape my lips," he said. "I will ask about their theories on the other net, but I'm not risking being thrown in the nuthouse for questioning them about an extinct prehistoric shark."

"Fine." Chris airily gestured with his hand to wave off Jack's attitude. "I'll track down the workers when we get back and ask them myself. I don't need you to do it for me."

"That's great." Jack rolled his eyes until they landed on me. "What are you going to do?"

That was a good question. "I'm going to see if I can track down information on Clark and Shayne," I said finally, making up my mind. "There has to be a way to figure out what happened between them, even if their involvement was more than a decade back."

"Don't go anywhere that you're isolated," Jack warned. "If Clark is the bad guy, he won't hesitate to go after you to keep you quiet."

"I have no intention of going anywhere with Clark." I internally shuddered at the thought. "Trust me. He's the last person I want to spend time with."

"DO YOU WANT SOME COFFEE?"

Despite my best intentions, I ended up in the lobby alone with Clark between conference classes. He was almost decent when he didn't have an audience, and he threw me for a loop when he offered to buy a beverage for me.

"Um ... green tea is fine," I said finally, taking a long look around the empty lobby, hoping to find at least one other stray body for reassurance. I came up empty.

My plan was to track down Lily and Sarah so they could answer additional questions about Clark and Shayne. If there was anything worth knowing, they would have the inside track. Unfortunately, by the time we'd finished breakfast they were departing for classes. That left me alone in the lobby.

The first time it happened I was fine with it because it allowed me to start Googling the formerly romantic pair. I managed to find out that they both graduated from a Louisiana high school, neither with high grades, and Shayne was the winter homecoming queen. Unfortunately, the school didn't have old yearbooks online, so I couldn't search through photos and piece together a history of the couple. I could, however, pull the name of the class president because the website had a list of each individual who had filled that position.

I spent the next twenty minutes tracking down Augusta Benson. She married and changed her last name, but returned to her maiden name upon getting divorced. Ultimately, she was right back in her hometown and it wasn't hard to track her down. She thought I was a telemarketer when I called and hung up. I decided to wait a few minutes before calling again, but she didn't bother picking up the second time. I left a message, but I wasn't holding out hope that she'd call back.

By this time, the authors had finished their first classes of the day and were enjoying their break. It was too late to ask Lily and Sarah my questions before they disappeared inside the conference rooms a second time. I wasn't alone once the lobby emptied this go-around. Clark remained with me ... and I was unbelievably uncomfortable with the turn of events.

"Thanks." I forced a smile as he delivered the iced tea I'd requested. "Um ... what do I owe you?"

"Don't worry about it." He sat across from me at the table. "I'm a successful author. I believe I can afford a five-dollar tea for my new friend."

There was something about the words that set me on edge. "Um ... ."

"Oh, I love your face." Clark slapped his knee and gave in to raucous laughter. "You have an expressive face. Most authors would love writing about your face."

"Is that a compliment?" I really wasn't sure.

"It's not an insult."

And that wasn't really an answer, I mused. He was good at deflection. When he wanted attention, he knew how to garner it. He was fine being lewd and crude. In fact, if I had to guess, he probably got off on the power. Most women weren't comfortable with the things he said and walked away rather than continue listening. He took that as a win.

Well, I had news for him; I wasn't most women and I had no intention of walking away.

Of course, that didn't mean I was comfortable. Jack would be absolutely furious when he found out I spent alone time with one of our chief suspects.

"How did you get into writing prepper fiction?" I asked, changing the subject. "That sounds like a fascinating genre."

"Oh, it is." Clark turned serious. "I've always been interested in writing about the end of the world. I think preparing my readers is important. My knowledge will help them, and I'm all about helping people."

Everything I'd seen from him since arriving seemed to prove that statement wrong. "Are you married?"

"Are you interested?" He winked and made my stomach roll.

"I don't think I could live the prepper lifestyle." I opted for honesty. "I don't mind camping one or two nights — although it's not my favorite activity — but living the prepper life is probably out of my wheelhouse."

"It's not for the weak," he agreed.

Wait ... did he just call me weak? "I don't think it's about being weak or strong," I hedged, biting back my temper. "I simply prefer food that doesn't taste like cardboard."

"When the end of the world comes you won't care what your food tastes like. You'll only care about survival, the fact that the zombies aren't eating you and your neighbor isn't trying to steal your virtue along with a pantry full of canned goods."

Good grief. This guy was more ridiculous than Chris's Megalodon theory. "Well ... at least you know how you're going to approach the situation. That's what's important, right?"

"Oh, I'll definitely be prepared." Clark's grin was lazy as he leaned back in his chair and sipped his coffee. There was something predatory about his expression ... and I didn't like it. "You're with that group investigating the death of that paranormal fantasy author, right?"

Hmm. He didn't refer to her by name. He'd either already distanced himself from the girl he knew or he wanted me to believe they were barely acquaintances. I was leaning toward the latter. "Kind of," I replied. "I'm with the Legacy Foundation. We investigate unexplained deaths." That wasn't exactly true. It wasn't totally a lie either. Explaining what we really did often incurred laughter ... and in extreme cases, fear.

"We're here because there's a question about the shark activity," I continued. "Hey, maybe you can help us." I made up my mind on the spot. Clark and I were alone in the lobby, but that didn't mean I was vulnerable. There were hundreds of people only a few feet away behind closed doors. If I screamed, help would come. That meant I could push him, and I was dying to see his reaction.

"You think I can help you?" Clark's expression turned doubtful. "I don't know much about sharks, but I'll try."

"Oh, I'm not talking about sharks." I made a dismissive wave. "I'm talking about the fact that you went to high school with Elsie May Haymark." I decided to use her real name because I wanted him to understand that I was serious and not operating in the dark. "You guys used to date, right?"

I kept my tone casual because I wanted to appear as if the questions were standard and the situation entirely ordinary.

The look on Clark's face told me he felt otherwise.

"Excuse me?" His eyes flashed with something I couldn't quite identify. "What are you talking about?"

"You and Elsie May Haymark went to high school together," I repeated, refusing to back down. "My understanding is you dated. That must have made attending the same conferences throughout the year pretty stressful. Did you ever meet her kids? I hear she has five of them."

Clark worked his jaw, temper lurking in the depths of his brown eyes. Finally, when he spoke, it was to issue a denial. That didn't exactly surprise me. "I have no idea what you're saying."

I decided to lay it out for him as if he were twelve. "Elsie May Haymark is Shayne Rivers. You went to high school with Elsie, dated her even, and then fought with her on the internet in public forums. The thing I'm curious about is, did you fight because she refused to mold herself into the model you wanted for a partner or did you adopt that mantra after she became the primary breadwinner in her family?"

Clark's mouth dropped open. "What the hell are you talking about?"

"You believe women should stay home and not work, right?" I had no intention of backing down. "That's what someone said."

"I believe everyone should have the opportunity to provide for their family," he clarified. "Once married, women should provide for their families by having children and taking care of the house. However, if kids aren't on the menu right away, I think it's fine for a woman to have a job and contribute to the household budget, as long as she doesn't shirk her other duties."

Wow. What a peach. I couldn't believe how much I wanted to punch him in the groin. "How did Elsie take it when you told her about your world view?"

Clark narrowed his eyes. "I've told you, I don't know what you're talking about."

Interesting. He was sticking to the lie. That would come back to bite him. I rationalized that he could be panicking — unaware that anyone knew his secret — but that seemed unlikely. He probably thought he plugged that information hole when he asked Carter to keep his friends quiet. If Carter was as well-liked as everyone said, that meant he had power. Apparently that power wasn't enough to stop the gossip machine.

"Well, I guess I must have heard wrong," I said finally, grabbing my tablet and tea and getting to my feet. "Thanks for the drink. My friends are expecting me and will come looking if I'm late."

"Then you should definitely go." Clark's eyes were cold. "I'm sure we'll talk again."

I kept my smile serene and sweet. "I'm sure we will. I look forward to it."

TWENTY-TWO

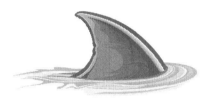

I was happy to make it outside even though the humidity was oppressive. Clark could suck the oxygen out of a room without even trying. Still, I'd left him feeling uncomfortable — I was certain of that — and it seemed prudent to relieve some of the building pressure if I didn't want him to blow.

The patio between buildings was empty except for a young author I recognized because I'd seen him hanging around over the course of the investigation. I'd yet to talk to him, and yet when I focused on his face I realized he'd been lurking in the shadows since I first started talking to Lily and Sarah.

I was intrigued enough by that realization that I decided to sit with him. I didn't wait for an invitation, instead grabbing the chair across the way and plastering a huge smile on my face.

"Hi."

He looked up from his computer, swiping his thick black hair away from his forehead and looking me up and down. "Hello, Charlie Rhodes."

He greeted me in a matter-of-fact manner, as if we'd known each other for years. I found his reaction interesting, if a bit disconcerting.

"Have we met?" I asked after a beat. "I can't help thinking I would remember."

"Because I'm memorable?"

"Because you're younger than most of the people here," I answered honestly. "Are you even old enough to drink?"

"I'm twenty-two."

"So ... barely old enough to drink. How did you get caught up with all these people?"

He shrugged, noncommittal. "I'm a writer. This is where writers come to hang out."

"What name do you write under?"

A small smile played at the corners of his lips. "Oh, any number of names. I don't stick to one genre ... or name ... or one game plan. I'm an experimenter of sorts."

He seemed open to conversation and yet I still didn't know his name. "You know who I am. What do I call you?"

"Max Thatcher." He extended his hand. "I know who you are because you've been hanging around Lily and Sarah."

"Are you friends with them?"

"Yes."

He wasn't the sort to volunteer information. I was going to have to drag it out of him. I wasn't opposed to that, but it made things easier if the person I was questioning blabbered. Thankfully, most of the authors I'd crossed paths with wanted to talk about themselves. Max was something different.

"What sort of things do you write?"

"Romance. Police procedurals. Prepper fiction. Space opera. High fantasy. Dark fantasy. Paranormal mysteries."

My mouth dropped open. "You write all of that?"

He nodded, amused by my reaction. "I told you I was an experimenter."

"Yeah, but you're twenty-two. How can you possibly have written everything you just listed?"

"I'm highly motivated."

"Because?"

"Because I have a certain plan for my life," he replied, turning his full attention from his computer to me. "I'm not set to one path and I don't want to spend my life struggling for money. That's how my parents live."

I could see that. Worrying about money was always a bummer. "How did you get involved in publishing?"

"I saw a news article on Lily Harper Hart when I was in my second year of medical school. It sounded interesting."

Medical school? "You're only twenty-two. How are you in medical school?"

"I finished two years of college while still in high school."

"But ... how?"

"Advanced placement. I've always been motivated. It only took me a year and a half to graduate from college, and then I headed straight to medical school."

I was impressed. "I guess you weren't joking about being motivated, huh?"

"Not even a little. I'm trying to finish up my rotations right now so I can get a full-time job and better streamline my writing schedule."

I was back to being confused. "Rotations? Wait ... you stayed in medical school even though you wrote all those books?"

He nodded. "I want multiple revenue streams."

"You have to be working sixty hours a week to keep up that schedule."

"More like ninety." If he was bitter about the hours he was putting in, he didn't show it. "It's not as bad as it sounds. There's a lot of downtime when I'm on rotation so I write my books on my phone between patients."

"You write books on your phone?" That seemed impossible. I couldn't write a clean text on my phone because my fingers were too fat. "What kind of doctor are you going to be?"

"A psychologist."

"Oh." Well, that was slightly different than what I was imagining. I thought he was trying to be a surgeon or something. I kept picturing the doctors of *Grey's Anatomy* trying to write books in their spare time between getting frisky in the on-call room and saving lives in the operating room. "And you're close to finishing?"

"I am."

"Will you actually set up a practice, with patients and everything?"

"I'm already looking at practices I can join when I'm finished."

I had no idea what to make of that. I couldn't imagine being that driven. "I guess that's why you're always the quiet one when the other writers are around. You don't have the energy to be loud."

"I'm quiet because that's simply who I am. I don't have a loud personality. Besides that, it's easier to fly under the radar if you're quiet."

Now we were getting somewhere. "And what are your observations, as someone who flies under the radar, I mean?"

"My observations on what?"

He was going to make me say it. I guess he had that right. "Shayne Rivers."

Max's lips twitched. "I figured she would come up eventually." He sighed. "Lily warned that you would sniff me out no matter how hard I tried blending in. I was hopeful that wouldn't happen."

"Why did Lily think I would sniff you out?"

"Because Shayne and I weren't exactly friendly."

"You didn't like her?"

"Nobody liked her," Max replied. "You must realize that by now. Has anyone said they liked her? If so, they're lying."

"Nobody has admitted to liking her."

"That's because she was toxic and it was essentially career suicide to align yourself with her. The only ones who cross the line are the newbies who don't understand the ramifications of what they're doing. Writers have long memories, like elephants."

I thought it was hilarious that a twenty-two-year-old was calling others "newbies," but he seemed so sure of himself I was convinced that he was twice the age he claimed. "What was your beef with Shayne about?"

"She outed me."

"Oh, you're gay?" I felt sorry for him. Not because he was gay, but because anyone would pry into his personal business and make things difficult due to his sexuality. "She shouldn't have done that. Your sexuality is your business."

He chuckled. "I'm not gay. That's not what I meant. She outed some of my pen names."

I stilled. "I'm confused," I admitted after a moment's contemplation. "She told people your pen names? Is that bad?"

"It depends what genres you write in," Max explained. "There's a fight of sorts going on in romance circles right now. Female pen names sell better. It shouldn't be that way, but there's a bias with the readers."

"So your pen name is female?"

"For romance," he confirmed. "The problem is that a subgroup of authors is making a big deal about males writing as females. They're saying it's abusive to women. In the current climate, what with the MeToo movement and everything, you don't want to be accused of being abusive to women."

I was confused. "I don't understand why it's such a big deal to have a female pen name. I thought that happened quite often."

"It does, and vice-versa. There's a bias toward female writers in science fiction, so a lot of the women have to adopt gender-neutral names or male pen names to sell in that genre. That readership is mostly male."

"Hmm."

"The problem with what's happening in romance is that a few unethical individuals started interacting with their fans as females, asking them personal questions and acting altogether skeevy," Max explained. "When it came out they were really men — something Shayne was also responsible for — the women being bamboozled were understandably horrified. They completely freaked out."

"Wow. That's ... I guess I don't know how to feel about that."

"I started selling well in romance. Shayne figured out who I was, and she outed me to my readership. They didn't react well, and that pen name is now essentially dead because of what she did. It's too bad. I made good money off that pen name."

"You're saying you had a reason to want her dead," I surmised. "You probably shouldn't tell me that because I'm with the group investigating her death."

"I've heard you're on the up-and-up so I'm not particularly worried."

"Fair enough."

"As for Shayne, I wasn't happy with what happened, but ... ," he shrugged. "I'm actually going to turn what happened into a psychology paper for industry magazines because I think it's a fascinating look at the psyche of a narcissist. In addition, it will make for interesting reading on gender politics."

He really was a marvel. "You have a good attitude."

"I have a plan," he repeated. "I'm not going to let anything derail me."

"You're a lot more put together than I am, and I'm a year older than you."

"Your path is simply different," he responded. "The thing is, I've been watching you. I'm curious about people, and you stand out in a sea of dramatic souls who want to spend the entire conference touting themselves.

"Before you think I'm disparaging my friends, I'm not," he continued. "It's natural to want to talk about the things that inspire you, and most of the people here are inspired by what they write. That's a good thing. It's rare that people can find inspiration in what they do, but writing is a creative outlet and for those who can make a living embracing the dream, well, they think they've hit the pinnacle of happiness."

"And what do you think?"

"That it's always prettier when you're outside looking in," he replied. "No life is easy. People who want to be full-time writers think their lives will be perfect if they simply get to the position where they can fulfill their dreams. Once there, they realize they have a new set of problems to deal with and it starts all over again."

"Well, that's profound."

Max merely nodded.

"It's also kind of a bummer," I added, causing him to laugh.

"I'm interested in how people interact," he admitted. "I've infiltrated a lot of the groups so I can learn what makes some genres tick. That's why I have so many names."

"Does anyone know all your names?"

"Nope."

"I guess you're playing it smart."

"That's how I like to see things," he agreed. "I don't participate a lot. I'm often an outsider, which I'm fine with. It allows me to keep track of what everyone is doing without drawing attention. I was even in Shayne's private groups under another name."

The admission sparked in the back of my brain. "What do you mean? What private groups?"

"Shayne had at least three private groups in which she communicated with her followers," Max replied. "You had to be invited in. She invited one of my pen names without realizing it was me. That meant I got to see the crazy firsthand and she didn't even realize it."

"Could you show me?"

He didn't hesitate. "Sure, but if someone asks, I'm not the one who gave you access."

"I wouldn't dream of ratting you out."

"Lily says you're trustworthy. I'll take her word for it."

MAX SHIFTED GEARS QUICKLY. He had me inside Shayne's inner sanctum in a few minutes, and the world I found myself immersed in was flabbergasting.

"Wow. Look at this. She's accusing some action adventure writer of having sex with one of her enemies and she was even in the middle of organizing a plan to have her followers email his wife in an attempt to implode his marriage. Why would she do that?"

"She's not a good person," Max answered, amused by my reaction. "I'm surprised you don't realize that. You're an investigator. You've seen the ugly side of life."

"I've been an investigator for two months. I guess it's closer to three. You're younger but have more life experience."

"I'm simply a student of humanity." Max's grin said he was messing with me. "This is hardly the only instance of Shayne trying to rally her followers to ruin people. Look here. This woman, Lourdes Henley, used to be one of Shayne's best friends. She distanced herself from Shayne when things hit the fan and Shayne decided to launch a full-out assault on her books as payback."

"Wow. Is this Lourdes Henley here?"

Max shook his head. "She's British. She couldn't make the trip. Before you get too sympathetic, I heard that Lourdes is just as terrible to deal with as Shayne. She simply hides it better. She does a lot of vague posting, attacking her enemies without naming names."

"I never knew there was so much vitriol among writers," I said.

"You're not seeing us at our best. Most authors — I would say ninety-nine percent of them — are perfectly fine. I won't say 'normal' because it's a subjective term and who's to say what is normal? But most authors have a few squabbles and go on with their lives like normal people. It's only a random few who make the rest of us look bad, and because they're almost always attention seekers, it seems like they're taking over. They're not."

"All these people in this group are jumping at the chance to do someone else's dirty work." I scrolled through the messages, my heart sinking. "I don't understand why they would get involved in something like this."

"The newbies simply want to be involved. It makes them feel important. They believe Shayne's diatribes about being victimized and bullied. They truly want to help. When they realize they've been used, they'll turn bitter and attack other authors. It's basic human nature."

That didn't sound like the sort of life I wanted to live. "That's just with authors, right?"

"No, but it is more pronounced with authors. It's that whole 'tortured artist' thing we've got going on. There are some writers who believe that if you don't suffer for your craft you're doing it wrong."

"What do you believe?"

"I like experimenting."

He was so easygoing it was hard not to like him. "What about Clark Savage? What can you tell me about his relationship with Shayne?"

"It wasn't pretty."

"That's it?"

He sighed and took the computer from me, scrolling down a long time before coming across the message he was looking for. When he did, he pointed. "That's Shayne explaining why Clark is attacking her on a community message board. She claims it's because he tried to control her even when they were teenagers. She fought back, put him in his place, and became a hero in her own mind when she did it."

"Do you believe the story?"

"I don't know. Shayne lied so much it was impossible to believe anything she said. And yet, I've met Clark. I can see him trying to control her."

I could see it, too. "People aren't only one thing," I murmured, my mind busy. "Shayne was a terrible person, but she wasn't always a predator. Occasionally she really was the victim."

"Very good." Max nodded approvingly. "You're catching on."

"That still doesn't help us figure out who killed her."

"I thought a shark killed her."

"Maybe. Her cause of death is impossible to determine because of the state of her body. I don't think she voluntarily ended up in that water. I've been on that pier. Falling seems out of the question given the way the railings are built. She was too narcissistic to kill herself. That means someone else either pushed her over the side or dumped her body after the fact."

"Which are you leaning toward?"

I shrugged. "I have no idea."

"When you figure it out, tell me. I think it will make a fascinating paper."

He really was too much. "I don't suppose you would let me screenshot some of these messages before getting out of your hair, would you?"

"Knock yourself out. Just remember, I didn't give you access."

"I won't tell a soul I know you."

"That's the way I prefer it."

TWENTY-THREE

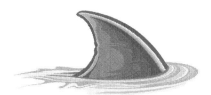

*J*found Jack and Bernard drinking iced coffee on the pier. They seemed to be in jovial moods, cracking wise, so I stood close to the railing and let them talk freely.

I spent a little time eavesdropping because ... well, I couldn't stop myself.

"Millie just messaged," Bernard offered. He was so chill that he often sounded lazy when talking. "She's been on the phone with Myron again. Apparently Laura refuses to let go of what happened this morning."

"That is so Laura," Jack grumbled, playing with the whipped cream on his drink. I couldn't remember ever seeing him get a frothy drink like that, so I was amused. "She's not going to win this one. Chris put his foot down. She should be afraid. She's not just messing with Charlie and me, but Chris, too. He has more power than she realizes."

"I never thought Chris had any power when I first started," Bernard admitted. "I was wrong. He's got a great personality and always wants to believe in the impossible. He's enthusiastic, a bit of a dreamer. He can also be tough when he wants to be."

"He can."

"He doesn't seem upset about you and Charlie. That's good."

Jack shifted on his seat and focused his full attention on Bernard. "Are you worried he'll be upset when he finds out about you and Millie?"

Bernard shrugged. "He loves her. He's an adult, but sometimes he reverts to being a kid with her. I think she spent a lot of time with him when he was growing up."

"Chris likes you. You have nothing to worry about."

"He likes me, but he loves his uncle," Bernard stressed. "I think, in the back of his head, he's still holding out hope they'll get back together. It might not be practical or realistic, but that kid thing he's got going for him isn't always cute."

"He'll get used to it," Jack offered. "He won't have the opportunity to do that unless you tell him what's going on, though."

"That's up to Millie. I agreed not to get involved with her relationship with Chris or Myron. That's really none of my business."

"You can't move forward until it becomes public."

"Yeah, well, that's becoming more and more evident." Bernard rubbed his chin. "It's not a worry for today. We're not going to fix it here."

"Definitely not."

"What about you and Charlie? Things seem to be going well with you."

I held my breath waiting for an answer. For some reason I turned into a total girl whenever talk of my relationship with Jack bubbled to the surface.

"Things with Charlie are fine ... other than the fact that she's trying to hide and eavesdrop."

I frowned when the words sank in, glaring when Jack met my gaze. He looked more amused than annoyed. I worked overtime to keep my face placid as I stalked to their table.

"I wasn't eavesdropping," I grumbled.

"Right." Jack tilted his drink toward me. "Want some? There's whipped cream."

"I've already had three green iced teas. I'm good for now."

"Where have you been?"

I told him about my run-in with Clark first. I figured if he was going to get angry he would blow up early and then settle when I told him about Max. As predicted, he wasn't happy with the turn of events.

"I can't believe you came right out and asked him about it," he complained, his eyes darkening. "That was incredibly stupid, Charlie. What if he's a killer? He could've taken you out."

I snorted. "We were in the middle of the lobby. He's full of himself, but he's not stupid. There was never any chance he was going to put his hands on me."

"You said the lobby was empty."

"Yes, but there were hundreds of people in the conference rooms and there are employees walking through the lobby all the time. He wouldn't have jumped me."

"I guess." He didn't look happy. "I think it's weird that he's denying going to high school with her even though that's easy to track down. He must have panicked."

"He sounds like a real piece of work," Bernard noted. "Everything you've said about him leads me to believe that he's capable of murder. Maybe she pushed him too far. Maybe he had some image of his life that involved her and he finally realized it was never going to happen and snapped."

"Maybe," I agreed. "The thing is, she has five children with her husband. It seems to me that if he was going to snap because of that he would've done it after the first two kids. Why wait this long?"

"Maybe she pushed him."

"Yeah, well, she was definitely pushing people." I pulled out my phone and highlighted some of the screenshots I'd taken with Max. "I found out she had a private group that she urged to attack her enemies. It wasn't something she did publicly, but apparently it was common knowledge."

"How did you find this?" Jack took my phone and started reading. "I looked all over the social media sites and didn't find this."

"It's a private group. I happened to stumble across a guy who is essentially an online ninja. He infiltrates all the private groups to keep up on the gossip." I told him about Max as he read. "He's like a genius or something. He writes actual books on his phone."

Jack was amused. "You sound impressed."

"He's younger than me and he's about to finish his rotations and be a full-fledged doctor. That's freaking amazing."

"That is pretty impressive," Bernard admitted. "You said he knew who you were?"

I nodded. "He's friends with Lily and Sarah, but he does his own thing. He admitted that Shayne outed him and he had to burn a pen name because of it. He didn't seem angry. I guess he could be faking it. If anyone knows how to mask emotions, it would be him. That's not the feeling I got."

"I'm going to run him anyway," Jack said. "Did you get his name?"

"Max Thatcher. I have no idea if that's his real name or one of his pen names."

"It's a place to start." Jack finished reading the screenshots and handed the phone back to me. "She was clearly the Devil. She played sweet and nice for the public but got off on screwing with people's lives. I guarantee that when we get to the end of this, whoever killed her is going to feel justified because she wasn't a good person."

"We still have a lot of suspects," I reminded him. "I bet there are more suspects out there than we're even aware of. If I was going to take down my enemy in a public setting like this, I would fly under the radar.

"The thing is, most of these writers can't fly under the radar because they're dramatic by nature," I continued. "They don't see themselves that way, but they clearly are."

"Definitely," Jack agreed. "It's like a soap opera except with writers. They stab one another with words instead of knives."

"We don't know that Shayne wasn't stabbed with a knife," Bernard said. "We have no idea how she died. Did the medical examiner say he was running a toxicology report?"

Jack nodded. "Yeah. They were going to message Hannah with the results when they returned. I'll make sure to ask her later if she's heard from them. If Shayne was drugged, that should show up. If she was using recreationally, that would show up, too."

"Why does it matter if she was using recreationally?" I asked.

"She might've accidentally fallen into the water under those circumstances."

Hmm. That made sense. "I think Clark is our best suspect right now. Shayne did a lot of nasty things to the other writers, but his beef with her was personal."

"I agree, but how do you intend on getting him to own up to his past with her? If he won't admit he knew her, we're definitely not going to shake him enough to cause him to admit he killed her."

"Well ... ." I didn't get a chance to finish because my phone rang. "Hold on." I didn't recognize the number. "It's probably a telemarketer. Do Not Call Registry my aching behind. Hello?"

There was hesitation on the other end of the call. I was close to hanging up when a voice finally responded. "Hello?"

"Yes?"

"Is this Charlie Rhodes?"

"It is."

"Um ... hello. My name is Augusta Benson. You called and left a message for me."

My heart skipped a beat and I held up a finger to silence Jack as I nodded. "Yes, Ms. Benson. That was me. I'm looking for information on Elsie May Haymark and Clark Savage. I understand you went to high school with them."

Jack fell silent, his eyes inquisitive. He didn't attempt to take my phone, and instead let me handle the questioning.

"I did, but I'm not sure how you found that out," Benson said. I could practically feel her squirming through the phone.

"I looked online," I answered honestly. "There's been an incident regarding Elsie and Clark in Florida, and there's some debate about their relationship."

Benson was instantly on alert. "What sort of incident?"

"She's dead."

"She's dead?" Benson didn't exactly squeal the question, but her voice ratcheted up a notch. "Are you sure?"

"She died several days ago."

"Did it hurt?"

The question caught me off guard. "I don't know. Her cause of death is ... undetermined ... at this point. Why would you ask that?"

"Because this conversation is going to be a lot more fun if I know it hurt."

Oh, well ... hmm. "She was discovered snagged in a shark net. She'd been fed on. There's a very good chance it hurt."

Jack and Bernard exchanged quick glances, clearly confused. They could only hear my end of the conversation. It was windy enough on the pier that I didn't want to risk putting her on speakerphone.

"That's what I want to hear." Benson brightened considerably. "What do you want to know about Clark and Elsie?"

"Well, for starters, I understand that they were involved. He's being evasive, and we're trying to ascertain how deeply that association ran."

"Deep," she replied without hesitation. "Very deep, in fact. They were involved all through high school. From when they were freshmen until they graduated."

"Really?" I didn't have many relationships in high school, but that sounded like an intense union for two teenagers. "What were they like when they were dating?"

"They were close. Clark was obviously in charge. Whatever he said, she did. She wasn't innocent or anything when all that stuff went down, though. She was simply better at hiding her involvement."

I was practically frothing at the mouth I was so excited. "And what went down?"

"You don't even know that?"

"No, ma'am."

"Well, it was a big deal here," Benson explained, warming to the subject. "Nancy Nelson went missing our senior year. It was rumored she'd been seen with Clark right before it happened. It was over by the track field and the team members saw them walking along the top of the hill. It was a big deal because Clark and Elsie were joined at the hip ... and other places, if you know what I mean."

I didn't need a diagram of the picture she was painting. "I get it."

"Nancy never made it home that night. Her mother called the police when she didn't show up, but they said there was nothing to be done until Nancy had been gone for twenty-four hours. So Nancy's mother started calling friends and someone told her about seeing Nancy with Clark."

My stomach shifted in a way that told me I wasn't going to like the end of this story. "Then what happened?"

"Nancy's mother tracked down Clark at his house," Benson replied. "She said he looked disheveled and seemed nervous. He denied being with Nancy and said that whoever told her that was lying. He said he was with Elsie, but when Nancy's mother tracked her down, she initially denied that.

"Nancy's body was discovered in the bayou the next day," she continued. "The cops said she was probably dumped there in the hopes the gators would get to her, but it never happened. She was intact, which was a small comfort for her mother."

I definitely felt sick to my stomach. As if sensing that, Jack rubbed his hand over my back. He was quiet and let me continue the conversation at my own pace.

"What happened with Clark?" I asked finally. "Was he arrested?"

"Nope. He told the cops he was with Elsie. The runners on the track team said they couldn't be one-hundred percent positive they saw him with Nancy, but they were eighty-percent positive. Elsie changed her story and said Clark was with her the whole time, and charges were never filed."

I was dumbfounded. "Was anyone else ever arrested in Nancy's death?"

"No. Everyone knows it was Clark. He took off right after graduation, and to my knowledge, he's never come back. Elsie comes back occasionally to visit her mother, but she stays to herself. She didn't try to hook up with any of us. I heard she was living in Baton Rouge, had some big house from her books or something, and insists her mother visit her there now."

I licked my lips, my mind going a million miles a second. "Do you know why Clark and Elsie broke up?"

"No. I heard rumors, but I don't know if they were true."

"What were the rumors?"

"That she was cheating on him with some guy at college. I believe it was the guy she ended up marrying. She was all meek and stuff in high school. I guess that changed when she got away from Clark."

"What about when they broke up?" I pressed. "How long did they last after graduation?"

"Not long. They went to separate schools, and by the first Christmas break she had a new boyfriend. I heard Clark was furious, but he didn't keep in touch with anyone, so I'm not sure how that word spread. It could be a total lie."

I knew how it spread. Shayne — er, Elsie — was a master at telling stories. She wrote her own narrative.

"Is that all?" Benson asked. "Do you need any other information?"

"No. That's it. Thank you so much for your time."

She hung up without saying goodbye. My hands were practically shaking with excitement when I shoved my phone back into my pocket. "You're not going to believe this." I told Jack and Bernard the story. When I'd finished, Jack was already on his feet.

"That is way too similar to be a coincidence," he said. "That's obviously his fallback plan. He killed that Nancy girl and left her for the gators to eat. Years later, he took out the one person who knew his secret and left her for the sharks to eat. His plan simply worked better this go-around."

"What are you going to do?" I asked, eyeing him with overt curiosity. "Are you going to tell the cops?"

"Eventually. First, I'm going to pull the police report on Nancy Nelson's death. There might be information in there that your phone friend wasn't aware of."

That sounded like a good idea. "What do you want me to do?"

"Stay out of trouble."

I frowned. "That's it? You don't want me to help you?"

"Actually, I do want you to help me." Jack changed his tune too fast to avoid suspicion. "I want you to keep Bernard company and talk to the shark net folks when they're finished. Chris will want information about that shark net no matter what we discover about Clark. I can trust you to do that, right?"

He had to be kidding. "I want to go with you and see the police report."

"I'll show it to you later. I need you to do this now."

He was clearly torturing me. "But ... ."

"No buts." He wagged his finger. "We both have jobs to do. You've done the heavy lifting so far. Now it's my turn. That doesn't mean your shift is over."

I was morose as I focused on the workers. "This is boring."

"It's also safe." He handed me the remains of his iced coffee. "I'll be back as soon as I find what I'm looking for. Don't leave until you have the information Chris specifically asked for. You'll be in trouble if you do."

"Whatever." I folded my arms over my chest and avoided eye contact.

"Oh, don't be like that," Jack complained. "It's not my fault. You can't pull the files."

"Do what you want."

He sighed. "I'll be back as soon as I can and I will share whatever information I find."

That wasn't as exciting as being part of the discovery process. "You're the boss. You have a job to do."

"I do. I'll be back as soon as I can."

"Have fun."

"Charlie ... ."

"Just go," Bernard instructed, waving him off. "I've got this. Believe it or not, I know a thing about wrangling feisty females."

Huh. That sounded like an insult. Apparently Bernard was bucking for a fight today, too.

TWENTY-FOUR

*T*he hunt for Clark Savage was on. The problem was, he'd disappeared right after our conversation.

No one knew where he was or how to find him.

"I think we should call the police," Hannah suggested once the group met in the condo she shared with Chris and Laura. That was hours after Jack left me to watch the people erecting the new shark net. "It's their job to find him."

"It's their job to find him, but we have no proof Clark is a killer," Jack countered. "We have our suspicions, a rather interesting set of facts from his childhood, a police report with gaping holes, but we don't have proof. We need to talk to him."

"I guess I don't understand what you're insinuating," Chris said as he stretched out his legs in an attempt to get comfortable on the couch. "What does Clark Savage have to do with Megalodons?"

I pressed the tip of my tongue to the back of my teeth and steadfastly ignored Jack's annoyed gaze as I tried to refrain from laughing. Jack really was one bad shark joke from killing the next person who mentioned a Megalodon.

"I don't think Clark has anything to do with a Megalodon, Chris," Jack said, his tone chilly. "I don't think a Megalodon was involved in

Shayne's death. In fact, I never thought a Megalodon was part of the equation. That was all you."

Unruffled, Chris merely blinked. "You saw the marks on her body in the medical examiner's office. The shark teeth were too big to belong to a regular shark."

Jack was exasperated. "Chris, Megalodons are extinct. There is no way a sixty-foot shark had anything to do with what we're dealing with here."

"Then how do you explain the state of her body?" Chris persisted, refusing to back down. "She was clearly eaten."

"By smaller sharks."

"You don't know that."

"I'm pretty sure it's a better possibility than a Megalodon. Bull sharks are prevalent in these waters. They go into feeding frenzies and are the most likely sharks to attack people. Tiger sharks are a close second. They're in this area, too."

"I hate to agree with Jack because ... well, I hate him right now, but it was never a Megalodon, Chris," Laura noted. "The odds of there being a human factor were always greater than you wanted to admit."

Chris's face told me there was a mighty struggle internally tearing him asunder. "We don't have proof of anything," he pointed out, managing to keep his voice calm. "We can't ignore the facts. There were huge teeth marks in Shayne's body. They couldn't have been made by a normal-sized shark. How do you explain that?"

"I don't know." Jack's tone was icy enough that I felt uncomfortable sharing space with Chris and him. "Megalodons are extinct. You must be reasonable. There is no way a Megalodon is roaming the waters. People would've seen it."

"The ocean is vast."

"A sixty-foot shark that, by your own admission, would be nothing more than a mindless feeding machine? It would impact the local marine population," Jack gritted out. "It would decimate dolphin and whale pods. There's only the limited orca population in the Gulf. You heard the guy on the ship the other day. We would know if there was a super predator hunting the waters."

Everything Jack said was rational. His theory made much more sense than the giant shark supposition. But Chris was a true believer. Until there was absolutely no reason for him to lose faith in the possibility of an ancient shark, he would cling to his ideals with jagged teeth.

"I guess we'll have to agree to disagree," Chris said finally. "I happen to believe it's a Megalodon."

Jack's face flushed with fury. "What about you, Hannah?" he asked pointedly. "Do you think it's a Megalodon?"

I understood what he was trying to do. Hannah was the pragmatic sort. Chris was totally devoted to Hannah. Jack needed Chris to see reason. She was his best shot.

He didn't take into account that Hannah was as loyal to Chris as he was to her. As much as she preferred science to whimsy, she wasn't about to crush the man she was sharing a rather intense relationship with.

"I think a Megalodon is possible," Hannah replied evenly, causing Jack's mouth to drop open.

"What?"

"You heard me." Hannah's hackles were up. "We have nothing that says it's not a Megalodon. We have several points of reference on a body that says it very well could be. I understand you don't want to believe it, Jack, but you don't always get what you want."

Jack's fury had teeth — jagged shark teeth — and he lashed out. "This is ridiculous! I don't understand how we can possibly be talking about a giant prehistoric shark as if it were normal. This is not the same thing as Bigfoot ... or the Chupacabra ... or werewolves. I didn't believe in those either, but at least they were small enough to hide in plain sight. A Megalodon is an entirely different story."

"That doesn't mean it's not real," Chris pressed. "I'm not asking you to believe. Why are you insisting that I stop?"

The question was simple, heartfelt. The look on Jack's face told me he registered what Chris was saying. He might not have liked the direction the conversation was heading, but he recognized the truth in Chris's words.

Jack being Jack, though, couldn't simply accept what his brain told him was impossible.

"Fine!" He threw his hands in the air and stalked toward the door. "Do what you want. You always do. When this blows up in your face, I don't want to hear one second of complaint. Do you understand me?"

"I will ask the same of you when I'm proved right," Chris replied.

"Ugh." Jack threw open the door with enough force it bounced against the wall. "I can't even deal with this. I just ... a freaking Megalodon! You people are nuts. Every single one of you."

He stormed out the door. I knew better than to follow him. He needed time to cool down. Laura was another story.

"Jack, wait!" She raced after him, almost desperate to get his attention.

I watched her a moment, unsettled, and then got to my feet.

"You should leave him be for a bit," Millie offered, solemn. "He'll calm down. He always does. He just needs time."

"I know. I'm not going after him."

"I don't understand."

"Laura," I explained. "She's probably a pile of mush on the sidewalk if she managed to catch up with him. He's already in a bad mood where she's concerned. If she tried to stop him, he probably unloaded a week's worth of annoyance on her. This Megalodon stuff has him firing on all cylinders."

"Fair enough, but why do you care about Laura?" Millie asked. "She tried to ruin your career this morning. I very much doubt she's going to apologize and make nice."

"That might be true, but I want to make sure. Jack lashes out sometimes without realizing the damage he's causing. I'm just going to check on her."

"You're nicer than I am."

That wasn't the word I would've used. *Nice.* I didn't feel nice. I merely smiled and nodded. Now wasn't the time for a lengthy talk on personality quirks. "I'm going to check on Laura and then head to the lobby. Maybe the other authors know where to look for Clark."

"And I'm going to talk to the cutter folks about returning to the water," Chris said. "I feel in my heart that we're on the right track with the Megalodon."

I almost felt sorry for him. He was as stubborn as Jack, just in a different way. "Well, be safe." I dragged my hand through my hair as I moved toward the door. "I'll text if I find anything that feels important."

"Good luck," Hannah called to my back.

"You're going to need it," Millie sang out.

I ignored them both.

I FOUND Laura and Jack on the sidewalk that led to the resort. They looked to be having an intense conversation, but it was one Jack clearly wasn't enjoying.

"Are you trying to make me be mean to you?" he exploded, his voice deep and harsh. "I don't want to talk to you, Laura. I don't want to hear one thing you have to say. Not one."

Instead of taking the hint, Laura pushed things to the point of no return. "I'm trying to help you. I agree with you. I want to make you feel better. I mean ... maybe we could get a coffee and sit down and talk. That sounds like a good idea, doesn't it?"

The look Jack shot her was withering. "No, Laura. That doesn't sound like a good idea. Why would I possibly want to talk to you?"

"Because we agree about the Megalodon. We're the only sane ones in the group."

"Don't lump me in with you."

"That was a compliment!" Laura's eyes filled with fire. "Why won't you take my compliment and put all the other stuff behind us?"

"Because you tried to get me fired this morning," Jack raged. "Why would I want to put up with you given that?"

"I wasn't trying to get you fired. Charlie is the one who needs to go."

I managed to bite back a hot retort, but just barely.

"Charlie does more work for this group than you ever have," he shot back. "Charlie is a doer and a thinker."

"Oh, right." Laura rolled her eyes. "She thinks it might be a Megalodon. She didn't say anything this morning, but you can tell she thinks it. It's written all over her face. She's a freaking genius."

"She's enthusiastic," Jack corrected. "She wants to believe. She doesn't really believe, at least not with this case. She understands what's going on here. She realizes that we have a human murderer ... and he's dangerous."

Jack took a step closer to Laura, glowering so hard that she took an involuntary step in retreat. "You're the problem, Laura," he hissed. "You want things your way no matter who you hurt. You went after Charlie this morning even though she's never done a thing to you. I won't stand for it a second time. I will remove you from this team if you ever try anything of the sort again."

"Oh, don't worry," Laura sneered, her real personality on full display. "It's been made clear to me that if I make another complaint against Charlie I'm the one who will go. Apparently Myron got an earful from Chris and Millie."

"Good." Jack wasn't so far gone he couldn't embrace welcome news. "I'm glad you got in trouble. You've had it coming."

"You see it as me being troublesome, but that's not what I'm about."

Jack snorted. "Oh, Laura, please tell me you don't believe that. You're not perfect by any stretch of the imagination, but one of the few things I could always say about you was that you were a realist. If you've floated into La-La Land we really do have a problem."

"I'm trying to help you." Laura was adamant as she planted her hands on her hips. "Charlie will drag you down. She's an idiot. She follows Chris's ideas without giving a thought to rationality. She's a complete and total moron ... and her goofy crush on you is suffocating."

"You don't get it." He slowly shook his head before shifting his eyes to me. He didn't appear surprised to find me watching them from twenty feet away. "Charlie is smart ... and strong ... and brave. She's overenthusiastic and leaps before she looks, but I find that refreshing."

His eyes never left me. "Does she occasionally drive me crazy? Yes." He bobbed his head for emphasis. "She embraces things before thinking them through. She races headlong into danger. She puts others before herself, especially when it comes to safety.

"That's not necessarily a good thing," he said softly. "It's not bad either. She's an authentic person living an authentic life. That's much more impressive than whatever you're doing."

"I'm better than her," Laura persisted. "I'm prettier ... and smarter ... and I'm a better choice for you."

"You're none of those things." Jack held my gaze a moment longer and then heaved out a sigh. "I need to take a walk. I can't be around people right now. Don't take it personally." He was talking to me now, and I understood his desire for space.

I nodded. "I'm going to the lobby to see if any of the other writers know where to look for Clark. Don't worry," I added hurriedly. "I will not go anywhere alone or risk running into him without backup."

He nodded. "Okay. Just ... be careful. I'm sure I will be calmer in an hour or so."

"Take your time." I flashed a smile. "Maybe get some ice cream or something. That always makes me feel better."

"I'll consider it." Jack turned to leave, but Laura grabbed his arm before he could take more than a step.

"We're not done talking," she snapped.

Jack's gaze was pointed as he stared at her fingers and then raised his eyes. "Let. Me. Go."

It was very clear he meant it. Even Laura recognized she was in a no-win situation and quickly released him. Jack gave me another lingering look before turning on his heel and stalking toward the beach. I knew he would sit in the sand, stare at the water, and stay there until he was relaxed. I had no idea how long that would take, but Jack was a man who relied on emotional stability.

Laura was furious when she realized he had no intention of turning around. "You're to blame for all of this. You know that, don't you?"

I was weary when I snagged her gaze. "How is this my fault?"

"You're ruining him."

"How?"

"He won't even talk to me."

I wasn't in the mood for a big fight, but I refused to be a doormat. It was time Laura and I got a few things straight, too. "He doesn't like you, Laura. I know you can't see that, but you're usually competent when it comes time to take the temperature of a room."

"Of course he likes me."

"No, he was indifferent to you when I first joined the group," I countered. "He didn't care either way. That indifference turned to dislike when you started with your full-court press. The fact that he didn't want to be with you wasn't a conspiracy ... or a commentary, for that matter. You're simply not his type."

"And you are?"

I held my hands out and shrugged. "Maybe. We don't know yet. This is new. We're just ... feeling each other out. The thing is, I don't try to turn him into something he's not. I don't try to make him bend to fit the mold of the perfect man I've created in my head. That's what you're trying to do, but he'll never bend.

"What you did today was ... horrible," I continued. "Jack expected it. He warned me. He knew what you would do and he was prepared to move when it happened. He had a plan, which I'm thankful for.

"You're like the scorpion in that old story, Laura," I said. "It needs to cross the water and it offers a deal to the turtle. It says it won't sting the turtle if it gives him a ride. The turtle agrees and, of course, halfway across the lake the scorpion stings the turtle.

"As he's dying, the turtle asks the obvious question. He wants to know why the scorpion did it. The scorpion only has one reply. It was in his nature to do it, and he couldn't fight his nature. That's you. You can't fight your nature."

Laura made a face that would've been funny under different circumstances. Unfortunately, I was deadly serious. "Are you saying I'm a bug?"

"I'm saying that you're trying to create a world of your choosing that no one else wants to live in," I clarified. "You want Jack, but it's not the real him you crave. He's a great man, but you can't see that. All you see is that he's handsome and protective. You want those things for yourself and you ignore what he needs. A relationship is not about one person."

"You sound like a simpering moron," Laura complained. "You're feeling full of yourself because you believe you've snagged Jack. He's quite the prize, so I don't blame you. Your relationship won't last, though, because he's above you."

"That might be true," I said. "Er, well, not the part about him being above me. I don't tend to believe one human being has more worth than another no matter their station. You're right about the possibility of it not working. That's why we're dating, to see if it will work.

"You'll never get to that point because you don't see him as a real person," I continued. "You see him as a prize, a thing to be possessed. No relationship will ever work under those conditions."

"Says you." Laura's eyes filled with annoyance. "I think I understand a thing or two about men that you can't even fathom. You're not smart enough to compete on my playing field. If you're smart, you'll bow out of the game."

"That won't happen."

"Then be prepared for Armageddon, because this is nowhere near over."

That's exactly what I was afraid of.

TWENTY-FIVE

*J*ack was capable of taking care of himself, and I had no interest in smothering him. I was mildly worried, but I knew him well enough to realize his burst of temper would pass.

Chris and Hannah were heading out on the Gulf ... again. I thought it was probably a waste of time, but it wasn't my place to order them around.

Millie and Bernard seemed fine entertaining themselves — which I was convinced would involve a trip to the tiki bar.

I didn't care what Laura did to pass the time. I was fed up with her attitude.

That left only me, and there was nothing I could do except question the other writers about potential locations for Clark, so that's what I did.

The courtyard was empty when I entered, except for J.D. and his wife, who appeared to be in a heated conversation close to the fountain. They didn't so much as look in my direction as I slowed my pace when I heard J.D. raise his voice for the first time.

"I can't believe you're being this way," he snapped. "This is a big deal for me, an important conference. This is about me!"

"Everything is about you," Christine shot back, her face hot with fury. "Our whole lives have become about you."

"I'm the one who got us out of that trailer park."

"I know that." Christine lowered her eyes and voice, stirring a waterfall of pity. "If you think I'm not happy about the change in our living situation, that I'm not proud of you ... ."

J.D. cut her off with an angry curse. "I don't need you to be proud of me. I need you to be supportive. I'm finally making something of myself, Christine. I'm finally going somewhere. If you want to hitch a ride you need to suck it up and realize my career comes first.

"I mean ... we would still be in that trailer if you had your way," he continued, his temper on full display. He either didn't see me or didn't care that I was listening. "You'd still be selling your potholders and afghans at flea markets so we could eat. Is that what you want?"

"I don't remember that being so bad," Christine hedged. "You've worked hard for us — you really have — but the money isn't everything. Some things are more important. That's why I want to go now. I think we should head home, spend some time together. You don't need this conference. You already know everything they're trying to teach you."

"It's not about what I learn, it's about who I meet. Conferences are about networking. The classes are ... unimportant. It's about the people. Why can't you get that?"

"I get that. I ... ." She broke off, her eyes slowly tracking to me.

I felt moronic for getting caught eavesdropping, so I offered a lame wave and pretended I hadn't heard them arguing. "I'm looking for Clark Savage. Have you seen him?"

Clearly done with his part of the conversation, J.D. trudged away from his wife. "I can't say I have," he said. "It's been a few hours at least. I'm pretty sure I saw him at breakfast, but that was a long time ago."

"You don't know where he's been spending his time when not attending classes, do you?"

"I don't pay that much attention to him. He's not my kind of guy."

I expected that to be a regular response when I started questioning the other writers. "Okay, well ... I'm going to head inside. See you later."

I was relieved to get away from them, but I felt Christine's eyes burning a hole in my back. She hadn't spoken to me, but it was clear she was angry that I had the audacity to interrupt them during an important conversation.

The lobby was packed with people, the authors split into the small groups. Those sitting on couches close to the back door were the first to catch my eye. Leslie, Abigail and Priscilla were among them.

"Oh, it's you." Leslie beamed as if I were her favorite person in the world. "I'm so happy to see you."

For a moment I thought she mistook me for someone else. Then I remembered she was crazy and plastered a smile on my face. The last thing I wanted was for her to start stalking me. Besides that, she might have information about Clark.

"It's me," I agreed, sliding into an open chair. I wanted her to believe we were friendly. "How are you guys? Enjoying the conference?"

"It's wonderful," Leslie intoned. "I've learned a great deal."

"I think it's kind of boring," Abigail supplied. "I could teach every class here."

"You think you could teach every class at every conference," Priscilla countered. "That's not always true. I think some of the things we've been discussing the past few days have been new and innovative."

Abigail snorted. "Like what?"

"Like in the craft class about opening chapters. The woman teaching it said the exact thing I've been saying all along. You have to write hooky. Hooky! It matters that you suck in readers, write intelligently for them, and don't put out drivel."

Abigail's expression was withering. "Don't you think that's a given?"

Priscilla shrugged. "If it was a given everyone would do it. Instead of having stupid books about women with glowing blue hands and moronic characters who say snarky things, we would have serious characters with a literary bent if it was a given."

"Yeah, but ... people prefer genre fiction to literary fiction. They think literary fiction is boring."

Priscilla balked. "You take that back!"

"It's the truth."

Leslie rolled her eyes as the duo continued to bicker, instead focusing on me. "Have you read the book I gave you? Amazing, huh?"

She clearly needed accolades. I could have offered them blindly, but if she questioned me about the plot of the book I'd be in real trouble. Instead, since he wasn't here, I decided to make Jack my sacrificial offering.

"I haven't read it yet, but I'm really looking forward to it," I replied. "My friend Jack has it. He says it's amazing."

"Really?" Leslie wiggled her butt as she preened. "So much better than James Sanderson, right?"

"I believe those were the exact words he used." I managed to deliver the statement with a straight face, but just barely. "I know he wishes he had more time to read, but we've been dealing with Shayne Rivers' death. I heard you knew her."

Leslie's lips curved down. "I knew her."

I waited for her to expound. When she didn't, I prodded her. "Were you friendly?"

"No one can be friendly with the gum found on the bottom of a shoe," she replied, her tone chilly. "There was nothing good about that woman. Ask anyone. If you find she had a fan here, that individual is lying because he or she is trying to avoid attention from law enforcement. That woman was hated."

"It seems she did quite a few things to be hated."

"She liked hurting people," Leslie agreed. "She wasn't happy unless she was ripping hearts out and stomping on them, leaving a bloody mess in her wake."

That was quite the visual. "My understanding is that she was brokering a deal with James Sanderson, one similar to what you have with him." It was a calculated risk, but I figured I might as well ask so I could see her reaction. If she flipped out I could always run.

"She was not writing with James."

Leslie's eyes flashed in such a way it made me nervous. "Oh, well ... a few people mentioned that she was working with him. In fact, someone — I can't remember who now because all the faces blur in my head — but someone said that he might have to drop you in favor of her."

That was a bald-faced lie. I was well aware of Leslie's position in the Sanderson writing pool. She was there because she was crazy and essentially threatened his family. Her place in his life was unique.

"Who told you that?" Leslie was furious as she leaned forward. Abigail and Priscilla finally broke from their conversation long enough to realize Leslie was about to lose it.

"I don't remember," I repeated, remaining calm. It would do no good to freak out. "Someone said that Mr. Sanderson was thinking about replacing your series with Shayne's proposed series."

"That is ludicrous." Spittle formed at the corners of Leslie's mouth, making me nervous. "I have a deal with James. We're writing soul-mates. He would never shove me aside like that."

Sensing trouble, Abigail cleared her throat. "You should know that Shayne was notorious for making things up," she offered. "She's been telling people for years that her books were being made into televi-sion shows and movies, but it never happened. She always came up with excuses after the fact for why the deals fell through, but none of them ever made any sense."

"So ... you don't think Shayne was telling the truth?"

"Not on this one. In fact, she didn't write mysteries or thrillers. There's no way James Sanderson would partner with someone new to the genre like that."

"That's right!" Leslie was still livid. "She was too stupid to write a mystery. That takes brains and talent."

"And a hooky writing style," Priscilla added.

"Oh, let it go, Priscilla," Leslie groused, shaking her head. "I'm so sick of the word 'hooky' that I want to smack you over the head with it. If you're not careful you'll end up with a different type of hook sticking out of you at the end of the pier. Do you want to end up like Shayne?"

The threat was pointed enough to set my teeth on edge. When I risked a glance at Priscilla it was obvious she felt the same way. She was furious at the words but leery enough of her friend that she didn't want to risk things flying out of control.

"Fine. I won't say the word again. Are you happy?"

"Thrilled."

I decided to take advantage of the momentary lull in the conversation to get to my feet and make an escape. I paused at the corner of the carpet to ask the question I'd almost forgotten about in my haste to get away. "Have you seen Clark Savage?"

Leslie furrowed her brow. "The prepper writer who thinks women should sit home doing dishes?"

"That's the one."

"Not since this morning. Check with Carter Reagan Yates. They're thick as thieves, although Carter isn't nearly as annoying as Clark."

"That's what I keep hearing." I kept my smile in place. "I'm sure I'll see you again later. I'll make sure Jack comes by to express in person how much he loves your book."

Leslie's smile was back to benign. "That sounds lovely. I'll see you later."

I FOUND CARTER DRINKING from his adult sippy cup outside the resort's main door. He was a good thirty feet from the door, and he had a Vape device in his hand.

"They make you come outside to Vape?" As far as opening lines went, it wasn't my finest. Carter looked amused, though, so I relaxed just a bit. We weren't the only ones outside. There were bellmen by the door. Everyone said he was the friendly one, but his association with Clark made me suspicious all the same.

"They have very strict no-smoking rules," Carter replied, puffing on the thin device. "It's annoying. There's a dedicated smoking area, but it's right behind a dumpster, so I come out here even though it's against the rules."

"Well, you have to get your nicotine fix somewhere. It's unfair that they essentially torture you to make it happen."

"Right?" His eyes flashed as he looked me up and down. He didn't linger on my legs or chest, which was a mild relief, and instead offered up a legitimate grin. "You're with the group investigating Shayne Rivers' death. I've seen you around."

"I've been making friends with your fellow writers," I supplied. "We met the other night at the tiki bar. I'm not sure you remember." I gestured toward his plastic cup. "You were re-filling that regularly, if I recall correctly."

"Well, what happens at the tiki bar stays at the tiki bar." He puffed on his Vape again. "You've been a busy little bee the past few days. I've seen you questioning a lot of authors. I thought you'd get to me sooner. I'm a little put off that you waited so long."

I wasn't sure what to make of that. "Well ... I didn't mean to put you off." That was true. I found him interesting. "You're usually surrounded by people that make me a little nervous." That also was true. "Like Clark Savage."

Carter's expression never changed. "He's not as bad as people think."

There was every possibility that he was worse than people thought, but I decided to keep that to myself. "He has a few issues," I hedged. "You must understand why women feel uncomfortable around him. He thinks they should be stuck at home handling kids and leaving all the available jobs to men. It's fairly insulting."

"Except he doesn't really believe that," Carter argued, serious. "Most of the people who read prepper fiction just want a good story. They like post-apocalyptic stories — even *The Hunger Games* and *Divergent* fit the bill — and they enjoy thinking about what they would do in similar situations."

"But?" I prodded.

"But there is a small subset of readers who take things a little too far," he conceded. "They like the political talk. They like our author personas to be a little rough around the edges. They like the idea that we would gut and kill zombies without blinking an eye ... or climb into the sewer system to take out a swarm of evil-doers. It's not necessarily a bad thing, but it is a hard image to live up to."

"You're saying it's not the truth. None of it?"

"I'm saying much of it isn't the truth," he corrected. "I'm a family man. I have four children and eight foster children, many of whom are grown. I live on a farm in Michigan. I have a big garden.

"Sure, I also have an RV that was built in the seventies because it can withstand an EMP attack," he continued. "I have four basement freezers that run on generators and contain enough frozen meat to get my family through a full year. I have other food rations that will last for five years."

I smirked. "Basically you're saying that you're a complicated guy."

"That's exactly what I'm saying."

"What about Clark? Is he a complicated guy?"

"He's many different things." Carter momentarily looked sad. "I don't agree that women shouldn't work. I don't think the things he says to people are okay. It's just, underneath that tough veneer I recognize that he's a soul in pain. He needs someone to stand with him, not another person to tear him down."

"I would argue that he's created a lot of his own problems."

"He has. He would never deny it. He wants to fix those problems. I can guarantee that."

That assessment didn't jibe with the man I'd met. "What about Shayne Rivers? Was he trying to fix that problem?"

"Shayne was beyond fixing. You must know that. She was a walking catastrophe."

"She was still a person, a mother. She didn't deserve to have her life ripped away."

"And you think Clark is responsible for what happened to her?"

"I think I know some people who want to talk to him," I replied carefully. "Speaking of that ... I don't suppose you know where he's been hiding all afternoon?"

Carter shook his head. "I haven't seen him."

I studied his face, trying to ascertain if he was lying. He was hard to read. "Okay, well, if you see him, give me a holler. I would really like to talk to him."

"Of course." Carter was charming when he wanted to be, his smile infectious. I could read the lie in his eyes, though. He would never betray Clark for my benefit. "If that's all, I'd like to get back to my Vape."

"Sure. I didn't mean to intrude." I held my hands up as I backed away. "Enjoy ... and I'm sure I'll see you later."

"I'm sure you will."

TWENTY-SIX

*J*ack sat at a table drinking green tea with Lily and Sarah when I returned to the lobby. He seemed much more relaxed than the last time I saw him. Instead of a polite look of mild interest as the two women chatted amiably around him, he seemed legitimately engaged.

Somehow, almost as if he sensed my presence, he shifted his eyes to me. He seemed bemused by the baffled look on my face and gestured for me to join them.

Lily and Sarah were all smiles when I sat in the open chair to his right.

"We were just spending time with your boyfriend," Lily supplied. "He's quite the charmer."

"Well ... ." Jack and I had yet to define our relationship. Calling him my "boyfriend" felt like overstepping. "He probably doesn't want you to call him that."

"What?" Sarah asked, her attention on her phone screen. "We didn't call him any embarrassing names, like pimento puff or cheese cuddles. That's what I call my husband and he hates it."

I had no idea she was married. That put me at ease ... at least a bit. "I meant the boyfriend thing. We haven't been dating that long."

AMANDA M. LEE

Jack cocked an eyebrow. "What would you call me?"

Uh-oh. The question felt like a trap. "Security smoothie?"

Lily chuckled. "Good answer."

"Don't ever call me that," Jack warned, though his gaze was playful. "Boyfriend is fine."

I was caught off guard. "Really? I've spent the better part of this week telling you I believe it's possible there's a Megalodon hunting the Gulf of Mexico, something you don't like, and now you're willing to claim me as a girlfriend?"

"Yeah, well, nobody's perfect." He graced me with an easy grin. "It's fine. But where have you been? I was a little worried when I couldn't find you in the lobby. I thought maybe you found Clark and confronted him."

"I was in the parking lot talking to Carter. He Vapes."

"Fun."

"No one knows where Clark is," I supplied. "No one has seen him this morning. I'm starting to think I might have been the last one to talk to him."

"What did you say?" Sarah asked, holding up her phone. "This is Mouse. He's my cat."

I pressed my lips together as I looked at the calico wonder. Finally, the obvious question escaped. "Why would you name your cat Mouse?"

"Why not?"

"Fair enough. I ... ." Before I could finish my statement she showed me another photo. "This is Potato. He's my other cat."

This one was black and it was hard to make out his features other than the lazy golden eyes staring back at me. "He's awesome. Why Potato?"

"I love potatoes."

"Of course."

Sarah wasn't done. She showed me another photo, this one of a tabby. "This is Colonel Chompers."

"How many cats do you have?" Jack asked.

"Just the three." Sarah shoved her phone back in her pocket. "I

240

would have fifty if I could. My husband says three is our limit unless I rescue a stray. It has to be an emergency. I'm always on the lookout."

I laughed. She was simply too funny not to encourage. "Well, it's nice that you've found your calling in life."

"Cats are better than kids."

I couldn't help but agree. "Anyway, Clark and I had a long talk this morning. I asked him about his relationship with Shayne and he denied knowing her when he was a kid even though we have proof they were involved. I don't understand why he would lie about that."

"He doesn't want anyone to know," Lily said. "I think he's embarrassed even though she was extremely pretty. What? I can appreciate that she was pretty even though I thought she was a psycho. She aged much better than him. She should've been the embarrassed one."

That brought up an interesting subject. "Do you think she was embarrassed?"

"I doubt it. Shayne wasn't the type to get embarrassed. She used their previous relationship as a weapon."

"Yeah," Sarah echoed. "A baseball bat wrapped in barbed wire and she'd ... ." She broke off, miming a violent beating on an invisible foe. "She really was the worst."

The way Jack's cheeks puckered told me it took everything he had not to laugh. Despite his earlier meltdown, he was having a good time. It was nice to see. "We found out some disturbing things about Clark," he offered when he regained control of his facial muscles. "It seems he was a suspect in a murder when he was in high school. The girl in question was last seen with him and then disappeared. Her body was found later in a body of water flush with alligators."

Sarah's mouth dropped open. "Seriously? Talk about Colonel Chompers, huh?"

"She wasn't gnawed on," I supplied. "Her body was intact."

"We think he might've gotten the idea to dispose of a body in predator-infested waters at that point," Jack volunteered. "Just because it didn't work the first time doesn't mean it wouldn't work a second. He's older now, smarter. He might've even seen the sharks in the water earlier in the day and that triggered the idea."

"We don't know if she was dead or alive when she hit the water, right?" Lily queried.

"No, but I don't know that it matters," Jack replied. "I think it's pretty obvious that Shayne didn't throw herself off the end of the pier. Everyone says she was a rampant narcissist. Narcissists don't commit suicide."

"She would never kill herself," Lily agreed. "It wouldn't even enter her mind other than as a device to make her enemies feel bad. But she certainly would fake a suicide attempt."

Jack tilted his head to the side, considering. "Like take some pills and then call the hospital herself?"

"More like claim she was going to commit suicide and then make up a lie about her husband finding her before she could follow through, thus saving her at the last second and giving her a new lease on life."

"What about the water?" I asked. "Do you think she would be stupid enough to get in the water after dark? I mean ... the shark net was supposed to be intact. She might've thought the area was clear of sharks. She could've been carrying out a public suicide attempt to garner sympathy and it backfired on her."

"I hate to say it, but that's a possibility," Jack said.

"Definitely," Lily agreed. "She was capable of doing it. I don't know that she would go that route, though. That's something she would have trouble controlling. She's much more the fake overdose sort."

"Well ... ." I tapped on my bottom lip, turning to look over my shoulder when I felt someone move in behind me.

"Hello, all." Millie shoved me so I was practically on Jack's lap as she yanked over a chair and joined us without invitation. "I wondered where you guys went."

"Welcome to the party," I muttered, massaging the hip she jolted.

Jack's eyes twinkled as he rubbed his hand over my back, clearly unbothered by the fact that I was pressed up against him. He was done hiding our relationship. Of course, there was always the possibility that he needed the tactile contact, too. He'd had something of a rough day.

"This is Millie," I offered by way of introduction.

Lily and Sarah introduced themselves. Millie was friendly enough, although clearly distracted. Once the pleasantries were out of the way, she launched in her news.

"So, I just got off the phone with James Sanderson," she started.

Lily widened her eyes. "You know James Sanderson?"

"Millie knows everybody," Jack answered, smirking. "She's a real people person."

"I am nothing of the sort," Millie countered. "My ex-husband was friends with him. I knew him well enough to call. He was interested when I told him where I was."

"I'll bet," I said. "Did you tell him Leslie Downs was here?"

"I did and he has nothing nice to say about that loon."

"Oh, I'm practically salivating," Lily said.

Sarah bobbed her head. "The only thing that would make this moment better is pimento cheese."

Millie snickered. "Oh, you're *that* girl. I've heard all about you."

"Should I be worried?"

"No. Charlie is worried the pimento cheese is code for something sexual. I tried to tell her it's a southern thing, but she won't believe me."

I was mortified, my cheeks hotter than lava, when Sarah pinned me with a look. "I didn't say it was code for something sexual," I said finally.

"Oh, you're kind of weird, huh?" Sarah didn't appear bothered. "It's fine. I would totally hit on you if I rolled that way." She patted my knee under the table and I felt Jack's shoulders shaking with silent laughter as he snuggled close to me. "Go on with your story, Millie. I want to hear all about Leslie the loon."

"Well, she's been warned three times about breaking the terms of her restraining order," Millie said, glancing around to make sure we weren't garnering interest from the crazy chick in question. "She showed up at Sanderson's old penthouse. But he'd moved, and they were very careful when buying property. They did it through a corporation he created just for that purpose."

"Wow. That's dedication," Lily mused. "Did she get arrested when she tried to get to the old penthouse?"

"Yes, and she was warned by the same judge who signed the restraining order. He told her if she did it again she would be in big trouble."

"Let me guess," Sarah drawled. "She did it again."

"She went back to the fishing cabin," Millie supplied. "He didn't want to sell it because it had been in his family for eighty years, but he'd upgraded the security considerably. There are cameras all over that property. They caught Leslie trespassing no fewer than three times."

"And the judge didn't lock her up for that?" Jack was incredulous. "I'm sorry, but what's it going to take? Does she have to kill him to make an impression?"

"Apparently she's got a zero-tolerance edict hanging over her head," Millie explained. "If she shows up anywhere near him again she's going to jail for three years. No ifs, ands or buts."

"I guess I'll believe that when I see it," Jack muttered, dragging a restless hand through his hair. "Did Sanderson say anything about his proposed partnership with Shayne Rivers?"

Millie nodded. "He said it's a load of crap. She did contact his agent, but was shot down before she even got her opening spiel out. James does not want to deal with another author, no matter who it is, playing in his pool. She was told it wasn't going to happen, so if she was spreading something else it was a lie."

"I told you." Sarah looked triumphant. "I told you that's what she was doing. There was no way he would've agreed to a co-writing arrangement with her. She never wrote a mystery or thriller in her life. That was all a way to drive Leslie around the bend."

"To what end?" I asked, legitimately curious. "Even Shayne must have realized it was dangerous to push Leslie too far. Why would she want to light that particular fuse?"

"Maybe she wanted to light it and send her in another direction," Jack suggested. "Perhaps she wanted to get Leslie going, make her believe she was talking to Sanderson, and then agree to back down if Leslie did something for her."

Now we were getting somewhere. "Like go after Clark," I surmised.

"That's a good guess," Jack said, "but she had so many enemies it's possible that she wanted Leslie to take out someone else. I'm willing to bet that Shayne hadn't made it far enough into her plan to turn Leslie. She was still in the agitating phase."

"I believe that." I told him about my run-in with Leslie earlier. "She hated Shayne."

"Is it possible she hated her enough to kill her?"

I answered without hesitation. "Definitely."

BECAUSE HE WASN'T IN THE MOOD to spend time with Chris and Laura — especially the latter — Jack suggested we return to the satellite resort restaurant for a private dinner.

I readily agreed, and this time we spent some time perusing the gift shop as we waited for a table to open.

"I've always liked ocean-themed stuff," I mused as I tapped a set of octopus wind chimes. "I think it's neat, and I always like the colors."

Jack watched me shop, amused. "Do you want those? I'll buy them for you."

"Thanks, but my apartment is on the ground floor and if I put them outside they'd be stolen within twenty-four hours."

His smile slipped. "You live on the ground floor? I didn't know that."

"You picked me up for our date."

"I know, but ... you came out the lobby door. I had no idea you were on the ground floor. You can't stay there."

"I'm perfectly safe. I've been there for months."

"Well, you're not staying." Jack was firm. "If I have to talk to your landlord myself, I will. You need to move to the second floor at the least. Maybe you should move to a different neighborhood. Your building isn't exactly what I would call modern."

"No, but I can afford it." I moved around the display I'd been looking at and focused on a shelf of colorful shot glasses. "It's not exactly easy to find an affordable apartment close to the office. It took me two full weeks, and when it came down to it there was only one that fit my needs. I have to eat Ramen noodles five days a week just to afford it."

Jack was so quiet I assumed I'd lost him. When I turned I found him staring at me with a serious expression on his face that made me nervous. "What?"

"Are you saying that you don't make enough to survive on?"

"I'm surviving."

"How close are you to being homeless?"

Oh, geez. I realized after the fact that I definitely shouldn't have brought that up. He wasn't going to let it go. "I'm fine, Jack. This job is a dream come true. It's just ... the area is a little expensive. If I have to get a second job, I will. Don't worry about it. It's not the end of the world."

"What second job will you get that allows you to travel with us for weeks at a time?"

That was a good question. "Maybe I'll see if I can be one of those internet assistants Lily and Sarah use. They might know someone who needs help. I could do that job anywhere."

"That's not as bad as what I thought you were going to say," Jack admitted. "Still, if the company isn't paying you enough I can talk to Myron."

"No." I vehemently shook my head. "That's not what I want. I agreed to my salary for six months. I can make it."

Jack didn't look convinced, but he let it go. "Fine. We'll talk about it when we get home." He turned his attention to the table in front of him. On it, a basket full of what looked to be huge shark teeth was on display. "Look at this." He grabbed one of the teeth and held it up. "It's a Megalodon tooth."

I frowned. He was mocking me. "That's not a real tooth." I snagged it from him, yelping in surprise when he swooped in and gave me a quick kiss. It was his version of an apology. I'm ashamed to say, I melted a bit. He had a certain effect on me I couldn't always explain.

"It's marble," Jack said when he was done kissing me. "It's supposed to be a decoration for shark enthusiasts. Maybe I should buy one for Chris. If he has a replica he might give up on the real thing."

"I don't think anything will make him give up on the real thing." I flipped the tooth over and ran my fingers over the edge. It was sharp. "Hmm."

"What?" Jack poked my side. "Do you want it?"

"You seem obsessed with buying me a gift. I don't need anything. It's just ... this is the size of a Megalodon tooth."

"I noticed."

"The wounds on Shayne's body were too big to be made by a normal-sized shark."

Jack understood where I was going and grabbed the tooth, holding it up in the light. "You don't think ... ?"

"I don't know. It's a possibility, right?"

"Someone would've had to buy it here, in the satellite resort."

"Some of the writers are staying here because it was cheaper," I supplied. "I heard a few of them talking about it. They were complaining about the walk between resorts."

"Which means someone could've bought this and tried to frame a shark for murder."

"That would be my guess."

Jack grabbed my hand and dragged me toward the checkout counter, the tooth clutched tightly against his chest. "Come on. I'm buying this and then taking some dimensions and sending them to Hannah. I want to know what she thinks."

"What about dinner?"

"We'll multitask." He slowed his pace. "As a Megalodon is my witness, you're not eating Ramen noodles again."

"I kind of like them."

"Never again."

"Yes, sir."

His smile was back. "That's better ... and kind of hot."

TWENTY-SEVEN

*W*e ate a quick, not even remotely close to romantic, dinner. The discovery of the marble Megalodon tooth was enough to tip things in an interesting direction, and apparently even Chris opted to listen when Jack called Hannah.

"I'm taking a photo," Jack announced, grabbing my phone. "It will come from Charlie so I can keep my line open. I'll message both of you." He was video chatting with both of them. "What do you want me to put next to it for scale?"

"Do you have a ruler?" Hannah asked.

Jack rolled his eyes. "We're on the beach. There are no rulers."

"Just come back here," Chris suggested. He seemed downcast. The knowledge that Jack had found a way to explain the Megalodon bite marks was almost too much for him to bear. "I want to see it in person, make sure it's actually as durable as you say it is."

Jack could've gloated. I thought maybe he wanted to because he seemed smug when we were checking out with the tooth. He managed to rein in his surlier impulses, though, and remain pleasant as he met Chris's gaze. "We're trying to find Clark Savage. He has to be around here, unless he checked out. I'm going to check with the front desk to be sure. Maybe I can get into his room."

"The hotel staff won't simply let you in his room," Chris argued.

Jack slid me a sidelong look. "Well, I might have a way around that. I can't guarantee anything. We need to look for Clark. This might be our last chance to find him."

"If he's the guilty party, shouldn't you leave apprehending him to the police?" Hannah asked.

Jack shrugged, noncommittal. "Maybe. The thing is, I'd like to talk to him. He's our prime suspect, but that doesn't mean he's definitely the guilty party. The evidence points toward him, but it's all circumstantial. Anyone could've bought a shark tooth."

Jack decided to place the call behind the satellite resort. From our spot on the beach, I could make out several people sitting at the tiki bar. I pointed to let him know I planned to head in that direction, but he grabbed my wrist before I could escape.

"Hold on, Chris." He ordered our boss to stop complaining and focused on me. "Where do you think you're going?"

"A few of the writers are at the tiki bar. I thought I might check with them to see if they've seen Clark."

Jack didn't look convinced. "We only think Clark is the killer," he reminded me. "We don't know that it's true. I think you'd be better off sticking with me."

"It's like four people ... and you'll be able to see me the entire time."

Jack flicked his eyes to the spot over my shoulder. "I know, but ... you should stay here."

"Jack is head of security, Charlie," Chris noted. "Do what he says."

That sounded like the last thing I wanted to do. "It's, like, a hundred feet away. He'll be able to see me the entire time. It will also cut down on the number of people we need to question once you're done sending tooth measurements to Hannah."

"That is true," Hannah noted. "She's being efficient, not reckless."

I wanted to crow, but managed to swallow the impulse. "I'm being efficient, Jack. How often do I get to say that?"

Jack scowled, but I knew I'd won by the way his shoulders sloped. "Fine." He released my arm. "Don't wander off. And don't tip our hand. Let them know we found the murder weapon. In fact, say it was discovered at a gift shop of all places, but don't say what it is or where we found it. I want them to sweat if it's one of them."

"I thought you were leaning toward Clark."

"I am, but I don't want to rule out the others."

"Fair enough."

I left Jack to measure his tooth and talk science with Hannah — seriously, could there be a more boring conversation? — and cut through the beach cabanas as I headed toward the tiki bar. The one at the satellite property was smaller than the one at the main resort, but the location was pleasant, and not nearly as loud as the bigger one.

"Can I have a rum runner?" I asked as I sat at the bar. I wanted to look as if I was merely hanging out.

"Sure." The bartender, who wore a name tag that read "Summer," flashed me a quick smile as she started mixing my drink. "Are you enjoying your stay at Gulf Winds Lodge?"

She probably had to ask that, customer service and all, so I nodded. "I am. We're having a great time. In fact, we just ate at the cool restaurant inside with the huge aquarium wall."

"Ah, yes, the food there is amazing. What did you have?"

"Scallops."

"Very good."

I risked a nervous glance toward my left, at the place where J.D. sat drinking and talking with someone I didn't recognize. Christine sat on a lounger behind him, those ever-present knitting needles clicking at a fantastic rate, Their fight from earlier appeared to have lingered, because they weren't speaking to one another.

"You still haven't seen Clark, have you?" I asked.

J.D., clearly annoyed at being interrupted, shook his head. "No. Why are you so obsessed with Clark?"

"He's simply a loose end we need to sew up," I answered. Remembering what Jack instructed me to say, I changed course. "We think we discovered the murder weapon. We found it in one of the gift shops, if you can believe that. Jack is confirming it right now. If everything holds together, we'll be able to say definitively that Shayne was murdered."

Christine abandoned her knitting for what had to be the first time since I'd met her. "Are you serious?"

I nodded. "Half of our group never believed we were looking for a real shark. The other half wanted it to be true, but it looks as if that's going to fall by the wayside."

Instead of reacting with worry or excitement, J.D. blew up. "No way! The police said from the start that it looked like a shark attack. A big shark. That's why I moved up the publication of my book. If a person did it, that won't help my book launch."

"Oh, well ... ." I hadn't even considered that. "I don't know what to tell you. The odds of it being a mega-shark were always pretty thin. Hopefully I'll have more answers as soon as Jack is off the phone. He's talking to our boss right now."

"Well, this just bites the big one!" J.D. snapped. "I had big plans for that book. If police prove it was a person instead of a shark that's going to suck. I can't freaking believe it. I have the worst luck sometimes. I swear."

I couldn't help myself from poking him. "I thought you were the miracle man who spun golden words from thin air."

J.D.'s frown was pronounced. "Haven't you done enough to ruin my night? Do you have to make things worse?"

He had a point. I sipped my rum runner and then craned my neck to see around Summer. "Where is the bathroom?"

Summer pointed to the building to my right. "There."

"Great." I hopped off my stool. "I'm going to leave my drink here. I'll be right back."

Summer waved haphazardly. "I'll keep your seat."

"Great." I shifted my focus to Jack as I trudged toward the bathroom, waving my hand to get his attention. He was clearly too focused on his phone — and mine, because he was using it to take photos — to notice where I was going. He didn't so much as glance in my direction, instead fixating on his task.

Ah, well. He probably wouldn't even notice I was gone. And, if he panicked Summer would tell him where I had gone.

I let myself into the small building that housed the bathrooms and glanced between the signs before heading to my right. I'd almost walked through the opening to the women's bathroom when a hand grabbed my shoulder from behind and spun me, causing me to widen my eyes as I faced the one person I'd been looking for all day.

"Clark!" Oh, crap. I found him ... and at the worst possible time. "What are you doing here?"

"I was just going to ask you the same question," he growled, his hair standing on end, as if he'd been swiping his hands through it the entire day and he no longer had control of how it looked. "Do you have any idea what you've done to me?"

"Me?" I was nervous, and I tried to take a step away from him. If I could make it inside the bathroom there was every chance I could lock myself in a stall and call Jack. Of course, after a few seconds of thinking that through I realized Jack had my phone. Still, I could hide until Jack decided to look for me. Summer knew where I was. She would send Jack ... just as soon as he stopped patting himself on the back for discounting a Megalodon as a killer.

"Who else would I blame?" Clark was beside himself. "You've been digging and telling people about Elsie and me. It's your fault."

I was frightened, a little off my game, but there was no way I would take responsibility for that. "You dated her," I snapped. "You fought with her online. You killed her."

Clark's mouth dropped open. "I did not!"

"You did. We know how you did it, too. We saw the huge Megalodon teeth in the gift shop. They're the exact size of the wound patterns. Did you see the teeth and get the idea, or did you kill her first and then stumble across the teeth and decide that was the best way for a cover-up?"

Clark made exasperated gestures with his hands. "I didn't kill her. Stop saying that. Why would I kill her?"

"You were upset that she broke up with you."

"That was more than a decade ago."

"Yes, but you had plans," I supplied, warming to my topic. "You thought she was going to play the dutiful housewife while you went out and provided for your family. It must have chafed your butt that she had that family with someone else."

He sputtered, his cheeks red with distress. "I didn't kill Elsie! As for breaking up, I was the one who wanted to end it. I tried to dump her before we even got out of high school. I started dating someone else ... although that ended in tragedy."

Something clicked in my mind. "You're talking about Nancy Nelson. We know all about her, too. You were seen with her the day she went missing and then her body was found in a bayou with alligators. That's how you got the idea for what you decided to do to Shayne."

I took another step back but the angle was wrong. I smacked into the wall instead of gliding through the open doorway. Well, crap.

"I didn't kill her." Instead of advancing, Clark dropped his hands to his sides. "I liked her. She was fun and totally sane. Do you have any idea how crazy Elsie was? I mean ... she was nuts. She made things ten times more difficult than they had to be."

I was taken aback. "You didn't kill Nancy?"

"No."

"The cops think you did."

"The cops are morons," Clark spat. "They questioned me for weeks. They never believed a word I said. That's why my father insisted I stop talking to them. He got a lawyer and told me to keep my mouth shut."

He sounded sincere. Most good liars have the ability to fake sincerity, though. He could've simply been playing his part. "If you didn't kill her, who did?"

"I think it was Elsie."

I wasn't expecting that response. "What?"

"You heard me." Clark increased the distance between us, allowing me room to breathe as he paced the small hallway. I now had an avenue of escape, but I didn't take it because I wanted to hear his theory on Nancy's death. "Elsie was upset. I'd broken up with her the previous day, although no one knew it.

"She kept bugging me, begging me to get back together," he continued. "One second she would be sweet and nice, promise me the world and that she would be a better girlfriend. The next she would be threatening, a territorial animal who promised she would rip out my throat if I didn't change my mind."

Sadly, that sounded just like her. I had never met the woman, but from what everyone said, she was a disgusting piece of work. "Did she know you were seeing Nancy?"

"I wasn't technically seeing her," Clark hedged. "I walked her home from school, talked to her a bit, and we hung out because she lived three doors down from me. I was gearing up to ask her out on an official date. I liked how easy she was to get along with. That's what made me realize that my relationship with Elsie wasn't normal."

"Definitely not," I agreed. "Just for the record, you're never going to have a real relationship if you keep up this nonsense that women are supposed to be seen and not heard."

"I don't care about that." He waved his hand. "That's to sell books. I like my women feisty." His eyes landed squarely on me. "If you weren't such a pain ...."

Oddly enough, that didn't make me feel warm and gooey all over. "I have a boyfriend."

"Yes, and he would kill me for touching you. You don't have to worry."

I relaxed, though only marginally. "How would Elsie have killed Nancy?"

"She had plenty of opportunities. My guess is she was watching my house, saw us walk home together, and then approached Nancy after. But I have no proof of that."

"Did you tell the police?"

"I didn't have proof and, truth be told, Elsie frightened me. At that point, I simply wanted to get away from her. The relationship continued, but in name only. I pushed her away, hoping she would find someone else at college. That's what happened, and you have no idea how relieved I was."

"You fought with her online," I pointed out. "Why would you do that?"

"Because the fear faded the older I got. I realized what she was — a manipulator — and I saw her hurting others. I wasn't about to let that stand, not a second time."

It made sense. Kind of. "Why not just tell the police all of this? Elsie isn't around to terrorize you any longer."

"The way she died echoed Nancy's death. You were right about that. I'm afraid the cops will think I held onto a grudge for twelve years and then tried to pay her back with a murder in shark-infested waters. I've been talking to an attorney. We're making plans to sit down and talk to investigators together, but I still have to get all of my ducks in a row."

"Oh." I licked lips. "Well, that sounds like a good plan. I wish you well in your future endeavors."

Instead of responding in kind, Clark glowered. "That doesn't change the fact that you've made things difficult for me. You've been pointing the finger all day."

"You can't possibly blame me. After we heard that alligator story you seemed the best possible suspect."

"You've been telling anyone who will listen that you've been looking for me," Clark argued. "Everyone knows you're here investigating Elsie's murder, so they assume I'm the guilty party. How do you think I'll be able to recover from that?"

It was a fair question. I didn't have an answer. "I don't know. Tell them I was wrong."

"It's a little late for that."

"Hey, if we find the real culprit you won't have anything to worry about," I pointed out. "That person's face will be splattered all over the news and you'll be able to paint yourself as a victim of the system you hate. You can write a prepper book about a man who gets a new lease on life after being falsely accused. When the end of the world comes, people will realize he's a hero, not a zero."

Clark worked his jaw. "I hate to admit it, but that's a good idea," he said finally. "I'm going to steal it."

"That's the least I owe you." I waited a beat, but when he didn't move to leave I pointed at the bathroom. "I don't want to be a pain, but I came in here for a reason and I'm not comfortable going knowing you're out here."

"I just told you I wasn't a killer."

"And I believe you." Mostly. "I still would prefer it if you weren't here when I did my business. I don't think it's too much to ask."

"Fine." Clark morosely trudged toward the glass door that led outside. "I'll be waiting in front of the building. I want you to tell your boyfriend I'm not a killer. He freaks me out more than you, if you can believe that."

I could totally believe that. Jack was intimidating. "I'll be done in a few minutes. I ... ." I forgot what I was going to say when the door behind Clark opened and Christine strolled inside, her knitting project clutched tightly in her hands.

It took her a moment to register what was going on, and when she did, her mouth dropped open.

"Holy crap! He's here!" Her voice ratcheted up a notch. "He's here! He's here!"

Whoops. Keeping Clark's presence under wraps was going to be more difficult than I'd envisioned.

TWENTY-EIGHT

*C*hristine's appearance threw me for a loop. The shrill noises emanating from her set my teeth on edge, and I wanted to quiet her by whatever means necessary.

"Chill out," I ordered, frustrated. "There's no reason to get all worked up."

"You were supposed to leave," Christine barked, her eyes on Clark rather than me. "You weren't supposed to stay. You were supposed to go." She flapped her arms for emphasis, the knitting needles flying in eight different directions. "Why are you still here?"

"Because I have things to do," Clark replied, annoyance evident. "Why do you even care?"

"You were supposed to leave." Christine was adamant. "You were supposed to run so the cops would follow."

I was confused and leery. "What are you talking about?"

She didn't look at me, instead focusing on Clark. "You were supposed to go," she said again, her eyes sharpening. "You were supposed to go and I need you to go. You weren't supposed to be here ... and you need to not be here now."

The shift in her demeanor was alarming. It was almost as if she'd become another person as she steadied herself. Instead of explaining what she was talking about, she simply reacted.

I realized what she was going to do when it was too late to make a difference, no time to reach out an arm and stop her. She raised her hand, one of her knitting needles clutched tightly, and jabbed it into Clark's chest. He didn't realize what was happening until the damage was already done. His eyes widened and he reached up to grab at the knitting needle embedded in his chest.

"What the ... ?" He didn't finish his sentence, instead listing to his right and hitting the floor with a hard smack.

My mouth dropped open as I slowly shifted my eyes to Christine. Part of me was convinced this had to be a dream, that I would wake up any second and start the day over. When Christine turned her eyes to me, I found madness waiting.

"What did you do?" I started to move toward Clark, some wild notion that she would see the error of her ways and help me bubbling up, but she shoved me hard before I could get to him, slamming me into the brick wall at my back and raising the second knitting needle to make sure I realized she meant business.

"I don't think that's a good idea," she drawled, her eyes serious as she looked me up and down. "I can't let you help him. I need him dead." Her affect was flat, as if she were already disassociating herself from what she'd done.

"He needs help," I said quietly, collecting myself. Clark's breathing was shallow, blood soaking his shirt. "He could be saved. I need to call for help."

"I don't want him saved."

"But ... ."

"I don't want him saved!" she shrieked, her eyes flashing. "Is your hearing bad? Do you have trouble comprehending the words coming out of my mouth? Do you need me to write it in crayon for you?"

The words were harsh; the emotion behind them harsher. Christine was clearly so much more than I'd thought. I needed to figure a way out ... for me and for Clark ... and I had to do it fast.

"I understand." I held up my hands in a placating manner,

reminding myself that she wasn't a trained assassin. I could take her if it became necessary. She had a knitting needle, but I had something more. I was hopeful I could talk her down before magic became necessary.

I licked my lips and collected my thoughts. "You killed Shayne Rivers, didn't you?"

Christine blinked several times. "Obviously."

"Why?"

"Why do you think?"

Was that a serious question? I couldn't be sure. "I don't know." I opted for honesty. "I can't figure it out. Was it because you wanted to help your husband launch the shark book he's been planning?"

"Partially."

"What was the other part?"

"You never met Shayne so you can't fully understand how evil she was." Christine took on a far-off expression as she shook her head. "She was truly evil. You have no idea how horrible she was."

"I've heard a few stories. I've heard about the things she did, the people she hurt. You weren't on the list of victims. Never once did I hear your name mentioned."

"That's because she usually ignored me," Christine supplied, scratching her cheek with the other knitting needle. She seemed confused, as if too much was happening for her to grasp the full magnitude of her actions. "She paid absolutely zero attention to me until that night."

"And what happened that night?"

"I heard her on the beach," Christine explained. "She was talking on the phone. I'm not sure to whom. She had a plan, though. She was going to write a series that was almost exactly like my husband's biggest-selling series."

"The shark series?"

"That hasn't hit yet."

"Of course."

She rolled her neck, the cracking sound almost deafening in the small space. "She wanted to ruin J.D. Not because he'd ever done anything to her, but because she enjoyed ruining people. She made no bones about it. She had a good time screwing with people."

"I believe that," I said. "Everyone I talked to said she was a horrible person and was only happy when being cruel to others."

"It wasn't just that she was cruel," Christine countered. "I can handle cruel. I've dealt with cruel before. She was much more than that. It was that she played the victim while victimizing others. That's what I couldn't stand."

"You confronted her, didn't you?" I tried to picture the scene in my head. "You couldn't let her ruin your husband. That was the last straw."

"I waited until she was off the phone," Christine agreed. "She didn't look happy when I called out to her. She called me names, made fun of J.D.'s weight, and then said we were going to end up back in the trailer park when she was done with us.

"I didn't really mind the trailer park," she continued. "I didn't think there was anything wrong with it. J.D. wanted out so badly, though, I knew the idea of going back would kill him. I couldn't let her hurt him so ... I hurt her."

She was so calm during the recitation that it sent chills down my spine. "What happened?"

"It was fast. I had my knitting needles in my hands and I just ... ." She mimed stabbing the needle into an invisible person, indicating she'd done the same to Shayne that she'd done to Clark. The needle was sharp but not very big. That left a few obvious questions.

"Did she die right away?"

"No. She begged for help. Tried to call 911 on her phone. I took it away from her."

"That was smart." I had no idea what else to say. "Did you consider calling for help?"

"You probably want me to say 'yes,' don't you?" Christine's green eyes were clear when they locked with mine. On some level she understood what was happening, what she had done ... both times. How she accepted her part was up for debate. "I wasn't worried about myself. I didn't let her die to protect myself. I just want you to know that."

"You did it for J.D.," I said quietly.

"I did," she agreed, nodding. "I was in a predicament. She was still alive and I wasn't sure her wound was life-threatening. I had to get rid of her."

"So you decided to follow the plot in your husband's book and dump her in the ocean."

"Not quite."

I jerked up my head, surprised. "What do you mean?"

"I needed help," Christine said simply. "I couldn't carry her myself. She was too heavy. Besides, I couldn't guarantee that she wouldn't somehow manage to swim to shore if I just dumped her over the side."

"I don't ... you ... what did you do?" I couldn't wrap my head around what she was insinuating.

"I called for help," she replied simply.

"She called for me," J.D. offered, moving from the shadows and filling the empty space behind his wife. I had no idea when he'd entered the building. He probably came looking for Christine when she was delayed. Ultimately it didn't matter. What mattered was that I was outnumbered ... and I didn't have a phone.

"You helped her finish off Shayne." I was mildly disappointed. "Why didn't you call the police, right the wrong your wife committed?"

"Are you kidding me?" J.D. made a face. "I didn't like Shayne any more than the next person. She was an evil little troll who got off on hurting people. Have you found one person at this conference sad about her death? I didn't think so. She was a blight on humanity and she deserved to be eradicated."

My hands clenched at my sides, and I debated my options.

"She thought I was going to help her at first," J.D. continued. "She ordered me to call the police. She didn't even ask, just demanded I do it. She kept saying that she was going to have Christine locked away for the rest of her life and she was looking forward to writing a book about what happened."

"We've already ascertained that she's a terrible person," I noted. "That doesn't mean she deserved to die."

"I wouldn't have chosen to kill her," J.D. offered. "But when it came to choosing between her and my wife, there was no contest. Christine is impulsive and often acts before she thinks, but she's a good person. You can't say the same for Shayne. She never did anything good for anybody."

Now wasn't the time to argue Shayne's merits. "She was alive when you got to the pier. Was she alive when you threw her in the water?"

"Yes, at least I think. She was unconscious, I definitely know that."

"Did she pass out from blood loss?"

"No." J.D. shook his head as he regarded me. "We needed her to be quiet. She'd started yelling, trying to attract attention from the tiki bar. We didn't know at the time, but Clark was there with one of his little friends, taking refuge in one of the cabanas from a rainstorm. He mentioned hearing voices, but he never went to check. Even though she was horrible to him, I think he felt guilty about that. He stayed with his prostitute while she died just one-hundred feet away."

I felt sick to my stomach. "How did you keep her quiet?"

"I injected her."

"With what?"

"Insulin." He reached into the bag he carried around his waist. "It was handy and I knew what would happen if I gave her an overdose. Hypoglycemia. She lost consciousness relatively quickly and never regained it."

"That allowed you to move her body without drawing too much attention," I mused. "Did you take one of the golf carts at the end of the pier?"

"They're very easy to hotwire."

I frowned. "So I've heard."

"We took her to the end of the pier. The initial plan was to simply drop her in and walk away, but I started to worry that she might wash back to shore intact and it would be too easy to identify what sort of weapon was used to stab her. Knitting needles aren't hard to identify."

"And your wife carries knitting needles wherever she goes," I added.

"Idle hands," Christine murmured, her eyes glassy.

"Did you already have the Megalodon tooth from the gift shop?" I asked. "How did you come up with that idea? It was genius, by the way."

J.D. beamed. "Thank you. I was rather proud of that myself. I bought the tooth in the shop earlier in the day. It was in Christine's knitting basket. We were sitting at the end of the pier, hoping I'd dosed Shayne with enough insulin to keep her under, and wondering exactly how we could cover up the wound. Christine stumbled over the tooth and it just sort of made sense."

"You had to push it into her body," I pointed out, disgust rolling through my stomach. "You had to stab her with it."

"Yeah. That was a messy business." He made a face as he shook his head. "We played rock, paper, scissors to see who would have to do it. She lost, but it turned out she didn't have enough upper body strength. I had to do it."

I pressed my lips together, horrified at the visual. "Did she wake up?"

"No. She was essentially in a coma. She didn't feel anything."

"You can't know that."

"I guess not, but I'm willing to bet she didn't feel anything." J.D. was blasé as he absently rubbed his hand up and down Christine's back. "I created two wounds, one directly over top of the wound Christine inflicted and the other nearby. By this time, Shayne was barely breathing. She might have stopped by the time I dropped her in the water. I can't be sure.

"Together, we lifted her over the railing," he continued. "She didn't sink right away. I thought she would. We could see the pink of her shirt bobbing in the surf and it made us both nervous. We watched her body for a long time, hoping it would be carried out to sea. We finally had to give up and return the golf cart. We couldn't afford for something that trivial to trip us up."

He didn't appear upset at his part in the story. In fact, he simply looked annoyed that he was forced to dispose of a body.

"She got caught in the shark net," I pointed out. "That's why she didn't float out to sea. That allowed for sharks on the other side to feed on her."

"Yeah. That was a godsend." J.D. beamed. "I heard there was so much damage to her body they couldn't discover a cause of death. That worked out really well for us."

I wanted to smack him. "She was a mother. She had five children."

"She was evil."

I shook my head, acid boiling through my stomach. "I can't believe you feel no remorse for what you did."

"Would remorse help? My wife is a good person. Shayne pushed her too far. No one will miss Shayne. I would miss Christine, even if she does cause a few problems from time to time. This one right here, this would be an example of a problem I don't want to deal with but have no choice." He gestured toward Clark's prone body.

"And how do you plan to deal with that?" I asked, dreading the answer.

"We have to kill both of you," he replied without hesitation. "Clark is already halfway there. You'll take more work — and we'll have to think of a good cover story. Perhaps you and Clark were having an affair and you took off together. I'm sure we can come up with something. I'm a writer, after all. Telling tall tales is what I do."

"Right." I shifted from one foot to the other. I sensed my time was running short. I would have to act ... and fast. "You know I'm not simply going to let you kill me, right?"

"You don't have a choice." Christine gripped her remaining knitting needle tighter as she regarded me. "We can't let you live."

"And I can't let you get away with this." I flexed my fingers, readying myself. "Part of me does feel sorry for you. I want you to know that. The other part is horrified. The depraved indifference you've shown Shayne and Clark is disgusting."

"They're both disgusting people," J.D. shot back. "They don't deserve to live."

"And what about me?" I asked the obvious question. "What did I do to you to deserve this?"

"You're simply collateral damage." J.D. took a step toward me. I didn't know what he was planning. He was big, probably strong, but he was in horrible shape and I was expecting him. When he reached out his arms I let my magic loose without even thinking about the consequences.

A terrible and biting wind exploded out of my chest, hitting J.D. with enough force to throw him into the wall behind him. His eyes went wide as his head smacked against the cinder blocks. He struggled to remain focused, but the blow was hard enough that he slid to the floor, his head lolling to his side.

It was over, start to finish, within three seconds.

"What did you do?" Christine screeched, her eyes going wide. "You killed him!"

"I didn't even touch him." That wasn't a lie. From Christine's perspective I went nowhere near him. "He probably passed out from the excitement."

"He did not!" Christine turned on me. "You killed him! You killed my J.D."

She waved the knitting needle around like the world's slimmest sword and managed to catch me on the arm before I could shift out of her reach. I yelped, instinctively reaching up to cover the wound, and thoughts of magic fled as she descended on me.

Instead of attacking her with the power pooling in my chest, I lashed out with my foot and caught her as she tried to stab me a second time, spinning her back hard enough that she bounced off the wall. She looked shaken as she attempted to regain her focus.

"I'm not going to let you get away with this," she hissed. "I'm not going to let you ruin my family. He's all I have. I'll protect him any way I can."

I recognized the truth behind her words. I also recognized she was a sad woman who'd probably long ago lost whatever shred of sanity she had clung to. "It's already over. You simply don't realize it."

"It's nowhere near over."

"But it is."

"No!" Christine screamed and lunged at me, the knitting needle directed at my face. Before I could release the magic begging to be unleashed, the door behind Christine popped open again to allow Jack entrance. He caught her before she could land on me, snapping her back and using his forearm to pin her against the wall as she fruitlessly struggled against his strength.

His gaze was incredulous as it bounced over Clark and J.D. and then latched onto me. "Are you okay?"

I nodded as I dropped to my knees to check on Clark, my breath coming in ragged gasps. He was still breathing, but his heartbeat was rapid and his breathing shallow. "What took you so long?"

"Why didn't you call me?"

"You had my phone."

"Oh." He was momentarily abashed. "Well ... you're okay. It all worked out in the end."

I nodded as I applied pressure to Clark's wound. "We need an ambulance ... and then I want to get out of this bathroom. This is not how I saw my night going."

"That makes two of us."

TWENTY-NINE

*R*esort security arrived quickly, taking custody of Christine and J.D. The police and emergency personnel were close on their heels, and Clark was briskly wheeled out so he could be transferred to the hospital.

When J.D. regained consciousness, he instantly began spinning a yarn about trying to protect me from Clark's advances. I had to give him credit, it was a fairly ingenious story and he took very little time to dream it up. Jack and I had already related our stories, though, so the police didn't fall for it.

"It was my fault," Christine announced as she was placed in cuffs. "I did it. J.D. had no idea what was going on. He's innocent."

"Listen to her," J.D. encouraged. "She's telling the truth. I'm an innocent victim here."

The way he turned on his wife made me dislike him even more than before, if that was even possible. Still, I followed Jack's lead and kept my disdain to myself as he was dragged off. It was unlikely the cops would believe him given the information I provided, but it was on them how they planned to proceed.

"Are you guys okay?" Chris asked when we exited the building. He stood to the side, the other members of our group close. "They wouldn't let us in to check on you."

"We're okay," Jack replied. "I ... ." He grunted when Laura raced to him and threw her arms around his neck.

"I was so worried," she gushed, her voice wavering. "I thought for sure Charlie dragged you into another ridiculous situation. You could've died."

Jack wrinkled his forehead as he pulled Laura's arms from around his neck and gave her a gentle shove back. "Charlie is the one who was in danger. I was on the beach when it went down."

"Not all of it," I countered, doing my best to ignore the way Laura batted her eyelashes. "You came in at the end and took down Christine before she could stab me with a knitting needle."

"That was after you'd already taken out J.D.," he pointed out. "You did the heavy lifting on your own. I don't know how you managed to take out a guy that big, but good on you."

I shrugged. "I didn't really do anything. He kind of did it to himself. I think maybe his blood sugar was out of whack or something." I avoided Millie's doubtful gaze. She knew how I'd taken out J.D. She would keep it to herself. "I got lucky. I wasn't sure you would come looking for me ... at least in time. I knew Clark didn't have long, so I was getting ready to fight Christine when you came in."

"Well, you still took care of yourself." He slung an arm around my shoulders, amusement pushing out the worry in his eyes. "You handled yourself well."

"Very well," Chris agreed, bobbing his head. "I'm still not sure how all this happened. Are we certain that J.D. and Christine killed Shayne?"

I knew what he was really asking. He didn't want to let go of the possibility that a Megalodon was involved. He would always be that way because he craved proof of the unknown. I understood his desire, yet it seemed silly to cling to the impossible given everything we knew.

"They admitted it," I said quietly. "Christine stumbled across Shayne plotting against J.D. and lashed out. She was still alive when

Christine called for J.D. to help her. He injected Shayne with insulin to keep her quiet and they dumped her over the side of the pier. It was all very clinical from their perspective."

"That doesn't explain the huge teeth marks," Chris persisted.

"It was the marble tooth, the same kind Jack bought earlier today," I explained. "Christine had one in her knitting bag. They used it in an attempt to cover up the knitting needle wound because it was so distinctive. They had no idea that sharks would do the bulk of their dirty work, but when that happened they decided to take advantage of the situation for J.D.'s upcoming launch."

"But ... it's a souvenir," Chris pressed. "How can we be sure it's strong enough to do the job?"

"They're made out of marble," Jack replied. "I left the one I bought out by the cabanas. We can collect it on our way back to the condos."

Chris didn't look happy with the suggestion. "I guess. I was really hoping it was a Megalodon."

"I know." Jack grinned at him. "It was never going to be a Megalodon, though. I think part of you always knew that. Ultimately, it doesn't matter. This investigation turned out to be a dud. You'll get just as excited for the next one, and that might not be a dud."

Chris brightened considerably. "That's true. There's always another case."

"There you go." Jack's fingers were gentle on the back of my neck as he slid me a sidelong look. "What about Clark? How did he get involved in all of this?"

"He was hiding in the bathroom. He blamed me for making things hard on him. He said he was talking to a local attorney and arranging a visit with the police because he had information he wanted to share."

"What information?"

"That he thinks Shayne killed Nancy when they were in high school and he was deathly afraid of her. He was convinced she did it, and that was why he was careful when he extricated himself from her a second time."

"Do you think he was telling the truth?"

I searched my heart. "I guess I do. He said he really liked her, that it wasn't until he spent time with her that he realized relationships weren't supposed to be as difficult as Shayne made theirs. He wanted out, but when Nancy died he was afraid Shayne would try to do the same to him.

"He knew he was a suspect in the murder. That's why he left the area, never to return," I continued. "He was afraid the similarities between Shayne's death and Nancy's murder would do him in. He was trying to arrange a meeting with the cops to finally tell them the truth."

"Well, that answers that question," he said as he linked his fingers with mine, ignoring the way Laura huffed and glared. "He's still a jerk."

"He is, although he says he's playing a part and doesn't believe half the things he says."

"Do you believe him?"

I shrugged. "I don't know. Does it matter?"

"No." He squeezed my hand and smiled. "You look tired."

"I feel tired. I'm ready for bed."

"Then we should head back." He gave my hand a little tug to keep me close. "I think we should get out of here early tomorrow. Not that I haven't enjoyed myself, but this humidity is enough to make me want to commit murder."

"We'll head home early," Chris said. "I want to see what new cases have crossed my desk."

"Sounds like a plan."

We lapsed into amiable silence for the walk back to the condo, and when we arrived I was surprised to find Sarah moving away from the front door. She didn't look guilty when she raised her eyes. Instead, she offered me a wan smile and waved.

"I wasn't sure when you would be back," she said, nodding at the other members of my group in turn before focusing on me. "Word is spreading about what happened at the other resort, your part in taking down J.D. and Christine. That's really weird, right?"

I nodded. "Very weird. I thought it was Clark."

"Yeah, well, he's the type." She gestured toward a bag she'd left on the front porch. "Pimento cheese and crackers so you can have a snack before bed. You'll probably need the energy boost."

I smirked. "What is it with you and pimento cheese? I have to know."

"It's the best."

"There has to be more than that."

"No, I simply like it."

I waited, convinced she would break and tell me. Finally, I merely shook my head. "Well, thanks for the snack. I promise to think of you when I eat it."

"That's all I ask."

"We'll be leaving tomorrow morning," Jack interjected. "We'll stop in the lobby so Charlie can say goodbye before we go."

"I'll be there." Sarah waved again before disappearing into the night.

Jack stopped in front of the door long enough to gather the snacks, grinning as he let our group inside and headed toward the kitchen.

"Where are you going?" I asked, weariness threatening to overtake me. "I thought we were going to bed."

"Do you really want to miss your chance to try this pimento cheese she's been raving about for the past few days? You promised her you'd taste it."

"I know, but ... ." Oh, well, what the heck? I didn't want to let her down.

By the time I joined Jack in the kitchen, he'd already placed knives on the counter and had the crackers open. "Come on," he prodded, prying the lid off the cheese. "You won't know unless you try it."

I was tentative when I spread the cheese on the cracker and raised it to my mouth. "If this is terrible I'll never be able to look her in the eye."

"Have faith. It might be as good as she says."

I bit into the mixture and chewed. Finally, when I swallowed, I spoke. "It's okay."

Jack grinned. "Are you saying it didn't change your life?"

"I'm saying that it tastes like cheese on a cracker."

"You'd better keep that to yourself when you say goodbye tomorrow."

"I'm not an idiot."

Jack sobered. "No, you're definitely not an idiot. You handled yourself well tonight, Charlie. You protected yourself and didn't freak out. I'm proud of you."

The sentiment warmed me. "Did you think I would be anything but chill?"

"I had my worries."

I could see that. "Well, I was a big hero tonight. I expect to be lauded as such until we leave for home tomorrow."

Jack's grin turned mischievous. "I think I can manage that."

"Somehow I knew you'd be up to the challenge."

"Eat your cheese ... and then let's go to bed. I'm ready to go home and try another date."

That made two of us.

23691610R00165